Vampiric Crush

by

Frankie Sutton

The Wild Rose Press, Inc.
PO Box 708
Adams Basin, NY 14410-0708
Visit us at www.thewildrosepress.com

Publishing History
First Edition, 2024
Trade Paperback ISBN 978-1-5092-5703-4
Digital ISBN 978-1-5092-5704-1

Published in the United States of America

Dedication

Dedicated to my nana, Jennie.

Chapter 1

The putrid stench of Shae's latest victim in the Battle Realm wafted across her nostrils from less than a foot away. The din of clashing weapons echoed within the area. Kneeling, she peered over a thicket of bushes. Two male warriors tested each other's battle skills to the death. Vision blurred from a bead of sweat. She wiped both eyes, wishing she'd visited a much cooler region on this planet.

She flinched the moment an unwelcomed poke of a pointy object flipped her bandanna off. A breeze swept sweat-dampened strands of dark hair loose. *Ugh, gross!* She spit and scraped the tangled mess away.

The owner of the blood-stained blade laughed as he sliced her polyester pants. "Shame on you, distracted by those two fools."

Shae towered over him by two inches. "That was my favorite purple bandanna." She waved a hand out and a wide blast of a hefty gale tumbled him back. Shae swung her stained blade at him, severing his right arm.

She squinted and swung again before he could reach for a second weapon. The tip of her blade pierced his chest. His blood splattered everywhere as she wrenched the blade free. She stepped back, watching him fall into the dirt and the surrounding pool of blood.

Shae turned and clenched both hands around the handle of the sword, blade pointed at the ripple forming in front of her. But she eased back as Master Verties Crimshon emerged from the fading portal. He glanced up at the clear sky, rubbing his weathered hands through a grizzly beard. "I should have dressed more appropriately for this section." Then he rested his weary eyes on Shae. "But no matter. It is time to return to the Royale Hawse."

"I'm not done." She scooped up the tattered bandanna and turned to walk away. A heavy gale knocked her into the dirt.

"Today, you are." Long grayish bangs fell over his pale green eyes.

Shae grunted in protest. Her focus on staying alive in Battle Realm diverted her attention for two years. Refusing his extended hand, she rose and dusted off dirt from her legs.

Verties opened another portal into the third-floor hallway of the Royale Hawse, a Japanese-inspired palace. The Tatami floor buffered the sound of their footsteps. Shae removed blood-stained gloves and vest—handing them over to Verties, along with the soiled sword and bandanna.

"Take the weekend to rest. But be ready. The others are eager to hear about your excursion in Battle Realm." He held the items away from his outfit. "It's good to have you home."

She headed down the hallway and disappeared around a corner. Shae's shoulders sagged as she swayed into the privacy of the room. Each step toward the dark cherry oak armoire sent dull throbs from the soles of her feet to the top of her head. Her hands trembled as they curled around the shirt hem, grunting from the lack of strength to remove it. She almost stumbled to the floor while bending over to remove her pants and kicked them aside. Her arm banged against the doorframe upon entering the adjoining bathroom.

In the shower, each drop of water sent tingles to every nerve. Shae closed her eyes, savoring the heat and rejuvenating steam.

Finally, a hot shower. The only thing I've missed about this place.

A soft moan escaped her lips. *So not looking forward to all those intrusive questions on Monday. Battle Realm offers deadly opportunities if one isn't watchful, but I don't have to make small talk with my challengers. Just kill them quickly and move on.*

After a long moment, she flexed her hands open and closed. Raising her arms was no longer a chore. She found the rhythm in a usual shower ritual. While the water was still warm, her weight shifted from one foot to another, turning to let the water hit her backside. Another moan of pure satisfaction as the warmth of the water continued to soothe her. Once done, she exited the enclosed area. She shivered from an instant blast of cold air before drying off in quick movements.

After slipping into dark blue sweatpants and a thin shirt, she collapsed onto the bed, too exhausted to crawl under the single sheet and blanket for extra warmth. Rolling over, she stared at the pale gray swirls in the ceiling. A heavy sigh escaped as she turned onto her side, staring at the clock on the bedside table.

Shae let out a deep grunt, her fist pounding into a lumpy pillow as thoughts dwelled on Battle Realm. It was a dangerous place, filled with bloodshed. But it was also the only place where she felt truly alive. The rush of adrenaline that came with each victory was like nothing else in the world. It was also the only other place where she was safe from Gerard Jacquain.

Shae drifted off to sleep, cheek nuzzled against the pillow. Maybe she should take Verties' advice and rest for a few days. Allow some time to recover from the last battle. But the thought of spending even a moment away from the realm made her heart ache.

****

The next morning, Shae woke up feeling more tired than ever. The sun cast a warm glow that trickled through the small framed window. She sat up and stretched, feeling the knots in her back and shoulders unwind.

After slipping into tight-fitting jeans with no pockets and a solid purple long-sleeved shirt, she headed down to the dining hall on the first floor. Laughter and chatter from the other Deviants filled the room. The crackling fire filled the room with warmth and light.

She collected a tray containing a personalized meal and sat at a table between two other Deviants.

"Hey, Shae! How was Battle Realm?"

"It was fine," she replied, taking a sip of water, gazing across the table at Rozette. *My best friend. Even though I haven't been much of a friend lately.*

Rozette's coiffed bob framed her dark face as she looked hard at Shae. "You've been there for two years. You should really take a break. I could put in a recommendation to Lady Chastain on your behalf?"

Maybe Rozette is right. Maybe taking a hiatus from the Battle Realm is a good idea. But as she looked around the room at the other Deviants, she couldn't help but feel a pang of guilt. They were all passionate about the training and dedicated to their abilities. Could she really take a break while they continued to fight? "No. I have the weekend to rest. That's enough wasted time for me."

Shae finished breakfast: a plate of dry toast, stale cereal, and a bowl of watery oatmeal. The meal focused on nutrients rather than taste or aesthetic appeal. She carried the tray to the dispensing station, leaving the utensils and dishes in one bin, and the remaining trash in another bin. Then she set the tray on the top shelf, where a stack of used trays rested.

Back in the room, she sat in a rickety chair at the scratched old desk. Books and tomes rested in a stack in one corner. She opened a tome and removed a few sheets of paper used as a bookmark. The paper had almost illegible notes scribbled on it in familiar handwriting. The book left untouched was a history of Deviants—advanced Civilians that had mastered magic, such as raising or lowering their vibrational frequencies for open travel. Otherwise known as portals.

In her downtime, tomes laid open on the desk. *So what if I read them and write essays for fun. The other Deviants will never understand that.* Delving deep into the spell books to familiarize herself with any new undiscovered abilities, often became obsessive. Being one step ahead of Gerard Jacquain, if and when she ever engaged him face-to-fang, was the goal, determined to be prepared.

An intriguing spell caught her eye while flipping through some of the musty pages in the thick, leather-bound tome. The spell promised to grant the caster the ability to reveal the true nature of things. But she already knew Jacquain's true nature. *He's a very powerful vampire with a fetish for pleasure. Many Civilian women fell victim to his quest for ultimate pleasure. And Dorian's team had many brushes with the vamp.*

Shae's thoughts about Jacquain and Dorian, her fellow Deviant, were interrupted by a knock on the door. She closed the tome and rose from the chair to answer it. "Dorian?" *Well, that's creepy. Did he know I was just thinking about him?*

He leaned against the door frame, running a hand through his classic tapered hairstyle. "Lady Chastain requests your presence in the Throne Room. Mind if I escort you there?"

"Sure." Shae held the door open for him.

He entered and shut the door. "So…"

"Turn around or close your eyes. I need to change."

"Right, sorry." Dorian placed a hand over his ocean-blue eyes. "Better?"

"Yeah." Shae approached the armoire. She changed into an emerald-green jumpsuit with a fitted high waist matching sash and wide-leg pants.

"Other couples don't really hide from each other, Shae. You're gonna have to let me in some time."

Shae headed into the private small bathroom. "We're not 'other couples', Dorian."

"Tell me about it," he mumbled.

"I heard that!" she shouted as she combed her hair. Returning to the main part of the room, she saw him standing there with his hands at his sides.

"Can't you at least…try?" Dorian moved to the door, holding it open.

As Shae marched down the hallway, her footfalls created a soft echo that reverberated off the floors and walls. Dorian hustled, slowing down as soon as he caught up to her. They passed by other people in the hall, who moved aside, opening up an unobstructed path to the Throne Room.

Dorian's words rang out as they reached the imposing double doors of the Throne Room, desperation dripping from his voice. "After your meeting, maybe we could hang out at the market? Please."

Shae refused to look at him, gaze fixed firmly on the formidable entrance ahead. *I want to say yes, but...*

Dorian sighed. "Yeah, fine. I'll go find something else to do...again." He dared to lean forward and kiss her lips.

Shae stood there, stiffly.

"I really miss the early days, when it was you, me, Roz, and Keitan learning how to handle swords and magic in battle." He left her at the door.

****

Shae glanced around, taking in the formal décor and the Deviants scattered about the Throne Room. A few smiled and waved. She tilted her head once toward them in rehearsed, polite acknowledgment, then knelt on the blue carpet at the foot of the throne.

"Shae, thank you for joining me. I trust you slept well?" Lady Chastain was the picture of pure elegance in the shimmering, sky-blue gown. The woman sat on the large throne, a grim expression on an ageless yet ancient face accented by a pixie cut. Lady Chastain wore no crown, an aura the only indication of a royal status.

Shae smoothed out her jumpsuit and sat in a chair next to the woman. "It is I who should thank you, Lady

Chastain, for allowing me in your presence."

"Let me begin by welcoming you back home." Lady Chastain leaned forward. "Verties and I had a discussion over breakfast. We both agreed to revoke your visits to Battle Realm." She raised her hand to halt Shae's protest. "Young lady, you are becoming much too like him."

Shae narrowed her eyes at the insinuation that she was turning into another Gerard Jacquain.

"You're teetering on the verge of dark pleasure. And your excursion added fuel to the fire. That is not our intention. You were meant to learn to accept this life—not revel in it."

Shae grumbled as an uneasy feeling rolled through her.

"I know this will be difficult for you, but it is for the best. Unfortunately, your vacation will have to wait." Lady Chastain retrieved a document from the small table on the left side of the throne. "A strange request arrived this morning from Anisa. Her team went out on a surveillance mission two weeks ago. We'd lost contact with them until now. This request is in her writing, but it seems off. She asked only for you, but I want you to go with a team to retrieve them."

"But I'm not on the Retrieval Squad anymore. Not since I turned my badge in before in the excursion." Shae shifted in her chair, the thought of being part of a group again stirring a feeling of unfamiliar discomfort.

"My decision is final, Shae. Rozette will lead this time instead of Finley. I figured you'd be more at ease with her around. And she's promised me to finish this mission before Gerard gets wind of you being beyond the Royale Hawse."

Shae feigned interest at the armrest farthest from the revered leader to hide a shudder at the mention of the feared vampire. Not wanting to think about the monster obsessed with her, Shae changed the subject. "Is...Dorian joining us?"

Lady Chastain leaned back. "No, I have chosen Ruthie and Brodie. Their skills are more appropriate for this mission. Although, it would have been the perfect opportunity to become more comfortable by working alongside him."

Shae stood in a flash.

"Oh, come now, my child. You're not being fair to Dorian."

She glanced away and shifted her feet. Before she could dwell on how Dorian wanted to start a family with her, Rozette and the twins entered the room. "We are ready, M'Lady. Has Shae been briefed?"

"Let's just get this done." Shae snatched an offered jacket from Ruthie and shoved past the twins.

"Hey, that's not very nice," Ruthie huffed, adjusting the pink barrette in her blond hair.

"Shae." Brodie approached her at the door of the Throne Room, his shoulder-length curly locks bouncing. "You are forgetting this."

Shae turned to Brodie and snatched the old badge from his fingers. She pinned it to the collar of the long olive-colored jacket, in the same spot the others had theirs. They bowed to Lady Chastain and hustled down the hall into the main lobby area.

"This is a retrieval mission. We won't need any weapons. Magic only." Rozette spoke again.

Only the twins nodded in agreement. Shae stared straight ahead as they gathered in the elevator.

"Good, then we leave after dinner tonight." Rozette punched the button for the first floor. They dispersed into the dining hall. Shae collected her meal and retreated to a far corner. She paid no attention to the crowd.

****

The darkening of the late evening sky triggered lights attached to the buildings, illuminating the street. The group approached the toll booth guard at the end of the street. Their badges allowed them free passage onto the train.

Shae watched the sleek, black bullet train emerging from a portal as they walked down the platform. When it stopped in front of them, the doors slid open with a hiss. The group filed into the train and took their seats. Shae sat elsewhere. The bell chimed, and the doors closed. Before the train reached the tunnel, Rozette raised her hand. A dim glow formed, shifting the color of the portal the train swiftly rolled into.

"So…this is the great Shae that Jacquain is just so obsessed with?"

"Ruthie," Rozette barked at the girl.

Instead of hushing as Rozette ordered, Ruthie dared to approach Shae. Rozette reached out to stop her but only grabbed air.

"Shut up about him." Shae stood, diminishing any leverage Ruthie had. As the air around Ruthie's fist cackled and glowed, Shae's head tilted. "Sure you want to do that?"

The train announcer's voice blared the city's name from a speaker above. Rozette stood between them. "I said magic only as a defense. And definitely not against a teammate." The train doors were open for two minutes before Ruthie relented and sat back down with a sulk, mumbling something nasty about Shae. Rozette caught Shae's gaze. "Give them time to get used to how you are now."

Shae ignored Rozette's apologetic expression and returned to her seat.

The bell signaled that the sliding doors would close in thirty seconds. An older figure entered and moved to the bench seat opposite Shae. The rustling of clothes as the man sat down made Shae uneasy from the closeness. She noted his wet dripping hair and the puddle his shoes tracked from the door to his seat. The bell chimed again over a clap of thunder. Darkness surrounded the moving train as it left the city behind. The twins were quietly napping. Shae opted to ride in weary silence, keeping tabs on the figure until the train reached the group's destination.

After a while, Shae's eyelids felt heavy. But she refused to cede to their need with someone unfamiliar in the immediate area, even for a minute.

Shae felt a kick, and she jerked awake. The dark of the tunnel gave way to the morning of this city. The figure loomed over her. She gripped him by the throat.

"Whoa, lady!" the man choked out. "I was just seeing if you were okay. You were mumbling in your sleep." The other hand had formed into a fist but she hesitated, processing what the Civilian said.

"Shae!" Rozette's voice broke through the tense situation.

Not Ruthie—but just a concerned Civilian. Shae's grip unclenched, almost dropping him to the floor of the train car. He nearly tripped over the gap between the train car and the platform as he retreated. Rozette motioned for the others to follow her to the streets. Shae didn't even apologize. The twins dared not to comment.

"C'mon, let's just get to the diner. That's where Anisa said she'd be, but she doesn't have much time," Brodie said before leaving the train station entrance.

****

The walk past the first block was in silence. Midway past the second block, the noise from the park they had just passed caught Shae's attention. She recognized the park as a memory of two young Civilian's darting around the park in a game of chase. The group's footsteps grew feint, while Shae stared at the giant play fort—with slides, ladders, bridges, and an attached swing set. The vision of a slightly older man sitting on a nearby bench, as if waiting for the children, gave her pause. *Why do I feel like the three of us visited this park often? Why does this memory make me want to smile?*

"We don't have time for Civilian spectation." Rozette's concerned voice broke Shae's concentration.

Shae glanced again at the park, but the two kids running around and laughing were a boy with a buzz cut and a girl with a reddish-brown ponytail. She rejoined the others waiting at the corner crosswalk. When the hand signal permitted, the group crossed the street, passed one building, and reached the diner.

Chapter 2

Rozette pushed open the doors to the 50s diner. The metal hinges squealed like a hurt animal. Shae and the twins followed behind. Their casual outfits each had a small pendant pinned to their collars.

Shae scanned the dining area, locking eyes with a man buttering his English muffin. Everything around him faded to a dull gray. A dish shattering broke the mood. Shae tore her gaze away, struggling to decipher the moment.

"Looks like we're early." Ruthie chose an empty corner booth, large enough to accommodate the group. Brodie sat next to his sister and discussed the different flavored jellies in a bowl on the table. Rozette stared out the window, keeping watch.

"So, Keith...did you see the news last night?" Keith's coworker added one packet of sugar to his black coffee.

Shae tuned out the banter between Brodie and Ruthie as she felt drawn once more to Keith, the man from earlier. Shae noted the gray business suits both men wore.

"About Jacquain, right?" Keith set the English muffin down and nodded as he wiped the knife clean. "I barely caught it last night. Wasn't it something about a woman he was seen with having turned up dead?" Keith's partner mumbled an agreement.

A woman turned up dead? That is hardly news about the immortal. Shae bit the inside of her lip and ran a hand through her dark silky hair to keep from butting into the conversation. *I'm on the outside now, so I'll have to be careful.*

Brodie tossed an empty grape jelly packet onto the table, licking his fingers. "More Civilians are getting wise about Jacquain. How long before there's chatter about us?"

"Don't worry. We won't be here long enough for that." Rozette turned away from the window.

A waitress approached their table with menus in hand. The group went through the charade of ordering breakfast. Shae opened the menu, eyes drawn to a scribbled note taped inside. She slipped it into her pocket and closed the menu. "I'm going to the restroom."

Rozette nodded while scanning the menu. Brodie and Ruthie were too busy marveling at various jelly flavors.

****

A petite woman emerged from one of the two stalls.

"You're not Anisa," Shae asked, watching the woman turn the water on full blast. "Why are you wearing her uniform?"

The figure giggled.

"And why are there bloodstains on the collar?" Shae's fists clenched, charging up a hefty, magical punch.

"Shae Taizer? You're just as he described." The vampire scowled, speaking in a low voice, but still loud enough over the sound of the running water.

Shae raised her fist. "He?"

"I've been ordered to hide out here until you showed up. The Deviants going AWOL was his doing. To lure you here."

The magical charge fizzled out. "Jacquain." Shae latched onto the woman's arm. "What's he up to now? And who are you?"

"He let us feed from your friends. They were delicious." The figure licked her lips. "I wonder if you're just as tasty."

"I should throw your ass out into the sun for that." She tugged the woman's arm. "Now. One last time. Who are you?"

The vampire's wig fell off, revealing silver hair. "Doesn't matter who I am."

"Fine. But I'm here with my team. And it's our job to capture you."

The woman yanked free from Shae's grasp and ran out the door.

Shae gave chase, but Ruthie's appearance in the hallway—the division between the bathroom and dining areas—stopped the vampire from escaping into the men's room.

"Roz sent me to check up on you, but instead I get this." Ruthie clamped her hand around the vamp's throat and shoved her against the wall.

"That's not Anisa. Just bait to get me outside of the Royale Hawse," Shae hissed, snatching the vampire back from Ruthie's firm hold.

"If you kill me, you won't get your friends back," the vamp snickered.

"They're already dead," Shae coldly replied. *Mostly because Jacquain probably got bored with them.*

Ruthie blinked at Shae. "How can you say that? If we have a chance to save them, we gotta take it!"

But Shae wrapped her arms around the vamp and portaled out to the back alley. The female vamp sizzled and burned like a marshmallow on a campfire.

"What the hell do you think you're doing?" Rozette rounded the side corner of the building, with the twins right behind.

"This mission was a bust." Shae stared down as the vamp became a bubbly, gooey blob before disappearing into a nearby drain.

"I guess it was too much to ask for you to work with a team. I had hopes for you, Shae." Rozette shook her head. "C'mon, back home we go for debriefing. We'll see how Lady Chastain wants this handled." She then looked pointedly at Shae. "I have no choice but to recommend teamwork training for you instead of a vacation."

They opened a portal back to the Royale Hawse in the privacy of the alley.

****

Rozette sighed. "Everything went smoothly until after we arrived at the diner. Anisa was a no show but—"

Shae heaved out a long, frustrated sigh. "It was a trap. Not sure how Jacquain knew I had returned from Battle Realm."

"I should have seen this coming." Lady Chastain stood. "I suspect he'd taken Anisa and her team to lure you out."

"Well, the vamp in the bathroom said she was waiting for me," Shae recalled.

"I see." Lady Chastain glanced at Rozette. "Is there

anything you would like to add?"

"We were planning to interrogate the vamp. Shae killed her in daylight in public, in full view of everyone."

"We were in the alley, and it was empty," Shae snapped back.

"That was after you used a portal to get there."

"Rozette is still in charge. Show her some respect." Lady Chastain moved to stand in front of Shae. "You are dismissed. But, Shae, my dear…"

"Thank you, M'Lady." Rozette bowed and left the room.

"Now. For the blatant disregard of safety, there must be consequences." Lady Chastain stood, hands planted firmly on her hips.

Shae braced herself for whatever Lady Chastain had in store.

"But first, I need to know why you did that."

"It would have been pointless to bring the vamp here as a prisoner. She said all she was going to say to me in the diner restroom."

"What exactly did she say?" Lady Chastain moved to sit back on the large throne.

"She was wearing Anisa's jacket, and it had blood on the collar. The vamp boasted that Anisa and her team were tasty."

"And you believed your fellow Deviants were as good as dead?"

Shae nodded.

"Well, nothing can be done about any of this now." Lady Chastain pursed her lips and stared into the distance. "Shae, you are to attend two weeks of Teamwork Training. Also, you will be grounded. That means you must stay within the confines of your room, no wandering the Hawse, and your meals will be delivered. Any visitors must have clearance. You will be scheduled for all of Master Crimshon's classes, not just the one he requested you to join on Monday."

Shae dared not groan out loud. Being grounded like a child was embarrassing and frustrating. But she had to accept Lady Chastain's decision or risk making her punishment worse.

"After the two weeks are up, we shall hold an evaluation to see if you need an extension." Lady Chastain gave Shae a stern look before standing again. "Now go on! Get yourself cleaned up before dinner." She motioned to the door, an unspoken dismissal in the gesture.

"Yes, M'Lady." Shae bowed and hustled from the Throne Room.

As Shae stomped down the hallway, thoughts swirled in her mind. *Why had Jacquain gone to such lengths to lure me out? And where was Anisa's body? Surely, if she had been killed, there would be some evidence.*

Shae brushed aside these swirling thoughts and flopped down on the bed, feeling the soft sheets caressing her skin. *Two weeks of Teamwork Training...ugh!* She had been through worse.

Three sharp knocks on her door shattered her thoughts. "Come in!"

The door opened, and in walked Lady Chastain.

Shae sat up. "M'Lady, I thought you had dismissed me."

"I did," Lady Chastain said, taking a seat on the bed.

Shae sat up straighter, confused by Lady Chastain's unexpected visit. "Is there something else you need, M'Lady?"

Lady Chastain put a hand on Shae's arm, looking at her with genuine concern. "I just wanted to make sure you were okay. This punishment was necessary, but I don't want you to feel isolated."

Shae was surprised by the sudden display of concern. "Thank you. I'm fine, just a bit frustrated."

"I understand that, dear. But please know that we're all here to support you, even when it doesn't seem like it." Lady Chastain gave Shae's arm a comforting squeeze before standing up. "I'll leave you to your thoughts. Do take care of yourself, Shae." Lady Chastain walked toward the door, giving one last glance back at her before leaving the room and shutting the door.

Shae stared at the closed door for a few moments before heading for the bathroom to use the facilities. Back in the main part of the room, she exchanged the fancier clothes for something more casual to lounge in. The pajamas may have seemed thin, but the material kept her warm. After selecting a book off the nightstand and settling into bed, she flipped to the bookmarked page. The words blurred as thoughts wandered to the mission events. *Jacquain must be pleased with himself, even if he didn't get me this time.*

She shook those intrusive thoughts away and tried to focus on the words, but failed as the memory of the playground flooded her mind. The lingering smell of the wet grass, the laughter of the redheaded boy giving chase as they ran around. *But that's just impossible. I would never play and have fun like that.* She forced her mind to focus on the words in the book.

****

A tray of unflavored chicken cutlets, boiled potatoes, pickled cabbage, a small loaf of bread with a pat of butter, and bottled water were delivered to her room at dinner time. The combined smell of the food was acrid and sharp. *At least it doesn't look as bad as it smells.* Shae ate the meager meal; an experience made more uncomfortable by the lack of dining furniture.

A soft rap on the door, followed by a low voice, interrupted. "Shae? It's me, Roz. Can I come in?"

She stared at the door. "You better have a good reason for coming to my room."

"You're not still mad at me, are you?" Rozette pleaded. "C'mon, Shae."

"Okay, okay…come in."

"Thanks." Rozette glanced around the room, stopping her gaze on the pile of books on the floor. "What's with all the books?" She sat on the bed.

"What else am I to do here? Stare at the wall?" Shae threw a blanket over the pile of books and papers. Then she sat back down to eat.

"Sorry. And I'm sorry for interrupting dinner. But I really wanted to hang out with you. At least that is still allowed."

"Yeah, as part of my teamwork training." Shae shoved a forkful of unflavored chicken cutlets into her mouth, washing it down with a big gulp of water.

"I can understand why you'd want to keep your distance from the twins. But why are you pushing me, Dorian, and Keitan away?"

Shae was silent for a long time. That part of her mind seemed blocked. Slowly, she set the fork down and turned to face Rozette. "I can only explain why I stopped at the park on the way to the diner during the mission."

"Okay."

"There was...Shae paused. "I've been there before."

"For another mission?"

"As a kid. Playing with another kid." Her brow furrowed. "I was laughing."

"Oh." Rozette tapped her chin with a finger. "Well, we do let the younger Deviants visit different realms. Maybe that was it."

"It...felt like more than just a visit." She squirmed as she attempted to confide to her best friend.

"Let's talk about something else," Rozette offered.

She stared at the plate of half-eaten chicken. "Can you just leave me alone now?"

The bed squeaked as Rozette stood up.

Once the door opened and closed, Shae glanced at it and rubbed her eyes. *I know you're my best friend, Roz. But I'm doing this alone.*

She stood up, crossed the short distance, and opened the door. It was too busy in the halls at this hour to safely leave the room undetected. Shae closed the door and turned in early. Perhaps she would get a little more sleep than the previous night.

****

Most of the Royale Hawse residents spent Sunday mornings in the market or hosting impromptu tournaments. *Now I can take advantage of the library.* Shae snuck into the library in the front half of the second floor of the Royale Hawse. Out of the eight laptop stations set up in the middle section, only one was being used. *Tera, studying as hard as I do.* She sat at the station on the opposite end.

She booted up the laptop and typed in a password. Then simply sat staring at the internet home page. *All I have so far is that park memory. But I can't just search for a redheaded boy. He won't even be a boy now. And the guy we were with, he'll be older too.* Frustrated, she leaned back and ran a hand over her face.

"Try your name and the name of the city the park is in."

She sat upright and glanced around. The girl at the other computer was scribbling something in a notebook before shutting down the laptop and running off. Besides, the voice in her head sounded more like a male voice. There wasn't anyone else near Shae to offer such a suggestion. And sure, the Deviants had abilities, but none had shown any telepathic abilities.

She stared at the computer monitor. *Am I going crazy now? A side effect of spending too long in Battle Realm?* A finger hovered over the power button of the computer. *Is it exhaustion from too many late nights playing Battle Realm?* A gut-twisting sliver of fear settled in her soul. *Whoever it was, they gave an excellent suggestion.*

In the search bar, Shae typed in 'Jupiter'—the name of the town where the park was located and clicked Enter.

Page after page of references to Jupiter, the planet, or blue-colored things popped up, but nothing that fit what she needed. An hour later, she was five pages deep into one article about ancient gods. *I have to get back to my room before someone finds out I'm missing.* She let out a frustrated sigh with the pointer finger touching the power button.

"*Just one more page, Shae.*"

Again, she paused, looking around. Still just herself in this area of the library. "Okay." She sighed, not bothering to question the mysterious voice this time.

From the top of the sixth search page was a linked headline about an elementary school play. The name of the school was Jupiter Academy, or as the Civilians knew it, Pio Pico. Shae recognized her younger self in the large colored picture under the article headline. "Jupiter Academy fifth-graders perform a universal comedy to a jam-packed audience." *I was in a play? With others?*

She recognized the male figure standing in the picture. "That's him." A name in the caption under the picture caught her attention. "Nickolas Azura?" She leaned back from the screen, scratching the side of her head. "Funny how Azura sounds like azure. Another link to Jupiter. Maybe more like weird, not funny."

She continued reading another name. "Key...Kiran Varron?"

Another memory was unlocked—flashes of a young girl in a grape costume, performing opposite a boy with fiery red hair. The girl messed up a line and the audience laughed. The image faded as her younger self struggled to continue.

"Woah." Her fingertips touched the computer screen. "So...the boy is Kiran? And the man is Nick?" *This is too much.* She closed the window. "But why do I get the feeling Master Crimshon knows about this?"

She went back to the search engine, pairing her name with Kiran's. No real hits.

Then again but with Nick's name instead of Kiran's. The link at the bottom of the first page was an old wedding announcement for him and a woman named Diane Ashby. After clicking the link, the date of the wedding ceremony was above the picture. "1997. Two years after I became friends with Rozette, Keitan, and Dorian. And one year before I went through the Arrangement Ceremony with Dorian."

That ceremony was a Deviant tradition. When Deviants proved they could handle Battle Realm, they got matched up with another Deviant. *Roz and Keitan's personalities complemented each other. But me and Dorian—we don't mesh well at all.*

Shae stared at the image of Nick. *It's just an image, but when I stare at Nick—his eyes—I feel this pull toward him. Why?* Nick, in a full tuxedo, posed next to a woman with a wolf-styled haircut dressed in a glittering blue dress. *Blue. Azure. Azura. There's that connection again.* She leaned into her hands. *This is too much.*

Images of her younger self standing next to Nick in a backyard, surrounded by kids in party hats, a table of presents next to him as they watched a magician. The colors of the Happy Birthday lights from a banner strung across two poles blinked on and off. Shae's long dark hair, olive-tinted skin, and lithe figure fit perfectly with Nick's sandy brown hair, peach skin, and tall figure.

Dark eyes darted between Nick's bright gaze and the fake magic tricks being performed by a man in a tacky suit. She stared at the group of entranced kids while tugging at her earlobe.

However, there was no accompanying sound in this

memory as Nick's gaze became concerned while his lips moved.

"I bet it's those alluring chocolate eyes never failing to make women melt."

Wait, what?

"Shae, there you are."

The chair fell backward, making a loud snap as it hit the floor. She flinched, then smashed the 'X' button to close the internet window. "How'd you know I was here, Dorian?"

The worry in his eyes grew more pronounced the closer he got. "I've been looking for you."

"I was just passing time here." She adjusted her fallen chair.

He crossed his arms. "You're supposed to be in your room, remember? If Master Crimshon finds out—"

"He's going to have more to worry about than me skipping out on my punishment." She logged out of the system.

"What?"

Shae took his hand, leading him out of the library. "Never mind. I should head back."

****

Shae entered the classroom earlier than the others that Monday morning. The scent of chalk and home-brewed coffee invaded her senses. Verties stood at the board, writing a few last-minute class topics for the hour. Each of them wore their Deviant uniform.

"Ah, good, you're here."

"Yeah," Shae grumbled and set her satchel on the student desk closest to his teacher's desk.

Verties frowned. "Are you feeling all right?"

Shae shook her head and long strands of hair flailed. "I did some research in the library yesterday. Had a very disturbing session while on the laptop."

"So, you weren't in your room?" He motioned with his hand. "Please, continue."

"The mission to Jupiter was a failure, but then it wasn't." Shae watched him sit at his desk, but she remained standing. "There was a park we passed on the way to the diner…that sparked a memory of me being there. In that recollection, I was playing with a boy, while a man watched over us."

Verties pulled open a desk drawer. "Perhaps this conversation should be held later. Class will begin soon."

She stomped her foot, hard. "No. We're having this now. Because I found out their names. Kiran Varron and Nickolas Azura. Why are they important to me, Master Crimshon?"

Verties' eyes widened, but he regained his composure, "Straight to the point." He sighed, shut the drawer, and opened the middle one. "I had hoped to have this conversation later, but here we are." He pulled out a square wooden box and set it on his desk with a thunk. "This box contains the answers to your questions, Shae. I suggest you read what's in it after class."

Shae reached out and ran her fingers over the box. "I need a key?"

Verties retrieved a key from his chest pocket. "This enchanted key in your hand is the only way to open the box. It was Lady Chastain's way to keep the contents safe until you were ready for it."

The black onyx key felt warm and smooth. The

teeth of the key were normal, but the other end had a large blue jewel. *No, not blue. Azure.*

Sounds of students approaching filled the near-silent air of the classroom.

Shae stuffed the key and box in her satchel before moving to an assigned seat.

Having graduated from this class almost ten years ago, she spent the next hour half paying attention to Verties' lesson. She couldn't shake the memories of Kiran and Nick. Scribbling their names and the details of the memories in her notebook wasn't helping.

Chapter 3

At the end of class, some of the students approached Shae as she packed items into her satchel.

She paused, glancing at them. "Can I help you?"

One student, a tall, lanky boy with thick-framed glasses, stepped forward. "Yeah, we were just wondering, what was it like living in Battle Realm for two years?"

She scanned the group, stalling for an answer they would be satisfied with. She didn't want to give away too much. "It was challenging," she said, "but I learned a lot about survival and fighting."

Verties broke up the little pow-wow. "Shae. I'd like a word with you."

"Uh-oh." A freckle-faced girl giggled, and the group dispersed.

Shae hoisted the satchel over her shoulder and returned to his desk. "Yes, Master Crimshon."

"I noticed you weren't paying attention during class. I'll let it slide, but try to be fully present next time."

"I will."

"As for the box, take your time with its contents. Some things may be difficult to process."

Unleashing a pent-up sigh, she stepped out of the classroom, away from prying eyes and gossiping tongues. With quickened steps, she rushed down the hall and turned the knob to her room with a shaking hand.

After throwing the satchel onto the bed, she paced with nervous, jerky movements. The key was clutched against her chest as she stared at the satchel as if the box inside was a hidden snake. Taking a deep breath, she retrieved the box. The key felt heavy when inserted into the hole,

The jewel glowed, allowing her to turn the key. With a soft click, the box unlocked. Inside was a note in Lady Chastain's elegant writing on a stack of various folded papers and pictures. Her eyes scanned the note first, before fully reading it:

"My dear Shae,

if you are reading this, then it is time for you to learn the truth. The truth about your past, your family, and most importantly, your destiny. I have kept this information hidden, especially since you showed the promise of a different path after returning to us. You buried your memories of the Civilian life you grew up in and embraced your Deviant nature. But with the memories returning to you, it is clear that the time has come. I urge you to read the information within this box with great care and caution. Some of it may be difficult to accept, but I assure you that it is necessary for you to understand who you truly are. Trust in yourself, my dear. And remember, you are not alone in this.

Always,

Lady Chastain."

She read over those words twice before a baby picture caught her eye. 'Baby Shae' was written on the top white border of the picture. *Look at those pudgy cheeks and toothless grin. If it weren't for the caption, I would have mistaken this as someone else.* She set it aside and picked up the next picture. Keitan, Dorian, and Rozette posed with fierce expressions as each held their chosen weapon. The pre-teen Shae in that picture had sadness and uncertainty in her eyes. "Only thing I remember about that day was feeling sad about something. I'm guessing now that it was Kiran and Nick I was missing." The next item wasn't a picture, but frantic scribbles in Verties' writing.

Avia had another vision that triggered early labor. The following is what she shared after giving birth to our daughter—a beautiful little bundle we named Shae Taizer.

"Wait…what?" She wasn't sure she'd read that correctly, but a second skim of it was clearer. "Avia and Verties are my parents?" She never questioned it before, always being more focused on adhering to the Deviant ways. A teardrop blotted the corner of the paper. "I'm NOT crying." She wiped her eyes before closing them and using meditative training to recenter the conflicting emotions. Then she continued reading.

A succession of nickels fell onto a solid blue surface surrounded by darkness. Three, fourteen, eleven, nine.

Followed by flashes of orchids in a field.

Then came an image of a sterilized hospital room with a bassinet filled with wind-up chomping teeth.

Finally, blue food coloring squirted out of a tube, drawing out multiple sapphire gems. What we found out was that the bassinet represented our daughter. And the chattering teeth were a warning that we deciphered to be Gerard Jacquain. The nickels and the numbers spelled out Nick, but scrambled. The blue food coloring and the drawings were clues to where we would find Nick—the Civilian town, Jupiter.

As a result, we heeded the vision and placed our daughter in the care of Mr. and Mrs. Zenovia, who had been on the waiting list for three years to adopt a child. They lived across the street from Nickolas Azura.

But the shocking part was the orchids from the vision being connected to fertility.

The way the vision unfolded left us with no doubt that our daughter is meant to develop a deep bond with Nickolas Azura in hopes that she will be strong enough to resist when Gerard attempts to claim her as his ally in his thirst for pleasure.

Shae's jaw fell open as she stared at the paper. "Holy shit."

****

A knock at the door snapped her from sitting there, staring at the box and its contents.

"You in there, Shae?" Keitan's muffled voice spoke.

"Uh…yeah, just a second." She rushed to stuff all the papers and pictures back into the box, locked it and hid the key in the bottom desk drawer. There wasn't enough room in any of the desk drawers to hide the box. Shae stood between the desk chair and the bed, wildly glancing around. The armoire caught her attention. Opening it, she crammed the box on the bottom shelf under a pile of clothes.

Another knock and this time it was Dorian. "We're coming in! You better be decent!"

"Dorian!" She heard Rozette' scolding him.

Shae answered the door just as Rozette playfully swatted Dorian as part of the 'scolding'. "Hey."

Dorian entered the room first, to get away from Rozette's teasing anger. Keitan shut the door for them.

"What's going on?" Shae uneasily glanced at them.

"We're taking you to lunch in the courtyard," Keitan announced.

Lunchtime already? I've been sitting at my desk zoned out for that long?

Rozette clarified, "Master Crimshon let us be the one to inform you that your time has been served!"

I know why he lifted my sentence. Shae's expression remained neutral.

Keitan had moved over to her stack of tomes. "Were you doing extra credit work again, Shae?"

She moved over and shut the tome he tried to open. "No. Just some personal reading."

Dorian dared to hug her from the side, but she squirmed away. He pouted, so Shae allowed their fingers to intertwine. "Well? Let's get going!"

They stepped inside the dining hall, full of warmth and the smell of freshly cooked meals. At the counter, Shae asked for lids to cover their trays so their food would stay warm on the walk to the courtyard.

The air was thick with the sweet scent of rose and cherry of the blooms from a large tree, almost saccharine in the crisp autumn afternoon. A few birds fluttered in and out of the branches, chirping cheerfully.

The stone blocks provided a flat ledge as the perfect spot for them to use as a low table.

Keitan snuggled up to Rozette, who cuddled into his side. Dorian shifted awkwardly next to them, glancing at Shae before he turned his attention to his tuna sandwich. Shae avoided eye contact and watched a nearby fountain, its waters streaming down from ridged tiers and spilling over into small pools.

Shae lifted the lid off her tray, revealing a small salad neatly arranged. Peering in closer, she could make out pieces of cucumber, tomato, and radish, all showing off different hues of the rainbow. She speared a piece of lettuce with a fork.

Keitan finished another outlandish tale with dramatic flare. "And then, just as I was about to give up hope, a group of friendly dragons swooped down and offered to help me find the lost treasure!"

"You never cease to entertain me, Keitan," Rozette said with a smile.

"Yeah. Too bad we deal with vampires, not dragons." Dorian chuckled.

But Shae's mind was preoccupied with the prophecy as well as some of the memories that had resurfaced. *I wish I could tell them, especially Dorian. But they wouldn't believe me if I told them I was raised as a Civilian.* Shae was startled when Dorian reached across the stone block and took her hand. While Rozette and Keitan continued their lively discussion, she felt a wave of conflicting emotions: surprise, gratitude, fear, and hope all vying for attention at once. A voice demanded her to pull away.

"Is everything okay?" Dorian asked, his voice soft and sincere.

Shae hesitated before giving him a weak smile. "Yeah, just thinking about some stuff."

Dorian squeezed her hand, concern still evident in his eyes. "You know you can talk to us about anything, right?"

"I know," Shae replied, gaze dropping to the large-sized salad again.

Keitan interrupted, slurping up a noodle. "So, are you going to share what you've been reading, or what?"

Shae swallowed a mouthful of salad, hesitating for a moment before deciding to share. "It's just some old spell books I found in the library. Nothing too exciting."

Rozette raised an eyebrow. "Just some old spell books? You're already a Rank 1. You can't advance any higher than that."

Shae shrugged. "Yeah, I guess."

Dorian squeezed her hand again. "You should be next in line to lead the DeviMagi's, not me. I'm only Rank 2."

"Can't help that I love swingin' my sword around."

"Who knew the quiet Shae can crack such great jokes!" Keitan set his soup down.

"Not that funny." Rolling her eyes, she couldn't help but crack a smile.

As their lunch progressed, a sense of unease crept up on Shae. The birds had stopped chirping and the cherry blossom seemed to be wilting. A cold breeze swept through, sending shivers down her spine, leaving the courtyard in an eerie silence.

"What was that?" Rozette's voice trembled as her gaze darted around the area.

"It's too quiet now." Keitan stood in a defensive stance.

Shae glanced at the others. *Did they see the tree wilting too?*

"You shouldn't be here, Shae. He's not the one for you."

When the voice mentioned 'he', Shae had been staring at Dorian. She also remembered this same voice speaking in the library over the weekend. She pulled away from Dorian.

"Shae, what's wrong?" Dorian stood as well.

"You know what must be done."

"I have to go," she mumbled while turning to make her way back inside.

"Shae, wait!" Keitan called, but she didn't stop.

The voice held a resonating power she couldn't resist. She almost ran to her room.

The voice was dark and alluring, drawing her in like a moth to a flame. *The same erotic tone as Gerard's. I don't understand. If it was him, how is he able to reach me here?* Shae worried that Lady Chastain's protection spell was fading.

She closed the door and locked it. Inhaling a deep breath, she tried to calm her racing heart.

"No way it's Jacquain." She entered the bathroom and turned the tub faucet toward hot. *All I need right now is a relaxing bath and some meditation.*

****

An hour later, she redressed in a short-sleeved top that exposed the scars on her arms—remnants of Battle Realm. There were recent scars and old ones serving as a reminder. *I know I'm not infallible, even if I pretend to be invincible.* Donning the jeans previously worn, she cleared a spot in a corner of her room for meditation.

She closed her eyes and focused on blocking the sounds beyond the bedroom door. The rustle of feet against the tatami mats in the hallway, the hum of electricity, the hiss of her breath escaping from her lips in controlled intervals. But she could not focus completely on her breathing.

"You know fulfilling the prophecy is your best chance against Gerard."

Ignoring the deep voice, she delved deeper into the meditation, trying to reach her core of inner peace.

Another memory of Kiran unlocked—two young children laying on a patch of a freshly mowed lawn, watching the stars. Crickets chirp from their hidden homes. She rolled over on the blanket that was recently washed in lavender detergent and faced him. Kiran pointed out different constellations while she leaned against him, head on his chest. They were best friends living such a simple, oblivious life.

Nick emerged from the back door of a two-story house. A place where she spent more time than her own home across the street.

As she opened her eyes, the memory of Kiran and their friendship lingered in her mind. But the voice from before had only grown louder, more insistent.

"The prophecy will come to pass, whether or not you like it. It's only a matter of time."

She gritted her teeth, trying to block out the voice. But it was no use. The moment was ruined. She couldn't clear her mind now. Not with the voice's intrusion.

Though half of the punishment was nullified, she was still banned from Battle Realm. Letting out a long, defeated breath, her eyes shifted to the left. The treasured sword mounted on hooks against the wall gleamed softly in the light. Clenching her fists tightly during a moment of solace—at least she could still practice with it.

She snatched it off the wall and retrieved the scabbard between the mattresses of the bed. She sheathed the weapon and hustled to the open training area behind the Royale Hawse.

Several practice matches were already underway on the field as she approached. She joined the small row of those waiting their turn. The field may have been large, but there were only a few battle squares to have a match against someone.

Thoughts of Kiran fluttered within her mind. *Does he still think of me?*

"Next!" a loud female voice boomed.

A wounded challenger hobbled past and whispered, "She's too good."

Yeah, we'll see. Shae clutched her scabbard and took position on the challenger side, across from the unfamiliar opponent. The woman was tall, with muscular arms covered in tattoos.

"Ready when you are," the woman said, twirling her sword.

The challenger took the first swing, and she parried it easily. But something was off. The woman's movements seemed too practiced, too calculated. She wasn't fighting with reckless abandon like most of the other fighters did here. It was as if the woman was testing her.

As they continued to exchange blows, the memory of Kiran resurfaced. *Would he be excited seeing me fight like in all the sword-fighting movies we used to watch every week?* Shae faltered a bit as the new memory of Kiran zapped her concentration. A pang of sadness bubbled, but she pushed it aside and focused on the opponent.

The woman lunged forward with a swift strike.

Shae shifted her stance, evading the attack meant to

knock her down, and kicked the woman's stomach. Her opponent stumbled back but quickly regained her balance. *We're both testing each other.*

"What's the matter?" she taunted. "Is that all you've got?"

The woman's eyes narrowed and then launched herself at Shae with intense speed and strength. There was barely any time to react as the woman's sword came down on hers with a loud clang. The force of the blow traveled up her arm and shoulder.

Now this skirmish mirrored her time in Battle Realm. Shae's excitement grew as she shifted to a more threatening stance—ready to kill.

The woman's movements became more aggressive as well. They continued to exchange blows, neither one backing down. Sweat dripped down Shae's forehead and her arms burned with exhaustion. *I'll win, no matter what.*

They continued to fight; the surrounding air charged with the intensity of their battle. Shae could see surprise in the woman's eyes as she landed a clean hit, knocking the sword out of the woman's hand. In that moment of victory, a surge of power soared through Shae, like she was capable of anything. She walked up to the woman, the tip of the blade pressing against her throat, not quite enough to draw blood.

Shae recognized the warning cackling sound and stepped back from the woman just as a wave of energy zipped between them.

"That is enough, Shae." Verties angry tone reverberated through the room, causing everyone to stop what they were doing.

She noticed all eyes were on her as she turned to

Verties, her chest heaving from the exertion of the fight.

Verties looked at her with a mixture of disapproval and concern. "No killing in the training area. This isn't Battle Realm."

She looked at the woman she'd been fighting, seeing the fear in her eyes. The buildup of her primal rage faded. Shae dropped her sword and fell to her knees. "I'm sorry," she whispered.

Verties walked over and extended a hand to help her up.

She accepted it, feeling the weight of her actions heavy on her heart.

The woman stood up and bowed. "You are skilled with a blade, but the heat of battle easily consumes you."

Shae huffed and stormed off the training field.

Keitan approached her in the hallway of the living quarters. "Hey, I saw what happened out there. Pretty scary."

"Yeah, sorry about that," she said, unable to look him in the eye.

"It's fine," he said, smiling. "I'm just glad you're okay."

She shrugged but was grateful for Keitan's understanding.

"There are a few hours before dinner. Feel like joining me and Roz in the market?"

She thought for a moment. "Sure."

Keitan threw his arm around the back of her neck, resting on her shoulders as they walked to the market. "And don't worry about things. This is just like before, just friends hanging out at the market. Only difference

is we're just older and taller now."
      She couldn't resist a small smile.

Chapter 4

The afternoon spent roaming the market area outside of the Royale Hawse had been one of Keitan's better ideas. They moved through the bustling streets, looking at stalls selling fabrics, spices, trinkets, and souvenirs alike. No one had kept track of time until Keitan mumbled something about the sky.

The group stopped, mesmerized by the heavenly canvas. The vibrant reds and oranges reflected off the windows and walls of the Royale Hawse.

"We best get back to the dining hall." Rozette led the group back to the front steps of the Royale Hawse. On the way to the hall, Dorian met up with them.

Rozette and Keitan walked into the large room together, hand in hand. Shae and Dorian entered the room behind them also holding hands. The room was bustling with Deviants finding their seats or leaving the hall. A few Deviants entered the hall, absently bumping into the two couples.

Shae struggled to ignore a few stares from the others near them. Some of them had been in the training fields and seen her aggressiveness, while others had only heard of the situation.

"Don't let them bother you, Shae," Rozette whispered.

Shae turned to Rozette, trying to smile. "Thanks, Roz."

The sound of laughter and clinking glasses disrupted the dining hall, usually a place of peace and respite from the daily hustle and bustle of the city. As everyone settled down to their meal, deep in conversation and the pleasant anticipation of a delicious meal, the door opened and a group of rowdy Deviants came stumbling in.

Lestor, a tall man with a bushy beard, led the motley crew. Each of their Deviant uniforms held remnants of their boisterous personality—bright colors flared at the collars and sleeves. Despite the differences in their appearances, they all carried an unmistakable air of mischief, their laughter echoing off the walls as they walked in.

The room fell silent as Lestor's crew made their way to the section of the table where Shae and her friends sat.

Lestor sneered at her. "Well, well, well, what do we have here? The little princess finally decided to join us for dinner?"

She gritted her teeth, anger boiling within.

"Back off, Les," Dorian intervened.

Lestor let out a snort. "Or what, pretty boy? You gonna protect your little wifey here?" He gestured toward Shae. "Why don't you let a real man handle her?"

She felt the blood rush to her face, her fists clenching underneath the table. She wanted to stand up and give Lestor a piece of her mind, but didn't want to cause another ruckus so soon. Yet, the primal rage within her rumbled.

Rozette reached out and grabbed Shae's hand, giving it a reassuring squeeze. "Ignore them. He's still mad you volunteered for the excursion."

"Yeah, well…I was top pick until she submitted her name." Lestor fumed while his group made crude gestures toward her and Dorian.

With a swift movement, she stood and faced off against Lestor. Her lips curled into a snarl, her voice dangerously low as she commanded, "Tell your cronies to shut up."

Lestor scoffed. "My group is right. You should have been paired with me and not wussy little Dorian here. I would be past the puppy love stage with you already."

"Dorian handles me better than you ever could."

He chuckled. "Yeah, sure. I've seen you—always holding hands. Hell, Roz and Keitan act more like a real married couple than you both."

Her hand shot out, clenching Lestor's throat.

"Make him suffer for that comment."

What? No.

"Yes! Crush him."

No!

But still, her fingers continued squeezing Lestor's windpipe.

Lestor gasped and tried to pry her hand off, his eyes bulging in fear. His group stepped forward, but Keitan and Rozette stood up, their intention to protect Shae clear.

"Shae, stop it!" Dorian said, his tone firm but soft. "You don't want to do this."

Her rage was too strong and growing uncontrollable. Adrenaline pumped through her veins. Her grip tightened further, feeling Lestor's struggles weakening. His group tried to pry her off him, but Shae pushed them back with an invisible force.

One of the girls from his group then charged at Dorian, her fist connecting with his face. That distracted Shae enough for her to release Lestor.

The fist fight broke out, escalating by the second. The surrounding Deviants formed a ring around them.

Shae and Lestor seemed equally matched. Punch for punch, kick for kick. Each landed heated blows enough to spill blood.

Keitan and Rozette fought off the rest of the group with grace and precision, but it was clear they were in defensive mode.

Dorian focused on getting Shae and Lestor to stop. But the two were locked in a dangerous dance, each trying to outdo the other with their strength and aggression. Dorian saw an opening and he lunged forward, separating the two fighters. Shae stumbled back, her breathing heavy and labored. Lestor collapsed to the ground, coughing and gasping for air.

The room fell into an icy silence, punctured only by the heavy breaths of terror and ravaged sobs. Her knuckles were covered in purple bruises, her hair a wild and tangled mess. Everywhere she looked, Shae saw ruined food and drinks scattered around the floor like pieces of broken promises. The fear and awe radiating from the group made her body tremble with discomfort.

Lestor stumbled out of the dining hall, flanked by his group as they escorted him away. His face was drained of all color beneath his numerous bruises. When Lestor finally disappeared from sight, everyone's eyes settled on Shae, bearing down with a paralyzing mixture of fear and admiration.

Dorian stepped forward and placed his warm hand

on her shoulder. "Come on, let me take you to the infirmary."

She cringed in pain at his touch before reluctantly following Dorian out of the hall. As they passed Verties in the doorway, a deep sadness settled over his weathered face, which heightened her humiliation.

In the infirmary, the healer took one look at Shae's battered knuckles and swollen cheek before immediately tending to them. Then the healer worked gently on Dorian's black eye before helping them both to their feet.

"Well, you certainly have been a ball of excitement since you returned from Battle Realm," Dorian said once they were alone. "What happened to you? What did it do to you?"

Shae stared at the cold, sterile floor. "Not here, Dorian." She slid off the infirmary cot. "Let's talk in my room."

****

Much like when she confronted Verties, Shae opted to remain standing while Dorian sat on the comfier mattress.

"Okay. Let's talk." Dorian echoed her earlier statement.

But Shae paced the room. She couldn't bring herself to sit down and be comfortable in the face of what she had to say to Dorian. Every step felt heavy, as though dragging a weight behind her.

"I don't even know where to start." Shae's voice shook.

Dorian's expression was serious. "I know. And I'm sorry if I've made you feel uncomfortable in any way. That was never my intention."

"It's not that," Shae said, resuming her pacing. "It's just…"

Dorian stood up. "Shae. I care about you."

Shae paused and faced him. She could see the sincerity on his face, and for a moment, everything else faded away. The voice in her mind was eerily silent.

"You do?" she asked in a quiet tone.

His hand felt warm against hers, and for a moment, all Shae could do was savor the warmth. "Of course I care about you. And not just because of the Arrangement. But maybe…I could love you the way you need to be loved—if only you'd allow me to prove that to you."

Her heart skipped a beat at his words. *Should I dare let my guard down for him?* But another part of her was determined to remain cautious, still unwilling to let anyone in. *I want to…* She closed the distance between them, her lips finding his in a soft caress.

The warmth of his body threatened to undo her self-control, pushing away any rational thought that remained in her mind. Their kiss deepened as she completely melted into him.

"You insolent little vixen!"

The anger of the voice struck the silence in her mind. She flinched in fear, turning away to feign interest in a book on the desk.

"It's okay if you're not ready," he said, his tone gentle. "We can take things slow. I just know that being with you is what I want. I hope it's what you want, too."

"I know you want us to have a child together." *If this was any other situation, Dorian and I could make this work. Who knew kissing him was so amazing!*

"Yeah, but that can wait. I would want time with just you and me."

She bit the inside of her cheek to keep from breaking down. "I need to tell you something." Shae mustered the courage to look him in the eye.

"Okay, what is it?" Dorian held her hand again.

She pulled away and opened the armoire. Then she retrieved the box and the key.

"It's where I have to go." She sat down on the bed.

Dorian furrowed his brows in confusion. "What do you mean? Where do you have to go?"

She unlocked the box and poured the contents onto the mattress behind her.

"What is all this?" He sat down and fumbled through the pictures.

She handed him the prophecy Verties had written down. "I'm supposed to be with another. And the bond we would create is enough for me to face Gerard—so that his plans to corrupt me would fail."

Dorian's expression shifted as he read the words on the paper. "This is serious," he said, looking up at her. "You have to go through with this?"

"I don't know." Shae handed him the newspaper clipping. "After I was brought back here, he wound up marrying another woman. How am I supposed to fulfill this prophecy if he's married?" Distress enveloped her entire being.

"Maybe he's not married anymore. I mean," Dorian held up the marriage announcement "this article is pretty old. Civilian marriages don't often last as long as our Arrangements."

"Some of them do," she countered.

"Yeah, I guess." He exhaled.

"But this is to stop Gerard."

"If Lady Chastain only let my team do their job, this could have been avoided." He stood up. Now it was his turn to pace.

"Dorian." She moved and stood in his way. "We're still friends. You, me, Roz, and Keitan."

He stopped pacing and looked at her, his face softening. "Of course we are. That won't change, no matter what happens."

Shae nodded, "Thank you. I really needed to hear that."

Dorian reached out and squeezed her hand. "Whatever happens, we'll be there for each other. That's what friends do."

"That's very noble of you."

Dorian and Shae turned to see Avia and Verties in the doorway.

"Thank you, Lady Chastain." Dorian stood and bowed.

"Please excuse us. We'd like to have a chat with Shae." Verties patted Dorian on the shoulder. Avia moved over to the pile scattered on the bed.

"I see you have opened the box." Her voice was gentle but authoritative.

"Yeah." She stood stiffly on the other side of the bed, farthest from the door.

"Don't forget what I said, Shae." Dorian left the room.

Shae stared at her parents; decision made. "So…Mom, Dad…nice of you to visit my room." Her voice strained.

"We understand your anger, but you must still respect us," Verties scolded.

She bowed her head. "Sorry."

"Forgiven," Avia responded.

Shae's shoulder heaved as she inhaled and exhaled. The tension in the air was suffocating, and She wanted nothing more than for her parents to leave her alone. The disappointment in their eyes was clear, and it made her want to scream.

"Look," she began, her voice shaky, "I know you don't approve of my recent behavior—"

"Perhaps your time on Battle Realm—" Verties began, but Shae raised her hand to cut him off.

"Yeah, yeah, I'm becoming just like him now." She pointedly stared at Avia. Then she let silence fill the air for a few seconds. "I've decided to do it."

"The prophecy?"

She nodded at her mother's question. "Yeah." She pushed around the papers on the bed. "But none of the documents gave an actual address, and Jupiter isn't a small town. It's a place with a major city center."

"The address has been in the box the whole time, my dear." Avia held up the paper about the vision.

"It's 3529 Azure Lane." Verties pointed to the numbers in the part about the nickels falling.

Shae's eyes went wide. "These vision deals are really something." *If I had visions, could I handle it like Lady Chastain? Knowing my future and having to avert it. No, that would be too much.* She pulled out her cell phone and entered the address into the maps app.

"I've already given you clearance with the station guard." Avia indirectly revealed her permission for this mission.

No time to pack. She turned away from her armoire.

"Shae!" Avia called out.

She turned around in the open doorway and saw her mother holding out her cherished sword. "Oh, right. My sword." She took the weapon from Avia, but paused. "Just one more thing. Dorian and I agreed to separate."

Verties rubbed his bearded chin. "Hmmm, unfortunate but necessary."

"We'll deal with a new Arrangement for Dorian. You just stay focused out there," Avia added.

Shae bowed—a more familiar action rather than hugging her parents like she should have done. Then she left the room.

Chapter 5

Shae boarded the train once more to Jupiter. The portal's glow was changed to reach the designated town station. Once outside the station, she checked the map app, and then stared up at the dark sky.

As eager as she was to meet Nick, Shae opted not to portal to his doorstep. She blamed it on still being sore from the fight with Lestor instead of her growing nervousness to meet the man of her dreams—or rather, her memories.

Inhaling a deep breath, the smell of grass and flowers permeated her senses. Taking one last look around, she steeled herself and made her way toward Nick's home.

Most of the neighborhood was asleep this late at night. After walking a few blocks, she paused to check her app. *Oh, one more block to go.* A flash of shadow disturbed her peripheral. *What was that?* She put the phone away and glanced around as a swarm of vamps ambushed her. *No, I cannot have this nuisance when I'm so close.* The scraping of metal against metal of an unsheathed sword echoed as she settled into a long-point stance. A gust swept up, but Shae ignored the chill stinging her exposed flesh.

The vamp leading the group bared his fangs and his taunt was carried along the breeze. "Play with us!" The group closed in on her, undaunted by the flash of her weapon.

Yeah. Playtime. Only I'll be doing all the playing.

The first vampire lunged at her and his icy fingers dug into her shoulder. She grabbed his wrist with her free hand, smirking when he struggled to get free. Shae stretched out one foot toward his knee, only to have a second vamp leap from the left side. He was too fast, though, and a second vampire emerged from the right before another one rushed in from the front.

She stumbled back, colliding into yet another vampire. *Just how many vamps does Gerard have?* She clamped both hands onto the handle of the sword, chest heaving from the exertion.

Snarls echoed around them and mocking laughter filled the air as they formed a circle, trapping her with their numbers. The temperature had dropped so low, it froze the breath in her throat. Terror laced with doubt consumed her as she shivered involuntarily against the cold. They attacked again as one, but this time with more ferocity than before.

She slashed wildly but struggled as the vampires clawed anywhere they could and pulled her hair. She crumbled to her hands and knees beneath their weight. *Shit...to...retreat.* Whispering a chant, she summoned forth a portal. A few of the vamps snuck through before the portal closed. They crashed onto a random front lawn from an exit portal. Tucking her body into a roll before jumping to her feet, beads of sweat trickled down her forehead, despite the cold. *Where's my sword?* A gleam of metal flickered from the sidewalk. With an outstretched hand, the sword levitated back to her grip. She turned and hobbled between two houses, approaching a tall wooden gate door. *Please don't be locked.* It opened, granting her entry to the backyard.

While she rested a moment against the door, her ears were on alert for any signs the group gave chase. Only the whistle of the wind replied. *Are they just toying with me?* Shae left the backyard through the same entryway. No sign of the group at all. *Can't worry about them. If Jacquain shows up now, I'm dead.*

Heaviness devastated her conscious thoughts as if invisible hands peeled her brain into burned strips. As she fell backward and screamed in excruciating pain, she dropped the sward on the grassy strip between the sidewalk and the street.

"Shae…sweet, sweet Shae…"

A cold, slimy, bony hand trailed down her body. Her gaze traveled along the arm of that hand, locking eyes with a sinister creature with a wicked smile. "Ja…Jac…" Shae struggled but failed to inch away from him.

The moonlight sailed over Gerard's face, mirroring his evil smile. "You have finally decided to be with me, my dear."

His grotesque fingers fluttered across her cheek and down the curve of her body. *Don't touch me!*

Gerard kissed her neck, sending shivers down her spine. "You know you want this just as much as I do," he whispered in a voice that often terrified his victims.

The twisted, intimate moment was shattered when a dagger pierced his hand clean through. She flinched back before the tip of the blade touched her. Anger flared in Gerard's eyes. He grunted when he removed the blade from his hand. A figure landed with expert precision between her and Gerard.

Shae's body shook with ragged breaths, but she

refused to beg for Gerard's mercy. *Get out, Roz, or he'll kill you to get to me.*

"Best leave now, Gerard." Rozette flared her satin cape, hands resting on the sides of her curvy posterior. "The shadows are just waiting to reveal my Deviant companions."

Gerard frowned. "You're bluffing."

"Are you willing to take the risk?" Rozette dared a threatening step toward the vamp menace. Shae still clutched her head with one hand, while the other shakily brushed against Rozette's hamstrings.

"No matter. Considering the neighborhood we are in, I know where she is going." Gerard smirked and then faded into a mist.'

Rozette kneeled at Shae's crumpled figure. "It's a good thing I arrived when I did." She caressed Shae's hand.

After a few more moments, Shae's vision cleared. She blinked a few times and sat up, groaning in pain while touching the side of her head. "Is he gone?"

Rozette nodded with a grave expression, a hard gaze staring at the spot where Gerard had been. "For now, yes. But you need to get to Nickolas quickly." She helped Shae to stand up, and they stumbled up a random driveway and onto the sidewalk. "I really can't believe you endured that. Hell, I would've passed out the moment it started."

"How did you even know to come here?" Shae's mind was clear enough to question her friend.

"Dorian filled me and Keitan in on what happened after you both left the dining hall."

"Oh."

"You know we got your back, Shae."

"Thanks, Roz."

"Now get going!" Playfully, Rozette nudged Shae in the direction of Nick's house. "Azure Lane is just the next street over."

Shae parted ways with Rozette. It would be best to encounter Nickolas alone. Her steps slowed as she rounded a corner, not just from the piercing wind. *One house, another house. Gotta keep movin'.* Nick's address in large sticker numbers on a mailbox at the curb appeared. *Fuck, it's about time!* Shae forced herself up the walkway. Instead of knocking, she collapsed like a rag doll on the porch of the house.

****

Shae's eyes snapped open, and leaned away from a warm smile and an outstretched hand. *Wha—where am I?* Ignoring the sting of her wounds, she tossed the quilted blanket aside. She stared at the man in blue jeans and a gray t-shirt before forcing her gaze away from his brown penetrating eyes. *Could this really be him?*

"I didn't attack you, if that's—"

"I know." She stared at the rips in the knees of her pants.

"Okay, so what brought you to my porch?" He withdrew his hand and sat up. "And don't tell me it was the wind."

She sighed. *I shouldn't have come here. What the hell was I thinking?* Dorian's offered suggestion about Civilian marriage lingered in her mind. *Is the wife still around?* Out of the corner of her eye, she stole a glance at him. He was still waiting for a response. *It's him, I found him.* "I…"

"How 'bout you start with a name?" he suggested.

"I'm Nickolas Azura, but you can call me Nick." He held out his hand again.

She stared at it, fearful that a certain connection between them would be awakened. *But that's exactly WHY I came out of safety to find him!* She shook his hand. "I think we already know each other."

"Your wild, wind-blown hair can't fool me. But you're not the cute little girl that I once helped raise." His lips twitched in a half smile. "Shae, it's good to—"

She remained on the opposite side of the bed, but turned to face him. "Things have changed. I've…changed."

"I also brought your sword. It's over by the wall." He motioned toward that direction.

"I am grateful that you allowed me to rest a bit here. I must go now." She didn't care that she was chickening out after already agreeing to the prophecy.

"So soon?" His eyes crinkled as he blocked the door. "You're still dirty and bloody…and your skin is cold. Whatever attacked you might still be out there. You're not ready for that, Shae." Displeasure dripped from his words.

She stepped back onto the heels of her feet, a lone tear zig-zagging down her right cheek. It felt good to let go. "Nick…"

"Easy now." He caught her swaying figure in his warm embrace. "You need more rest."

When he attempted to get her to sit on the bed, she stiffened. "I'm fine." The icy tone of her voice returned. She limped over and picked up the sword. "Those bastards are gonna pay."

Nick frowned again. "Shae?"

She brushed him off and started for the door.

"Please stay."

She stared at the door handle. "I cannot." Her grip on the sword loosened, clattering as it landed on the floor.

"Shae!?"

Breathe, Shae, breathe! She crumpled against Nick as he held her head. This time, Gerard's mental attacks were brief—as if taunting her. Shae straightened up moaning. "I guess I could use a warm shower."

"The bathroom is yours to use. I'll get fresh clothes."

Shae glanced up and down the hallway, searching for the right path until Nick pointed in the correct direction. *Look at me. I'm disgusting. How come he didn't say anything about my disheveled hair and torn clothes?* Her knuckles throbbed, revealing barely healed scars.

Her hands swiveled the knobs until the temperature of the shower was suitable. The water pelted numerous minor cuts, but she adapted to the stinging. Dried blood and soap suds trickled down her body and swirled around the drain before disappearing. Shampoo suds soon replaced the blood, but her mind would retain those images for just as long. *Before I forget, I should check in with my—with Master Crimshon and Lady Chastain.* The shower ended once the water turned brisk. Finding a fresh towel, she dried off with an injured hand.

A knock on the door interrupted a search for a hair dryer. "Shae? I have…fresh clothes for you. And I must apologize, but these are some of Diane's old clothes."

She accepted them before slamming the door in Nick's face. A tumultuous amount of disgust rolled through her. *Well, better than my previous blood-stained outfit.* She grunted while tugging on each part of the outfit. *The sleeves are too long and constricting. These jeans have too many loops for the belt for anyone to grab. And since these are Diane's old clothes, does this mean she's not around anymore?*

"If he still has her old clothes,...then he hasn't let go of her."'

Trying to ignore the disappointment of the sinister voice, she wrenched the sodden strands of hair away from her paling face. Taking a deep ragged breath, she emerged from the bathroom into the hallway, where Nick's penetrating gaze awaited her. In silence, she followed him with uncertain steps down the hall toward the bedroom.

"I...remember being in this room. But it's different." The quilt used for the bedcover, the paint color on the walls, and even the picture frames had changed.

"Yeah, sometimes you slept over when your parents had to be out of town."

"Mr. And Mrs. Zenovia." This was the first time she'd spoken their names aloud. She leaned over and brought the sword to her lap from off the floor, fiddling with the pommel as a distraction.

"Yeah. After you disappeared, they just...moved. Guess they couldn't stand to be in that house anymore." After a bit of silence, he continued. "I had soup made for—"

She tightened her grip on the sword handle until her knuckles went white.

"Please don't do that." He unclenched her fingers around the handle and it fell to the hardwood floor at their feet. They winced from the obtrusive clatter. Hands touched again as they both reached for the sword. She flinched back, leaving Nick to pick it up. He leaned forward, propping it up against the wall closest to them.

At that moment, a young girl sporting ringlets of golden-brown highlights that framed her cherubic face entered the room without even knocking first. "Dad? I'm back from the roller rink. Mum said you were in here." The girl stopped short upon seeing Shae. "Oh...hi."

"Guess I spoke too soon. The wife IS still around."

Shae ignored the voice this time, fearing the underlying threat from its eager tone.

Nick turned to the younger girl, "Riley, this is Shae."

Riley brightened. "The girl you used to take care of before meeting Mum?"

"Actually, we were neighbors." She corrected the younger girl.

Nick stood up from his chair and walked over to Riley, wrapping one arm around her shoulders. "That's right, kiddo. Shae lived in the ranch house across the street."

Riley beamed at him, then turned back to Shae. "That's so cool! Did you guys hang out a lot?"

She shifted under the girl's eager gaze.

Nick answered for her. "Kinda. I seem to recall driving you and another kid around to places when your parents were busy."

Kiran. But she was hesitant to ask about him.

"Anyway." Nick reached out to touch Shae's shoulder. "Shae's going to be staying with us for a little while."

Riley's eyes widened with excitement. "Really? That's awesome! I can pretend you're like, my older sister! I've always wanted a sister."

She stared at Nick's hand as if it were Gerard's.

"Go ahead, Shae. Kiss him. Who cares if the kid is watching."

She pulled away from Nick's reach, trying to hide how the voice unnerved her.

"Don't worry about Riley. So young. She'll be easy to remove."

Shae's gaze whipped to Riley. *What the hell? I…could never hurt a child.*

"Not even in Battle Realm? If we just left her there, she could fend for herself."

NO. I—what, no. Just, what the hell? She first assumed the voice was Gerard, but now she's theorizing that it's the effects of enduring Battle Realm. Remnants of war.

She turned her attention to the forgotten bowl of soup and reached for it. After a few tastes, she mumbled, "This is…nice."

"Tomato basil. It was your favorite," Nick replied.

Shae stared at the liquid. *Ironic that it resembles blood.* She stirred her spoon around and slurped two spoonfuls of soup. "The last time I had it, was dinner that night with you."

"The last time I saw you."

The bowl teetered within Shae's loose grip as tears threatened to fall.

Nick took the bowl from Shae and turned to Riley. "Take this to the sink." Soup all over the floor was avoided.

"Yes, Dad."

"And you can tell me more about the roller rink later," he called out to her retreating figure.

"Okay, Dad!" Riley shouted as she headed to the kitchen.

There was silence in the room. Shae spoke up, fumbling a compliment. "She's pretty. And she...as the stepfather...you've done a good job." *Oh, real smooth there, Taizer.* She recalled that familiar phrase Dorian always teased her with when they first met. *Ah, hell. Now of all times, I'm missing Dorian's teasing? What the hell is wrong with me?* She tried to summon anger, but fragments of a happy childhood tugged at her emotions.

"Guess I'm good with kids." He tried to make a joke, but Shae wasn't laughing. He cleared his throat. "Well...I can't honestly say that...because you're so different from..."

That did it. A tear fell from her eye, and she turned away.

"I'm sorry. I didn't mean to-to cause you pain."

"No...no, it's okay." Shae wiped her eyes. "You don't have to apologize, Nick." At that moment, Shae yawned.

"Oh, yeah, get some rest. If you need me, I'll just be in the other room. And when you wake up, you can meet Diane...and Riley again."

"Good. We'll meet the wife, then we can assess how to deal with the woman."

She shivered again, more from the ominous threat of the voice, and curled up on the bed.

Shae awoke with a jolt, not having time to adjust to the pitch darkness of the room. Gerard's malicious mind attack seared through her skull like scorching hot flames. She writhed around like a wild animal, trying to escape the depths of his cruel torture.

She endured the 'brain scorching' sensation alone until it faded, then held still to ensure it was truly over. Not wanting to turn the lights on, she stumbled to the bathroom.

With a shaky hand, she adjusted the handle at the sink, bracing herself for the icy water that flowed out. The shock of the water temperature did nothing to diminish the lingering throb just above her left eye. She turned the water off, dried her face with a towel, and stared at the mirror. She returned to room and crawled into bed. *Do I dare try to sleep or will he attack again?*

When her eyes opened a second time, Shae noted the sunlight pouring through the window and Nick's hand just below her knee. "Hey…time for breakfast. We'll wait for you." He nudged her legs before leaving the room.

Chapter 6

Shae stepped into the kitchen, breathing in the homey scent of breakfast. Nick and Riley were already sitting at the round wooden table. He had a cup of steaming coffee in one hand, while Riley was busy sipping orange juice from a glass.

"Good morning," a woman said with a booming voice. "My name is Diane. My husband told me you're our guest for a while. Well, I hope you like my cooking." She placed a glass of orange juice in front of Shae's plate.

Shae's eyes raised to Diane, a voluminous woman in her mid-forties sporting a shaggy black wolf-cut hairstyle.

She pulled out the chair between them, perching on the edge as they resumed their conversation, voices rising and falling. Her gaze traveled to the hot plate, where each item had been artfully arranged. Scrambled eggs nestled beside three strips of bacon, and buttered toast cut into diagonal strips, all served to tantalize the senses.

Though her stomach grumbled in anticipation of devouring the meal, Shae stayed still for a moment more, taking in the room's warmth and the low rumble of conversation.

"Better eat the food before it eats you." Nick joked with her.

"What?" She blinked at him.

"Nevermind. Just enjoy the breakfast, Shae."

"Um, okay." She wasn't sure where to start. Every bite of scrambled egg, toast, orange juice, and bacon was exciting. Shae bit the inside of her lip to maintain an emotionless state—but the conversation and succulent taste of breakfast made it difficult.

"At least someone likes my cooking," Diane mused, sending a teasing glare to Riley. The young girl smirked but rolled her eyes.

"Why wouldn't you like these foods?" Shae was serious, failing to understand the teasing banter.

"Riley's not a fan of eggs. Right, Riley?" Nick set his glass of juice down. "All right, time for school. My turn to drive you."

Shae watched as Diane shuffled at the fridge while putting the orange juice away.

"When I get back…we'll find something to do today. I have the day off from work."

"*Now is the perfect opportunity to deal with Diane.*"

Shae froze. A bad feeling crept over her. To give herself something to do, she gathered the remaining dishes and brought them over to the sink. She flicked the kitchen faucet on, only to have Diane motion to the dishwasher.

"No worries. All I do is rinse them off and put them in there."

Shae was familiar with such machines but was raised at the Royale Hawse to perform the task of building character and habitually accept the responsibilities of living. However, any Deviant residing in the Royale Hawse was required to at least learn how to use Civilian equipment.

"By the way…you can stay in the guest room for as long as you need."

"Th-thanks." Shae couldn't shake that ominous sensation. She picked up a stack of brown paper lunch bags off the counter.

"Oh, you can put that into the pantry." Diane motioned to the small door next to the fridge.

She opened the door to the medium-sized pantry and set the bags in an empty spot on a shelf at eye level. A colorful cereal box caught her attention. The box sported an image of a cartoon captain wrapped like a mummy. Above the captain, were the words 'Halloween' in large orange font, and 'Crunch' in equally sized white font—both words had a black border for each letter.

"That's Riley's fav cereal of the moment."

Shae flinched at the intrusion of Diane's voice.

Diane excused herself to attend to some errands out of the house. Shae relaxed a bit once Diane was gone. Curious, Shae dared to investigate the area. Family pictures were scattered everywhere—walls, bookcases, and various other places in numerous ways. She avoided the room Nick shared with Diane and instead invaded Riley's room. Riley had enough materialistic items to keep Shae occupied until she decided to return to more familiar tasks.

****

The gloomy afternoon weather provided the perfect atmosphere for meditation. Shae settled in an Indian-style position on the lawn at the edge of the backyard patio. Her figure faced the small cluster of trees beyond Nick's property, and the cool breeze ruffled her hair as an invitation into the calming rhythm of nature.

A sense of serenity flooded her senses. The smell of rain in the air evoked an aura of tranquility. However, only a small handful of minutes passed before an intrusive pressure on her shoulder broke the meditative state. Shae snatched the hand in a crushing grip. Why is he smiling? Oh hell, it's so damn cute though.

"Uh, sorry. I didn't mean to startle you," he said, rubbing his hand.

She let out a breath, unable to shake the fear. "No, it's okay. I just…" Shae released Nick's hand, stood, and smoothed her shirt out. "You should be more careful when you approach me."

"Right, got it." Nick wiped a splatter from a large raindrop from his cheek. A few more large raindrops fell. "It's raining…C'mon inside, Shae." A breeze rustled strands loose and Nick tucked the hair behind her ears. She recoiled from his hand. "Relax, Shae…don't you know I'd *never* hurt you?"

"Sorry. I'm just not…never mind." She wanted to inform him that spending time alone with his wife and not him was upsetting, but she kept her mouth shut.

"It's okay." Nick led the way back inside the house.

Riley ran up to them, halting in her tracks before she collided with Shae. "I'm sorry I peeped into the guest bedroom this morning and saw your sword." She shifted on her feet. "I told Mitch about your sword, cuz he loves swords. He wanted you to come to the party so he could show you his collection. I said you might not show up."

"It's okay." Shae sighed. "I don't mind."

Riley hollered. "Okay then, meet you there." She dashed out the front door.

Shae continued alone to the bathroom, jumping in for a quick shower.

"Getting Nickolas away from the wife might lure him more toward our favor."

No. She dressed in fresh clothes and put her shoes back on.

They walked to Mitchell's house, a block over—a modest, brick bungalow. The same home where Gerard had ambushed her—now lined with cars along the curb. They followed the horseshoe driveway up to the house, curling around vehicles and kids in party hats running around the decorated yard.

Nick reached out to make sure she didn't stumble on the driveway. "You used to be so vibrant...and full of life," he whispered.

She shifted her gaze toward the front of the house. The bright helium balloons and streamers tied around the porch stirred memories of a childhood birthday party with a magician making doves appear from thin air. She looked at Nick for a beat, wondering if he remembered too, when Riley came barreling back into their conversation.

"Riley, what's wrong?" Nick hugged Riley's distressed figure close to him.

"Mitchell's mom told me that he ran off after being told his dad wasn't coming either. Now he's sulking at his favorite tree stump." Riley panted.

Nick frowned. "That's terrible." He made a move away from the front door, but Shae stopped him. "Shae?"

"Let me talk to him." She looked at Riley. "Where

is this tree?"

"At the empty lot down the street that way." Riley motioned with her hands. "It's the same set of woods behind our house."

Shae glanced at Nick before walking away. It wasn't that difficult to find Mitchell from the simple instructions Riley gave her, and soon she spotted the young boy. She approached him from the side. There were enough trees to give them both substantial coverage from the moderate rain. "What do you want?" he snapped and sniffled.

She stopped a few steps from him. "I'm Shae."

He looked at her. "Riley said you weren't coming." Shae looked at a house in the distance. "But I'm glad you did." She looked back at Mitchell to see he wasn't crying anymore.

"I wasn't sure if I should," she mumbled.

"Why not? Don't you like birthday parties?" He stood up.

"I haven't attended one in a long time." She was unwilling to share a conversation with an unfamiliar Civilian. "There's a group of people that miss you." She held out her hand to him.

He contemplated it and smiled. "Not much of a party without the birthday boy, huh?"

"I wouldn't know." She wanted to retreat from him.

He soured for a moment. "My dad wouldn't even talk to me on the phone. He only talked to Mom."

She stared down at him and said the first thing that came to her mind. "Take comfort to know he loves you…wherever he is."

They walked together in a comfortable silence until

they entered his house. Mitchell ran ahead, joining a group of kids at the gifts table in the living room. Shae observed the decorations and gifts adorning the table. A large rock fireplace took up one wall, the dancing flames casting shadows on the white paste and stone walls. Nick stood near the window decorated in yellow and red paper streamers, talking with another parent. She brushed her fingertips against his hand lightly, leaning in close to whisper, "Can we, uh…leave now?"

Nick excused himself from the conversation. "What's up?"

She shifted from one foot to another, eyes wandering around the loud, crowded space. "Mitchell seems nice, but I really shouldn't be here. I'm just gonna head back to your house and wait for you there."

"No, wait, Shae." He caught up to her at the front door. "Just let me check in with Riley first. Okay?"

"Okay." She stood alone for only a few seconds before sitting down on the bench seat at the front window, staring at her hands.

"Oh my god…Shae…is that you?"

She glanced up at a man with a familiar face and red hair. "Kiran?"

He approached the bench with a warm smile on his face. "Wow, you've really changed," he said, pulling her in for a hug.

She was too stunned to reciprocate. "We're not kids anymore, Kiran."

Kiran let go and took a step back, still grinning from ear to ear. "I know, I know. But you still look as beautiful as ever."

She felt her cheeks warm up. "What are you doing here?"

"I work at the warehouse on the riverfront. Mostly I'm in charge of checking in shipments. But sometimes I have to make special request deliveries." He held up a clipboard. "Where have you been?"

She took a deep breath and leaned back on the bench. "I've been all over the place. Trying to find my way, you know?" She wasn't ready to tell him the truth.

Kiran nodded. "Yeah, I get that. Life can be tough sometimes."

If only you knew, Kiran. She sighed.

"Oh, now that I know you're back,…do you want to attend an Arts N Crafts market this weekend?"

NO!

Shae's eyes narrowed, and she chose to defy the voice. "Yes."

"Cool!" Kiran stood back up. "Well, I should get back. See you this weekend, Shae."

"Is this guy bothering you?" Nick rejoined them.

"No." She snatched Nick's hand and stepped back before letting go, hoping Kiran didn't notice. "Bye, Kiran." She was grateful that Nick followed her out the open door.

****

Shae checked in with Rozette the following afternoon, knowing she'd report the conversation to her parents. She forced a cheery voice, opposite of the rigid way she sat on the bed in the guest room. "Hey, Roz."

"How's the bonding going?"

Getting right to the point, huh, Roz? She sighed. "Things are…awkward here, Roz. I don't know if I can do this. He's married. Has a stepdaughter. Maybe I should have stayed with Dorian and worked it out. Let him have the kill Jacquain moment."

"Stop second-guessing yourself, Shae. You made your decision. Now, stick to it. As for your bonding situation, it's a tricky situation for sure, but what other choice do we have?"

She bit her lip, nodding. *Rozette is right. There's no turning back now, not when I'm already here.* But still, the thought of being with a married man made her stomach churn. "Okay, I'll try to make it work. But what do I do? How do I deal with the attachments he has?"

"Have you tried kissing him? Test the water, Shae."

Shae's heart skipped a beat at the suggestion. "Oh. Okay, I'll try it." Shae's voice was barely above a whisper.

"Just remember, whatever you decide, I'm here for you. We're all here for you."

She glanced up to see Nick in the bedroom doorway, tapping his watch. "Roz, I gotta go. We're picking up Riley from school."

"Okay. Stay safe, Shae. And don't forget—"

"Don't remind me." She groaned.

Nick had been leaning against the guest room door frame, but then stood up straight after she hung up. "C'mon, Riley is gonna wonder where we are." He took one step but turned back to Shae. "What did you want Roz to not remind you about?"

"Just that—" Shae froze as a sickening pain shot through her skull.

Nick mumbled something that sounded like it should've made sense, but a roar replaced his voice. This time, it felt like a heavy chain was pulling in and out of the cells of her brain. The world blurred, and she doubled over, heaving with the sensation of nausea.

"Shae!" He placed a hand on her upper back. She stood upright just minutes later. "What happened?"

She hesitated to explain, only to be pressured by Nick's glare. "Gerard knows I'm out here, out of the safety of the Royale Hawse."

He half snorted. "A vampire with a bachelor's lifestyle."

"Well, he's been trying to 'get to me' by chipping away at my mental defenses. That's what Roz was reminding me about."

"How long has this been going on?"

"Since the night you found me on the porch."

"I don't get it," Nick mumbled.

"What?"

"All the news reports have shown Gerard to be the kind of guy who simply takes what he wants. He makes a vague comment about a girl he has his eye on, then boom, they're pictured together having a public dinner!" He frowned. "Well, if he's obsessed with getting you…why is he wasting time with these 'mind attacks'?"

"I don't know." She changed her mind about withholding the truth from Nick. "No, I do know. Jacquain seeks someone to indulge his quest for pleasure." Shae paused before continuing, "Civilian women aren't engaging enough for him. He wants me to be by his side…as his mate for the rest of his undead existence."

Nick stared at Shae in disbelief. "Mate? As in…like a vampire bride or something?" he asked, incredulous.

She nodded slowly. "Yes."

"No. No way. Not you, Shae."

She understood his reaction. *A lot of the women Jacquain targets usually wind up missing. Cops will never find those women. Jacquain keeps up his innocence in order for them to keep flocking to him.* However, she couldn't tell Nick that it was Dorian and his team that cleaned up the bodies that Jacquain's lackey often tried to bury in 'inconspicuous' places.

Nick waved his hands up in retreat. "Let's just go pick up Riley."

She understood his ending the conversation about the deadly vampire leader. "Right." She followed him to the car.

"By the way,…I wanna know more about this Roz person." Amidst their conversation, they climbed into Nick's car. He was test-driving a brand new car the whole weekend for his job.

"Roz…Rozette. She's the one that helped me escape that night to get to you," Shae explained, avoiding mentioning Gerard.

Nick shifted the car in reverse out of the driveway. "Well, remind me to thank her for that." He drove past three blocks of houses and took a left before arriving at a main road.

"That's not a good idea."

"Why?" Once the traffic cleared, he made a safe right turn.

Because I would rather have you to myself, that's why! She turned away, blushing, and recalled Rozette's advice from earlier. *Just kiss him. That's all I gotta do.* Shae slowly turned to see Nick looking back at her. "What?"

"You're blushing."

"Am not?"

Nick chuckled, but he changed the subject. "So, Riley had her birthday last month. We just attended Mitchell's party. But yours is coming up next month—October twenty-first, to be exact."

She gaped at him, awed that he never forgot, even if she forgot him. "I haven't celebrated since returning to the Royale Hawse."

"Your real family doesn't believe in that thing?" He slowed down as he approached the school parking lot.

"No. I mean, they do. But I spent most of my time in Battle Realm—the days become a blur there. The only thing you can focus on is staying alive."

"I see." At the light in front of the school, Nick stopped the car. "Well, we'll have a big celebration—to make up for those missed years."

The light turned green, and he completed the turn into the parking lot. Shae shook her head. "I don't need a celebration."

"Everyone deserves a birthday party, Shae." He pulled into a parking spot. Riley had seen the car and walked toward it. "Don't worry, I won't hire a magician."

She heaved a sigh, refusing to let Nick know his 'joke' was amusing. When Riley opened the rear passenger door and got inside, Shae and Nick pulled away from each other.

That was too close. She feigned interest in the car radio.

"I figured you forgot about me," Riley quipped as she settled into the backseat.

Nick turned to Riley. "Couldn't forget you, kiddo!"

"I'm not a kid! I'm twelve!"

"Almost a teenager." Nick muttered, sending a bright smile at Riley before side-glancing at Shae. Nick put the car in reverse, backing out of the parking spot.

Riley unzipped her bookbag and retrieved a crumpled piece of paper. "Hey, Dad. Need you to sign this permission slip for a school trip to the museum."

"Alrighty! But wait ''til we get home." He shifted the car into drive. "I bet you're hungry, Riley."

"Yeah…starving!"

"How about you, Shae?"

"Not really." With Riley in the car now, Shae hid behind her familiar distant demeanor.

"Just wait until you smell the food," Nick replied as he maneuvered the car through the streets and headed home.

Chapter 7

When the weekend arrived, Diane suggested a visit to the Arts N Crafts market. "Perfect weather. A crisp sixty-five degrees with no threat of rain."

"Oh, I love the market!" Riley sprang to her feet, dashed upstairs, and returned with a jacket in hand. "C'mon, Shae. Maybe we can buy matching rings and be honorary sisters!"

Shae only fidgeted on the couch, trying to shake her arm free from Riley's lighthearted grasp. "Umm...thanks for inviting me, but I'm gonna pass."

"It's only a couple of hours, Shae."

Shae contemplated Nick's words before remembering having to meet Kiran there. She rose from the couch. "I guess I can handle a couple of hours." She grabbed slip-on sneakers from a rack underneath a bench near the front door and then retrieved her jacket from the coat hook above. She moved aside as Diane and Nick followed suit.

They still walked two blocks to the large grassy area where the market was held, despite nabbing the perfect parking spot. The number of cars Shae noticed paled in comparison to the crowded aisles with market stalls lining each side. Shae pressed back against Nick.

"You okay?"

"Yeah, just not used to crowds like this." Not a total lie. Shae had easily dealt with large groups in

Battle Realm, but they weren't having jovial conversations like now.

"C'mon, Shae." Nick nudged her arm. "We'll start here and work our way around."

A few of the vendors were getting a head start on Halloween—giving attendees a chance to have time to decorate their homes. Each booth had a mix of the usual hand-crafted jewelry, novelty artwork, or scented candles. They all had small sections of said items but Halloween-themed.

At one booth, Nick and Shae happened to be alone together. Riley and Diane were examining scented candles two booths away. She noticed a small hand-carved wooden statue of colored pumpkins—as if it were a snowman, but with pumpkins. While reaching for it, her hand collided with his. Their eyes met, and she was sure he felt the same jolt of electricity.

"Sorry…"

The heat of his apology wrapped around Shae, unable to look away or blink.

"*Hey, Dad*…can I buy this?"

Nick turned his attention to Riley. "What? Yeah, sure."

Riley ran back, snatched the offered ten-dollar bill, and dashed off again.

She heaved a sigh and wandered over to the next aisle. *How am I supposed to fulfill the bond when they keep interrupting us?* A food truck serving cider and donuts was parked in a spot normally reserved for three stalls. Next to the truck was a picnic table. There was only one figure sitting there at the moment. "Kiran?"

The figure turned around, in mid-bite of his donut. "Oh, hey!" He wiped his hands on a napkin and stood.

"You made it!"

She sat next to him, only to be reminded of the strange fluttering in her stomach. "Yeah, I did."

He reached over and grabbed a plastic bag near his feet, moving it to the table. "I got this!" He revealed a handmade scarecrow holding a 'Happy Halloween' banner. "I'm gonna hang this on my front door. I just love passing out candy on Halloween. It's my favorite holiday."

She took the item, turning it over in her hands— being careful not the break it—as she listened to him. "I don't have a favorite holiday. At least, I don't think so."

"You don't think so?" She handed it back to him.

Shae shook her head, staring at the scarecrow once more. Sadness trickled within her as she looked at the colored banner. The idea of a happy Halloween seemed almost foreign, a reminder of a simpler time—before she succumbed to a detached demeanor courtesy of the Battle Realm.

"You used to *love* Halloween. The way you took charge and mapped out the houses that gave the full bars. Even those teens that swore off the 'childish' festivities joined us."

"I never really had the chance to celebrate Halloween with my real parents," she said, a hint of bitterness lacing her words. "I was always too busy hiding from the real monsters."

"Like Jacquain?"

Shae's body tensed at the mere mention of the vampire's name. "Please, Kiran…" Her voice quivered. "I don't want to talk about Jacquain."

"Is he after you?"

Shae gazed at Kiran. His genuine concern and

curiosity were palpable, but Shae had no desire to broach the subject of Jacquain. "I can handle myself," she said, trying to keep her voice steady. "Let's just focus on Halloween."

Kiran's eyes flickered with something that looked like frustration, but he nodded. "Okay." He paused, then took Shae's hand in his. "But if you ever need someone to talk to, I'm here for you. Always."

She leaned in toward his lips, his body following the moment. Their lips met in a soft kiss, hesitant, but filled with promise.

The delicate moment was shattered as uneasiness churned her stomach.

"I…I can't do this," she stammered, backing away from him. "I'm sorry."

"Don't go," he whispered.

She wanted to remain in the moment, but reality beckoned. Taking a deep breath, she mustered the strength to speak. "I wish I could," she said, her voice barely a whisper. "But I'm…" *I have a prophecy to fulfill.*

Kiran looked' confused. "It's all right," he said softly, tone now laced with concern. "Will I see you again?"

Shae walked away, her heart heavy with unseen emotions—leaving him there. After a bit of wandering, she found Nick, Diane, and Riley.

"Is everything okay?" Diane spoke up before Nick could.

Shae paused for a moment, unable to give voice to the warring feelings inside of her. Instead, she simply said, "Yeah," and let out a deep sigh.

"We're done here, anyway. Time to head home."

Nick's voice conveyed more conviction than she could ever muster in the moment.

As they returned home, Shae was torn between a desire to hide and the feeling of safety that came with being near the family. *I don't understand why kissing Kiran made me so nauseous and fearful. I was fine talking with him, but kissing him...*

"C'mon, let's go to my room. I wanna show you what I bought!" Riley then talked incessantly about the trinkets she had found at the market that morning. Despite Riley's efforts to show off a growing passion for fashion, Shae couldn't help but focus on the fear that Gerard may try attacking her again.

She pushed food around the plate during dinner, creating an illusion she had been eating. Gerard could unleash his mind attacks at any point, and that thought intensified her anxiety.

As the night progressed, she only spectated while the family engaged in three rounds of game night before bed.

She settled under the bedsheet in the darkness of the guest bedroom. *I'm ready for you, Jacquain.* Yet, tonight they seemed more forceful and frequent. The pain was sharp. Dizzyness set in and the bed soaked with her sweat. *Keep trying, Jacquain. You won't break me.*

****

Riley packed her bag for a visit with her biological father the following night. Diane chose to go to bed early, nursing a headache.

Shae peeked out, seeing the door to Nick's bedroom was closed.

"Good. She's still asleep. Time to make your move,

Shae."

Inhaling a deep breath and letting it out slowly, her careful, deliberate footsteps headed toward the end of the hallway. She stood in the small archway, spotting Nick on the couch immersed in a late-night program. She glanced down at herself, proud of sneaking one of his long shirts to wear just for this moment. Long enough to hide the fact that she only wore her bra and panties underneath. *I am SO not ready...*

"But this must be done."

The illumination by the TV highlighted his figure. His arms were folded over his chest and he had such a peaceful posture that she was afraid to disturb him.

She tiptoed closer to Nick with nervousness and anticipation. *Weird how he sits at the opposite end of the couch. Is that his designated spot?*

"Nick?"

Taking in her appearance in his oversized shirt, his eyes widened in surprise. The sight of her body seemed to snap Nick out of his reverie, causing him to blink several times before offering an appraising look. "What are you doing up?" Nick finally asked after a long moment.

"I couldn't sleep." She blushed, trying to keep her voice steady through the emotions roiling beneath the surface. "And I wanted to talk to you."

Nick shifted in his seat. "Is everything okay?" he asked, finally tearing his gaze away from her legs.

She approached him with slow, tentative steps until standing right in front of him. She lingered for a moment before leaning and pressing her lips to his.

Nick was surprised at first, before melting into the moment. Shae's hands found their way to the back of his neck, pulling him closer, deepening the kiss.

Nick broke the kiss and looked at her with a mixture of confusion and hunger in his eyes. "Shae, what are you doing?" he asked, his voice hoarse with desire, in total contrast with his words.

She swallowed hard. "I want you, Nick," she whispered, failing to keep the anxiety she felt from shining through.

He leaned back, putting a slight distance between them. "Shae, I can't do this. I love my wife, and I am committed to her."

A pang of disappointment coursed through her, but she knew deep down that he was right. She couldn't ask him to betray his wife like that. She bit her lower lip. *Maybe if I tell him abou—*

"It won't work properly if you tell Nickolas about the Bond."

It won't? She glanced at Nick before looking away. She noticed the program on the TV—an animal mating documentary.

"Trust me, Shae."

"I'm sorry…I…" A growing sense of unease crept through her entire being. Her cheeks flamed. "Jacquain has me a complete mess. I risked a lot leaving my group." She drifted off with a heavy sigh before confessing about that foreboding feeling.

Nick nudged her shoulder. "Shae, about Jacquain. I know you've been suffering from his mind attacks. What can I do to help you deal with him?"

That's when tears threatened to fall. *Do I dare tell him? I want to, but I don't. Argh! Stupid Jacquain. If it weren't for you, I wouldn't need this Bond!* That foreboding feeling was pulsating again, urging her to reveal the truth to him. She paced, working to quell a rise of uneasiness before sitting on the coffee table in front of him. Neither cared about the documentary on the TV now.

"Talk to me, Shae. C'mon."

She retreated from him and turned her gaze to the floor. "Nick, I…" *I must hold strong for the sake of his family.* She grunted in pure frustration. *Why did you have to be MARRIED!?* She shivered from the wicked sensation laced beneath the last part of her thoughts.

"Shae?"

She heard the fear in his voice, matched by the concern in his deep, chocolaty brown eyes. His oh-so-sweet-and-kissable lips hid an angry frown. His hand was on hers again. A wave of warmth coursed through her, settling in her loins. There was a moment of silence until she slid away from Nick. *No, I can't do this.* Her expression remained flat. *But those dreams…or visions—oh hell to the part of me that wants to recreate them.* There wasn't enough corruption for her to use and drive Diane and Riley out of the picture. Solemnly, she retreated to the guest room.

She tossed his shirt onto the bed and headed toward the dresser drawer. After changing into a shirt and trousers, she reached out a hand toward her sword.

Nick appeared in the doorway. "Where are you going?"

"I cannot stay. I must return to the Royale Hawse. It isn't safe for me out here." Despite Nick's protests, she lifted her sword from against the wall by the door. "Thank you for letting me stay here." Shae opened the door and hesitated, but didn't turn to him. "It was good to see you again." Nick could only grunt in disbelief at that final sentiment. She stomped through the doorway.

Once she was on the front porch, Nick yanked her back into the house.

"No!" she squeaked in protest, dropping the sword before he pushed her against the closed door.

Any determination to leave faltered in the heat of his embrace. "Nick…"

His lips latched onto hers in a searing kiss while his hands traveled over her body, tracing every curve and dip with a hunger that made her dizzy.

Where is this searing need for him coming from? I feel it in him too.

As they kissed, his fingers slipped beneath the fabric of her blouse, teasing at the sensitive flesh beneath. But as the pleasure consumed them, a nagging feeling of unease began to creep up. *No, not now. This is too good. I want more.* Yet, the feeling persisted. *Dammit.*

She latched down on the sides of his upper arms, ready to push him away. "Nick, stop."

"What?" The glaze in his eyes faded.

"Not like this." She pushed him back and stepped out of his reach, still not comprehending this sensation, which slowly faded.

"Not like this?" he repeated. "Then how?"

How could I explain the chaos surrounding us? Or the voice inside my mind?

"Will you, at least, stay?" Nick broke the silence.

The moment Shae picked up her sword, Diane's voice screeched from the bedroom, "NICK!"

Shae followed Nick into his bedroom, finding Diane sitting up on the bed with a tear-stained face. Before Nick could ask what was wrong, his cell phone fell from her loose grip onto the hardwood floor with a thunk.

"Riley's been kidnapped!"

Chapter 8

Riley. He's got Riley just to get to me. I must take the bait. This isn't right. She is an innocent. Her eyes narrowed, fists clenching tight. *Gerard, you bastard. It's too soon!*

Nick turned from his kneeling position in front of his wife. "Shae?"

Diane sobbed. "Do something!"

"I'll get her back for you. Then I'm gone." Shae headed for Riley's room on the second floor, leaving Nick speechless.

"How do you plan to do that?" Diane followed behind Shae. It was clear that doubt shaded Diane's belief in Shae's ability to get Riley back.

"I have my ways. Now, please, stay out of this." A tentative pull on Deviant magic and a flick of her wrist shut the door in Diane's face. She gazed around the room, only half listening as Nick tried to console his wife.

Shae moved to the center of the room and sat down Indian style. She closed her eyes, muttering an incomprehensible whisper in a language native to the Deviants. A picture of Riley, Diane, and Nick peeled away from its place on the wall's bulletin board. The picture then ripped in half, separating Riley from the rest of the picture. The rest was discarded while the half with Riley floated near to Shae. With lips still moving in a whisper, the picture flipped and words appeared on the back.

Seek your answer in the hands of the Master.

Shae's concentration broke, and the hold on the door faded. She rose in distress, teetering dangerously close to the Darkness. Shae sunk onto Riley's bed—sinking deeper into a heavy decision. *Should I leave Riley to the monster...or turn myself in to become the monster?* Again, she cursed herself for seeking Nick out to fulfill the prophecy. Leaving the protection of the Royale Hawse was an end to her own life.

Nick opened the door. "Shae?"

Unable to hold back any longer, tears mixed with grief spilled down her cheeks. "I'm so sorry!"

Nick closed the door behind him. "You have nothing to be sorry for. It was him, that vampire, Jacquain, that kidnapped my daughter!" Nick radiated fear and anger.

Their proximity to each other made them both susceptible to the Darkness now. But it was his pain, fear, and anger she focused on.

"But it's up to me if she lives or dies." She covered her face with both hands.

"You won't let her die, Shae. I believe in you."

"That's not..." Shae became enthralled by his deep chocolate eyes and rubbed the palm of his right hand.

"Everything is going to be all right." His lips were so close to hers. It was all she could do not to close the distance and take what she craved. But he had a wife, who was just a few feet away in the other room, and Gerard had his daughter.

"NO!" she screamed with blazing eyes, sending Nick toppling backward onto the floor. Two trembling legs straddled each side of him as she looked straight into his eyes from her standing position. "Checkmate, Nick. He's got me." Tears welled in the edge of her eyes, but they wouldn't fall. Despite wanting to reach out and touch him one last time, she resisted.

He scrambled away from her and rose to his feet. "I don't understand."

Unable to meet his gaze any longer, she turned toward the door.

"Shae?" She heard him calling out to her in a barely audible whisper.

"You don't need to understand..." She almost said his name, but refused to say it now. "You just need to be with your family. Just forget about me." She moved into the front room with a deliberate coldness that belied the raw pain in her heart and spoke calmly to Diane. "You shall see your daughter soon." With those words, Shae walked out the door without looking back.

Shae emerged from the house, bracing herself for what awaited outside. Seven of Gerard's vamps lined up in the driveway, their eyes glowing like embers in the night sky.

The leader's pale fingers gripped her shoulder. "Move it. Boss does *not* like to wait."

Her eyes narrowed in defiance, stomach twisting in knots and heart pounding in tune with the heavy raindrops bursting against the pavement.

They ignored the heavy rain. Nick was shouting even as he got to the end of the driveway. But she tuned him out. There was no other way to reunite him with his daughter.

The group escorted her toward Gerard's large, dark mansion, set back from the road, half a mile from

Nick's. Most of it was hidden behind a dense curtain of trees. Two bright pulses of lightning flashed once they reached the main gate. She used the blinding moment, shaking free from the grip of two vampires, and unsheathed the sword. She portaled out of the center of the group and reappeared behind a vamp, slashing his throat. She eliminated two more vamps in similar fashion before jamming the steel blade into the heart of one more before he could react.

The leader ordered the remaining two vamps to hold her down. Shae's sword dropped from her grasp. She struggled against the hold, grunting as the leader quickly retrieved it. He then pressed the sharp point at the base of her neck. "Nice try. But it's over now. Time to deliver you to the boss."

"Is it? Are you sure it's over now?" She remained still, her lips moving in a low chant. Invisible hands grabbed the three remaining vamps and shoved them against a tall brick column, one of two that adorned each side of the main gate. Shae reached, drawing her weapon back. As she gripped the handle of the cherished weapon, she spun and slashed their heads clean off. The heavy rain washed away the thick blood splattered on her soaked skin.

"Oh, good. You already took care of them."

She turned to see Dorian. "You shouldn't have followed me."

"C'mon, Shae—you know I can't let you go in there alone." Dorian nodded toward the gate. "Now let's go take care of Jacquain."

She latched her hand on his shoulder. "No, Dorian. Someone is going to have to return Riley to Nick and Diane. That's your job. I'll take care of Jacquain." She handed the weapon over to him. "Take care of this for me." Then she portaled to the other side of the gate.

With her senses sharpened and alert, she made her way toward the house, attuned to any sign of Jacquain's vamps waiting to ambush her. She navigated between the dense foliage surrounding the den's window and peered in.

Gerard glided to the dying fireplace, his fingers reaching out to caress a photo frame. Shae's face smiled back at him, illuminated by the flickering glow of a restaurant's neon sign. *That was from one of the nights I went out to dinner with Nick and his family. Bastard was spying on me.* Somehow, she managed enough willpower to not succumb to the boiling anger from the invasion. She listened closely to their conversation, knowing her magic created an invisible barrier to eavesdrop on secrets.

"Are you going to change me?" Riley's voice was quiet as she addressed the older vampire.

The corners of Gerard's mouth turned up in a wicked smile. "No need to. The boy can barely contain himself when it comes to you." He shook his head and burst into laughter.

Shae could only describe the look on Riley's face as fear. Still, the girl tried to be brave.

"What's so funny?"

Shae ducked below the windowsill as Gerard's gaze swept past. She steadied her breathing and resumed spying.

He clasped his hands behind his back as he glided over to a leather chair across from Riley. His jaw was set firm and his mouth a grim line of displeasure as he sat like a king on his elevated throne. He glowered down at Riley with a condescending sneer that made Shae's insides churn with dread.

"You are, my dear." He stifled his laughter enough to answer as he stood and then knelt before the child. "What makes you think I will change you?"

"Why else would you kidnap me?"

"For food." His lips parted, and a wicked grin stretched across his face, showcasing his sharp fangs. "Don't worry. That is not my interest in you, either." He ruffled the child's hair. "No, you, my dear Riley…are bait."

"Bait!?" Riley's lower lip quivered like she would burst into tears at any moment. "I wanna go home!"

The fear in Riley's voice tore at Shae's already broken heart. But before she could formulate a solid rescue plan, two hands yanked her away from the window.

"Well, looky what I caught. A magical little birdie!"

Her eyes widened at the sight of a vamp dressed in biker gear. "If you let me go, I promise not to kill you."

"No way. I'm about to get brownie points." He dragged her along to the front door. Shae feigned a struggle, letting the vamp believe he had the upper hand. "Master Jacquain, I found your little birdie."

She failed to deliver an interesting quip when Gerard's eyes lit up with lust. In a blink of an eye, she stood face to fang with him. *Keep it together, girl.* Lucky for him, she refrained from hurling on his buffed dress shoes. His slimy hands brushed down her rigid arms.

"No." The tone she exhibited was dark and low, hiding an inner throb that begged for his smoldering touch again.

He chuckled in amusement and reluctantly removed his hands. "Set her down next to the child." When the biker vamp squeezed her arms too tight, Gerard snarled, "Gently. She's our special guest."

Poor Riley had to witness that.

Once seated, she placed a hand on Riley's shoulder to assure the pre-teen that everything would be all right. Riley nodded at the signal to keep quiet.

Gerard stepped closer still, his twisted seduction oozing from every pore. "I'm glad you could make it to our little intimate affair this evening," he said in a sickly seductive voice. "You have certainly made this whole thing much easier for me, my swe—"

"Let the child go, Jacquain." She glared at him. "She's done her job as bait. I'm here now."

"Um, Mr. Jacquain, sir?" Riley paused, waiting for the vampire's full attention.

Shae was shocked at the audacity this girl had. If it was any other situation, Shae would have been very impressed.

"I don't understand. Why is Shae special?"

"Please, Riley dear, just call me Gerard." He leaned forward. "There is no reason we cannot be friends, is there?"

"Friends?" Riley scrunched up her face.

"You will never be friends with anyone, Jacquain," Shae huffed.

Yet, Riley continued. "But I heard my best friend Mitchell's dad call you a monster once."

"Now that's quite enough!" Gerard's curled bony hand drew close to Riley's neck.

"Don't you dare touch her. Don't even think of

touching her or I'll—"

"Making threats to the Boss in HIS domain?" The biker vamp stepped forward. "I thought the all-great and powerful Deviant wasn't into protecting Civilians."

Gerard spun on his heel and spat in the vamp's face, "Be careful how you speak to her." He shoved the biker vamp toward the door of the den that led into the foyer. "Now leave before I decide to strap you to the chair for punishment."

"Yes, Master Jacquain." He quickly hustled out of the room.

Gerard glided over to a record player and slipped the needle on. Soft instrumental music filled the room. He approached Shae and slipped his arms around her waist, resuming their conversation like nothing had happened. "Why is Shae special, you ask?" He forced her to dance with him.

She tensed up and moved along with him, refusing to display interest—especially in front of Riley. She rested her head on Gerard's shoulder, toward his neck and away from Riley and Gerard's gaze, to hide the confusion that rolled across her face. *This sensation— being this close to someone so powerful.* She struggled to stifle the rush bubbling up within her. *Why do I feel such a craving to have him and his power?*

A rumble of excited purring escaped Gerard's lips, but he continued with his answer. "Certainly you have noticed. Have you not been living with her for a brief time?"

"Dad was worried a lot about her all the time. But she is scary," Riley recounted, glancing at Shae. "I didn't think you liked me." Riley looked up at Gerard, attempting to get on his non-existent good side. "Shae acted nice to me, though, and played along at being the Big Sister. But it was just to make Dad happy."

"Interesting." Gerard wrapped his arms tighter around Shae, spinning her out of Riley's view. But confronted by Riley's words.

Bastard wants more of a reaction out of me. Well, too bad. You won't get any. Determined to maintain composure, she forced a half-smile, but each second pressed against his body clashed against her defiance. She would rather die before giving him the satisfaction of desire.

"Tell me, young Riley, has Shae ever shown any real emotion at all while she stayed with your family?"

"Are you going to hurt her?" Riley shifted in discomfort.

Please stay seated, Riley. Shae mentally willed the child to not do anything brash.

Gerard's eyes blazed with passion. "You're going to help me save her!"

"What? How?" Riley gasped in shock.

"From your father," Gerard spat.

Riley shook her head vehemently at the accusation. "No way! He seemed so happy having her back. Why would we hurt her?"

"She belongs with me!"

Riley's gaze remained fixed on him as her body instinctively inched away.

"Enough of this, Jacquain." Shae's body went stiff from his arousal from behind and the sensations of his roaming hands. She peeked one eye open at Riley and saw fear. "It's gonna be okay, Riley."

Gerard's hand hovered just above the warm dampness between her legs. She wanted so badly to surrender. A wave of shame failed to negate any arousal. In a struggle of willpower versus desire, she snatched his hand in a firm grip.

Shae tried to spin around to face Gerard with a raised fist. He caught her wrist in his palm and chuckled. "Your fist against my face is not the contact you really want between us."

Before she could knee him in the gut, he coiled his hand around her arm. One final dizzying twirl and he pushed her forward, bent over one arm of the chair. Shae's face was close to where Riley sat.

Gerard leaned over, whispering in her ear, "I've seen the way you fought against my lackeys. Your fury is terribly exciting. But this…you are holding back in the presence of this Civilian child?" Then he glanced over at Riley. "She cares about you. Coming here to save you. And not even really fighting me."

She heard the dissatisfaction in Gerard's voice. But it was true. *You know damn well I could kick your ass— even if your lackeys came to your aid. You also know I won't fight you in front of the kid. She's been through enough.*

Gerard snarled. "When you see your father again…ask him who he loves more—you, your mother, or Shae!"

"YOU are a monster!" Riley began to cry. "I hate you! I wanna go home!"

Seeing the tears in Riley's eyes broke Shae. For the sake of the child's well-being, Shae trembled and gave in. "Gerard." She pushed herself upright from the bent-over position on the chair, and pulled free from his grip. Then she mustered up every ounce of inner gumption as she took his hand. "Gerard." This time, she injected more heat into her voice. "Let me get the child home. You have my sworn promise that I will return."

He scowled but relented, perhaps sensing her sincerity. "Right back here, my sweet. My servants have dinner prepared for us."

Shae ushered Riley to the main gate and met up with Dorian. "Take her home," she said in a firm tone.

He hesitated, looking at her with concern. "But what about you? Did you kill him?" He glanced toward the mansion.

"No. I…"

Horror flashed in his eyes. "Oh no, Shae. What did you do?"

"She has to have dinner with him. I didn't even know he could eat real food." Riley's voice trembled.

"It's nothing I can't handle. Now just get her home."

He sighed and then looked down at Riley, his expression kind and sympathetic. "Come on, let's get you home." He held out his hand, and Riley took it.

Chapter 9

She stood transfixed by the awe-inspiring grandeur of the entrance to the mansion. Her shoulders sagged from the crushing weight of defeat. Taking a deep breath, she twisted the doorknob and pulled the door open.

The warm candlelight illuminated the smooth marble flooring, casting dancing shadows on the detailed paintings adorning the walls. Each step resonated with defeated heart beats, a reminder of her fate.

In the center of the foyer stood two gaunt servants, eyes sunken deep with deprivation. The scars on their necks indicated they'd been fed on too many times. One held towels while the other bore an outfit that made her skin crawl—a mini skirt ensemble, its seams puckered where they'd been roughly stitched together. The top had an uncomfortable zipper running down its back, exposing her vulnerability in this situation.

She said nothing about the women drying her hair as best they could, but turned to one. "Which room?"

The woman pointed to a set of double doors at the opposite end. "He's waiting for you there." Both servants gathered the soiled towels and dashed off in the opposite direction.

She turned away from them and heaved a sigh. She strolled to the set of doors, but then stopped and glanced over her shoulder. *I'm not sure how many servants and lackeys are in this mansion, but I think I can spare the servants in my escape. They are only human. I can't say the same for the lackeys. It is, after all, my Deviant duty to get rid of them. I know I gave my sword to Dorian, but*...Shae clenched a glowing fist, cackling in blue energy.

'That would be an ill-advised move, my dear Shae.'

She whipped her gaze to the double doors, and the glow faded.

"Best let him have you. There's no telling what he would do to your precious Nickolas—or his family."

She stepped back and put a hand on her head.

"If you want revenge, you must enter the dining room."

No argument there. She did want revenge. *Jacquain is the reason for all of this. I have to end him. Even without the Bond.* She approached the doors, ready to push them open. *I must believe that even as a bloodthirsty monster...I would NEVER hurt Nick.* She stepped into the room, noticing that all the light was from candelabras hung from the walls. There was just enough light for Gerard to notice her. He sat at the end of the large dining table.

"Ah, my dear, you have arrived as promised. Please, have a seat. Dinner is about to begin." Gerard held out a hand toward a chair that a servant stood by.

The servant placed their food and drinks before them, but Shae barely acknowledged the help as she sat down. She watched in horror as Gerard arranged the raw bloody mess of a meal on his plate. The thick smell of blood made her stomach queasy and difficult to ignore, yet it was the smile he wore that made her ill.

He seemed completely at ease with enjoying such a barbarian meal. She studied his face, but still found no indication that he was the mysterious voice. *Then who was it?*

"I hope you enjoy the family duck," he announced with pride, digging into his meal with vigor.

Desperate not to show any sign of weakness, she reluctantly pushed the more cooked pieces of meat around the plate, yet allowed herself a small sip from the glass of dark red wine. Her defiance tasted sweet, but only temporarily.

He had taken a few bites before speaking again. "Are you not hungry?"

She set the crystal goblet down and stared hard at him. "Is it not enough for you that I am here? I have let my people down." Were it not for his thin and bony frame, Shae could imagine him as the handsome young man in the large, framed picture on the wall behind him.

"But you are fulfilling destiny!" He swished his arms out from him as he spoke. She turned away, breaking the gaze, and he set his hands back down on the table. The clanking of silverware against a dish in frustration filled the air. From outside, a low rumble erupted. "You should eat. You will need the strength."

To satisfy him, she reluctantly chewed a piece of the duck. She squeezed out a small smile to appease him, and he nodded before finishing his dinner. Despite many sips of wine, her glass still sat half full by the end of dinner.

The same servant returned to the room to clear the plates. Gerard waved her off in a cold voice. "Concern yourself with this later and do not interrupt us." The woman scurried away.

Lightning from outside lit up the room in an eerie yellow hue. Shae's insides fluttered with a mix of fear and anticipation, knuckles white from the tight grip on the chair. Gerard dragged her to the space between the wall and the large dining table. The loud crack of thunder shook the room. It sounded like laughter—HIS laughter. She gasped at his icy touch, internally screaming for freedom.

"Shhh…" He crushed her against him until she could hardly breathe. His hand cupped her chin toward his awaiting lips. "My sweet Shae…"

She grew dizzy with the desire to be in his presence. Her arms remained stiff. She had no idea when they'd dropped so helplessly into place of their own accord, but now they were there resisting any urge or desire she may have to touch him, let alone kiss him back.

She did not pull away, instead whispering, "Jacquain." Of their own accord, eager hands brushed his sides. The part of her that was opposed to his pleasure in the action, forced them back to his sides again.

"Do not be so formal, my sweet…" He breathed into her ear, and she shivered.

Before she could grip his throat, he shook his head and placed a kiss on her knuckles. Losing control much too fast, Shae longed for the sweet release of a well-placed lightning strike. But it didn't happen. She struggled to remember he was the enemy, when all she wanted to feel was the continued pulse of building pleasure between them.

The cool air sent shivers coursing through her. His

fixated gaze appraised her body with an intensity she had never experienced. Somehow, he unzipped the back of her outfit. When she reached for him, Gerard shifted around as if he sensed she might strike at any moment.

Shae moaned with pleasure as he lightly caressed her neck and shoulder, sending warm chills crawling down her body. She ached for his passion. A storm raged from the darkened skies outside of the mansion. Crackling thunder rumbled beyond its walls in sync with Shae's heartbeat; every other beat brought another surge of desire from deep within her core and into each fingertip.

He put a hand against her cheek as a tear spilled down to his thumb. "I can't control myself around you anymore. You're so beautiful, but I knew this day would come."

"Gerard." She pleaded for his hands to continue their dangerous exploration.

His chilled hands left a trail of yearning as he peeled off her top and skirt ensemble. When she couldn't hide from his assault any longer, she turned to face him, suddenly very aware of her nudity.

"Your sudden shyness is endearing, my sweet." He reached for his own buttons, undoing his dress shirt and tossing it aside. "But it's the other side of you I desire." He maintained eye contact as he unbuckled his belt, pulled the zipper down, and stepped out of his trousers.

His erection was much more noticeable now—even through his briefs. His pale figure bordered on being way too bony. It was hard to believe that this frail body had done major damage to well-built Deviant warriors. Shae recalled the few times that even Dorian returned home with more than a bruised ego.

Gerard captured her lips, the kiss more intrusive than she'd been prepared for. Fingers twitched and burned from wanting to push him away, but also itching to pull him closer.

As he pulled away, every cell in her body cried out for the ultimate pleasure his touch promised. "Why do you draw this out?"

He chuckled. "Such an occasion must be enjoyed, my sweet Shae." When he curled his fingers around the elastic band of his cotton briefs, she had to look away again. He made a show of dispensing with his final layer of clothing, throwing the discarded briefs over her head in dramatic fashion.

Shae gasped at the sensation of him moving to his knees, straddling her as she lay on the wooden floor in the dining room. As his hands slid over every exposed curve, she wished for the strength to push him away. With an all-knowing smile, he placed his cold hands on her untainted silk thighs, pulling himself closer. Any feeble attempt to scramble free couldn't fool either of them. It was her first time, but curiosity and the pleasure of his touch overrode any defiance she once had.

Gerard's hold tightened. "Just relax, give into it. I can feel how much you want me."

She fought the boiling desire. *This is wrong...yet it feels so right.* Her defiance broke from the momentary pain of his penetration, replaced with a feeling of fullness she'd never experienced. In their first time together, his movements were slow and tender, allowing them both to experience every inch of him. She soon mirrored his thrusts as they sought the zenith of their destined pleasure, toward a rapture beyond their imaginations.

"Gerard…" The whispery chant of his name echoed in rhythm with his thrusts.

His razor-sharp teeth pierced through the delicate flesh of her neck. A strange dizziness erupted, so strong she no longer saw the light. She stopped moving with him, failing another attempt for freedom. Hands slipped from his arms, colliding with the hardwood floor with a resounding thud, trying to prevent an unavoidable descent into the abyss that threatened her true self. Soon, Gerard's bony weight and his fangs embedded in her neck disappeared. The light she'd come to depend on was gone, replaced by a limbo of infinite darkness and a thundering, raucous laugh.

A hand broke through the darkness. She longed to take it and pull her to safety, back to the light. *I can't move. Why can't I move?!* The hovering hand dripped something cold and slimy onto her lips. *What…is this?* A bit of it fell into her mouth and she recognized the substance. *Blood. His blood.*

Shae had never felt such a powerful thirst before, never been so desperate for something. While swallowing those few droplets, more dripped onto her.

"Yes, take it. Take all of it."

The voice had returned. Or had it always been there, though mostly silent while she ironically did its bidding?

Soon she licked her lips to capture it. The darkness fizzled and Gerard's smiling visage filled her vision. She sucked the liquid from his wrists.

"Devour him. Consume him."

The monster within was unleashed after several more mouthfuls of blood. "More." Her words were delivered in a dark and enigmatic tone. After another few mouthfuls, she pulled away, only to distract him with a kiss.

He cupped her breast, its fullness crushed between them. She sighed in contentment, eyes fluttering shut as he shifted to top position. He leaned forward, pressing his lips against hers in a passionate kiss that spoke of a pleasure that had been absent for far too long.

She felt no need to keep them apart any longer, for the time for such efforts had long since passed. She invited him to explore its depths, and he eagerly obliged. His tongue swept through her mouth as his hands roamed from top to bottom.

He planted a trail of fervent kisses down her neck, blood smearing her body, but she didn't care.

She nipped at his shoulder, reveling in his moans of pleasure. "Gerard…" His name rolled off her lips in a coherent whisper, despite now having fangs.

He responded by pushing harder and faster, eager to explore deeper.

The rhythm of their lovemaking shifted and changed in perfect harmony. Each intimate caress and deep thrust of his hips was an extension of her own pleasure intensifying with his touch. His hands gripped her waist as she rocked back and forth.

The darkness of the night could not dim the fire that burned within them.

He claimed all of her with the perfect thrusts of his hips. She reclaimed position on top of him. A sensual, but no less intense roll of her hips and she lost control. An orgasm erupted, increasing the surge of darkness his blood had awakened. She wanted to extend the power through eternity, but exhaustion was inevitable. He jerked and spilled himself within her. Their eyes met and for a second, Shae saw her true self in his.

Gerard's hand brushed sweat and blood-dampened strands from her face, his touch too gentle to comprehend. "Sleep now, my sweet Shae."

She obeyed, her eyelids drifting shut as she surrendered to the enveloping darkness and pleasure.

****

Gerard rested on his side, his face and nudity illuminated by the pale candlelight hanging on sconces around the room. His breathing was slow and shallow. Shae shifted position; her gaze still fixed on him. She watched as he turned his head, his eyes now open.

"Good morning, my Queen."

She chuckled at his joke as one of her hands settled on his chest, leaning forward to nip at his right pec.

He sucked in a breath, sliding his hands to her sides. "Your fingertips against my inner thigh..." He let out a contented moan, his lips curing into a smile.

Shae's cheeks flushed as the heat emanating between them grew more intense. With the slow intensity of a smoldering fire, they explored each other with their eyes, their mouths, and their touch.

Silky fingers glided over the faint scar on his neck. *I fed from him last night. Why do I feel the urge for more than just his blood?* She drew herself close to that spot on his neck, jaw twitching in anticipation while she moved to straddle him.

Gerard held her still. "We shall go out tonight and you may select your first meal."

She heeded his wishes and noticed fresh clothes on a chair by the foot of the bed. She donned a black turtleneck and dark blue jeans before waiting by the door for him. His dark green sweater and black pants complimented her outfit, almost as if he wanted the world to know she belonged to him. He escorted her down the hall, their strides synchronized.

Once outside, she stepped away from him, staring up at the sparkles in the sky. The night was cool and refreshing, a welcome change after the intensity of the last few days.

A sleek black Lexus, with the back rear windows tinted, rolled up the circular driveway at the front door. Gerard reeled Shae's attention back to him. He motioned to the vehicle, and they took their respective seats in the back. In the privacy of the dark vehicle, she couldn't resist touching him. Maintaining eye contact, her hand wandered to his clothed form, ending up on his very interested cock. He sighed as she teased him with gentle rubbing.

"Just look at the fool. Complete putty in your hands."

It's so euphoric.

"Don't worry. We'll have him soon enough."

Play was interrupted when a servant announced their arrival. Gerard aided Shae's exit from the Lexus to the sidewalk. Brick buildings and parking lots lined the surrounding blocks. The moon glowed through the mist like a half-eaten mango in the night sky.

As they ventured along the streets, she inched a few steps ahead of him and scanned the area. It was late for those with daytime desk jobs, but early for those who liked to party. As it was, Halloween parties were already in full swing well before the holiday.

A man stepped out of a liquor store and leaned against the brick wall, lighting a cigarette that he pressed to his lips. He was tall, likely in his mid-thirties, and wore a navy blue suit. His hair was dark and slicked back, and his tanned skin suggested a life spent in daylight.

The sun. I'll never see it again.

But the loss wasn't enough to tame the inner beast. Her heart pounded and gums tingled in anticipation. She had never been asked to hunt a Civilian before.

Deviants don't kill humans.

"You're not them anymore."

She glanced over toward Gerard, desperately seeking his guidance.

"Don't enjoy him too much, my sweet." He gave an encouraging nod, "I'll stay here on this side of the street."

"Those will kill you," she whispered, attempting to sound sexy and inviting.

The man nodded. "Yeah. Guess I should kick the habit, huh?"

She sidled up close to him, pulse-pounding as she looked deep into his brooding gaze. He flicked the cigarette to the ground and watched it slowly burn out on the sidewalk. She noted how he kept patting his leg, each second stretched out between them like an eternity.

"SHAE!" Riley charged Shae with a hug while calling out, "Hey, dad, it's Shae!"

In the melee, Shae lost sight of her victim. The chance to give chase dwindled by the passing second. She couldn't move because of Riley's grip.

Nick emerged from the store with a plastic bag of snacks dangling from the fingers of his right hand. "Sweetheart, it's the middle of the night and you're talking loud enough to wake the dead."

"But, *DAD!*" Riley tugged Shae closer.

"Shae?" Nick nearly dropped the bag, but Riley took it from him.

The hunger grew and her jaw tingled in anticipation. She tried to remain still and calm, but the smell of his exposed neck only incited desire. She refused to say anything, lest it denied her the opportunity to keep emotions hidden from Nick.

Blinded by concern, Nick pulled her into a hug.

She struggled to get free, feeling slightly ashamed at the uncontrollable urge. "No!" she shouted, hoping he would understand that it was not him she was refusing, but rather the hunger within.

"Shae, what's wrong?" The worry in Nick's voice was evident.

She broke free but the hunger was stronger, grabbing Riley with shaky fingers. She fell to her knees with a sob.

"What have you done?"

Shae wiped her eyes, "Dorian…?" she choked out, fangs exposed.

"She's a vampire!" Riley scurried to hide behind Dorian, as far away from the monster Shae had become as she could.

"You son of a…" Nick's words died in his throat when Shae latched on to his arm.

Riley's voice rang out again. "It's the bad man!"

"Why don't you just leave?" Dorian mumbled in his native language and formed a psionic sword. He stepped between Shae and Gerard, keeping his attention on the vampire. "Nickolas, get her and Riley outta here."

"Yeah…" Nick turned to Shae. "C'mon, Shae."

"No…"

The protest was weak as Nick scooped her up.

"Please, no…"

Nick hustled to the car at the curb in front of the store. "Riley, open the back door." Then he called over his shoulder, "Dorian, I can't drive and hold Shae at the same time!"

In Nick's distraction, Shae lurched up, grasped his collar, and tugged him down. "Must…feed…"

"Shae, no!"

"Just get in the backseat and hold her down."

"Thanks, Dorian." Nick grimly turned his head as he settled into the backseat. "Riley?"

"In the front seat, Dad."

The entire ride home, Shae trembled and fought the urge to tear them all to pieces. It seemed the further away she was from the source of her darkness, the more the light pierced through.

"We're almost home, Shae." Nick's voice sounded far off in the distance as exhaustion settled in and she gave in to it.

Chapter 10

The silence was heavy in the small room, so palpable that it seemed to suck the oxygen out of the air. Tension radiated from her body, as if it were a living, breathing thing.

Shae stared at Nick, sensations of something stagnant stirred within. *The bond. But Gerard and I...* She became distracted as Nick's hand wildly moved across the page, filling it with a flurry of shapes and lines that she could barely make out. *He filled a whole page in an hour?*

She struggled to ignore unfamiliar urges from deep within. *I can't see him as a friendly neighbor from my childhood. This sensation...the thought of him being married...I should be happy for him and Diane, but I only have this crushing urge to take him.*

With those thoughts, she shifted from the bed to the low table he used for doodling and sat on his papers. Their gazes locked with a deep intensity that both scared and emboldened her. Eventually, she inched forward and delicately traced his lips., Her voice trembled, "I'm..."

"I know." He set his pencil down. "There's still time."

Her eyes grew wide and she squirmed, "How did—"

"When I kiss you, touch you—just being this close

110

to you…I have this…feeling. Like, something in the back of my mind. Like a memory that's been buried deep, but it's trying to resurface." Nick paused and shook his head. "I don't know what it means. But I can't deny it."

Her eyes widened. *He's feeling the bond!*

"Did you think he wouldn't?"

She flinched at the voice. *I didn't know what to expect.*

"What's wrong?" Nick asked.

She took a deep breath and leaned back, creating some distance between them. "It's complicated, Nick." She fidgeted, feeling the weight of the truth she had been hiding from him for so long.

"I know it is," Nick said softly, "But we can figure it out together."

She shook her head. "You don't understand, Nick. There are things that I haven't told you. Things that could change everything."

Nick's expression hardened. "What things?"

"That sensation you feel. The wanting me despite your Civilian commitments."

Nick's eyebrows furrowed as he leaned in closer to her. "What are you trying to say, Shae?"

"Don't say it!"

"I'm…I was supposed to form an intimate bond with you…" She glanced away, biting her lower lip. Despite the voice's warning before, it was eerily silent now. That was more unnerving than its shouts. *Why is it allowing me to talk now?*

"An intimate bond?"

"It was to protect me from Gerard."

Realization flashed in his eyes. "Is this why you

were upset at having to go to him to save Riley?"

A tear trickled down her eye. "Yes."

"Why didn't you tell me sooner? I'm sure if we explained it to Diane…"

"NO!"

The harshness in her tone caused him to flinch. "Why not?"

"My first time was supposed to be with you." Tears glistened, threatening to spill. "But instead, Gerard had the honor." Shae moved over to the window.

"Look, okay. You gave yourself to the monster to save my daughter. But you aren't totally his. Are you?" Nick wiped her tears away and linked their hands together.

"No." Her denial was weak, knowing the monstrous battle between the Light and Darkness that lay ahead.

"Do you trust me?" he asked, his voice low and husky.

She nodded, heart racing with anticipation.

"Close your eyes," he whispered.

She did as told, stumbling away from the window. Her legs collided with the side of the bed and her eyes fluttered open.

"I still feel like I want you too much. So, our bond is still alive, right?" He leaned in for a kiss—placing his hand on her back, tracing circles with his fingers.

She melted into the kiss, gripping his shirt tightly, and pulled him closer. The bond behind their attraction was faint, but strong enough to fuel their passion."I think we should lose the clothes." She meant to sound witty, sexy even. But it came out breathless and nervous. The anxiety of sharing herself with Nick bubbled through.

"Right." A smoldering grin slipped across his face, but their fervent desire was like wildfire. He removed their clothing, revealing gentle curves in her soft lingerie, and the hard contours of his body beneath his briefs. The intensity between them crackled like electricity in the air.

Their bodies intertwined as they lay in bed. Underneath him, Shae savored the weight of his body and his bulge pressing against her. Yet, he still wore far too many clothes. She reveled in the way his hips ground against her.

His open shirt revealed a well-toned body. She shoved an uneasy feeling aside as he groped one of her breasts. They kissed with intense passion.

The heat of the moment was shattered as the window to the room exploded inward. Instinctively, Nick pulled her to him, their modesty a secondary concern as they both prepared to face the intruders.

"Sleeping with the enemy?" There were two vampires on the edge of the shattered part of the wall. They couldn't rightly enter the room itself just yet. Nick frowned and was about to reply until Shae moved forward.

"Shae?" His arms were knocked aside as she drew away from his protective stance. He grabbed a sheet to cover his nudity as she strode further away from him toward the vampires.

She had been chanting a temporary spell to allow the vamps to enter the room. She continued approaching the group, but stopped and glared over her shoulder at Nick. "Foolish Civilian."

"What the hell?"

While observing the arrival of the others entering the room, Shae's eyes narrowed wickedly. She bared fangs at Dorian while briefly levitating. "How nice of you to join us." She smirked at Diane. "It's a pity that I must take leave now...just as things were getting so juicy with your husband." Darkness wrapped around Shae's figure.

"Shae, please..." Nick's voice was a shocked whisper coming from his crumbled cowering position as she settled back down on the rug. She took a step toward the door and the lackeys rose off their knees.

Dorian stepped forward, standing next to Nick. "That's not Shae."

As Shae stopped at the doorway, the lackeys moved to file out of the room via the hole in the wall. "You are of no use to me in this sorry state," she scoffed. A distracting glow of blue formed within her peripheral. She whirled around and there was Dorian, standing tall and determined despite his slight frame. The rippling muscles in his arms only begot her amusement, evil laughter rippling from within. "Oh, my foolish husband. Or should I say *ex*-husband. You want to play?"

Before Dorian could even react, she swept one of his legs with remarkable agility and he fell backward. Jumping atop him, she whispered a spell and sucker-punched Dorian with a heavy fist—knocking him out cold.

"MOM. DAD!"

Diane turned to see Riley standing in the doorway. "Riley!"

Shae slowly stood up over a now unconscious Dorian. She turned her attention to the girl, her breath coming in short, sharp bursts. "Foolish little Riley…"

"Riley, go back to your room." Nick's voice trembled, as he tried to warn his daughter away.

"Shae, stop hurting my family!" Riley, yet again, dared to face the danger.

"You are trying my patience!" Her rage was building. Shae took a swipe at Riley.

Diane snatched Riley out of harm's way. "Nick…do something!" She sent him a disappointed glance before rushing Riley out of the bedroom.

"Shae, stop this *now*." Again, Nick grabbed her upper arm. "Don't let Jacquain's path be yours."

For a moment, she hung her head, "Nick, please…" *Save me!* But Nick's hesitation was much too long. Their bond wasn't strong enough yet. She shoved him away with a snarl. "You try that again…and you'll lose a daughter." Then Shae vanished from their home.

****

Shae lingered in the shadows between large cement buildings on the waterfront. She watched as Kiran entered a warehouse. She approached the closed door, glancing up to see a giant bold number one. She entered the building just as he reached the stairs to the second floor.

His work uniform was fresh from last night's laundry. The keyring jangled as he spun it around his index finger until placed his foot on the bottom step. He clutched the keys in his grip and ascended the stairs. Kiran rotated through the choice of keys, choosing the correct one as he reached a storage room at the end of the hall.

Shae followed him up the stairs, careful not to alert him of her presence. She reached the top as he stuck the end of the key into the doorknob, only to be startled by a loud crash from outside. She slipped into a spare office as he spun on his heel and faced the hallway to the stairs.

"H-hello?"

"Kiran," Shae called out from the room.

His figure appeared in the doorway, shrouded in shadows. He flicked on the lights, illuminating much of the room, except for the corners.

Shae retreated further into the shadows. The door now wide open enough for light from the hallway to spill in.

"What do you want here?"

"No good…can't…back." Shae spoke in-between sobs and in an unknown language as she slumped down on her ass.

Kiran stepped further into the room. "Shae?"

"Stay away." She sniffled.

"Shae. C'mon. What's wrong?"

She eyed him. The hunger and the blood she could almost smell under his skin grew irresistible. "You…" Eyes closed tight, she whispered, "No."

"Did Jacquain do something to you?" Kiran touched her upper arm, flinching back when she jerked away. "Sorry."

With another sob, she sunk to the cement floor. "Kiran."

"Yeah, it's me." But then he frowned. "Shae…"

"I lied to everyone." She placed her hands on her knees, applying pressure as if punishing herself.

"You…lied?" He slowly sat on the floor nearby. "Hey, don't do that." She flinched from his gentle massage of her knee.

Shae stared at his hand. "To everyone. Including you."

"What did you lie about?"

"I said I could handle it. Him."

"Him?" Kiran tilted his head. "Are you afraid to tell me something? If you think it will hurt my feelings, well, I'm a big boy, I can handle that." He brushed his finger against her tear-stained left cheek.

"Don't touch me!" She snapped, pulling away from his reach.

Kiran withdrew his hand. When she moved again, he stood up. "Shae, let me help you." He moved to block her path.

She snarled and launched herself at him, shoving him against the doorframe.

"No, please...don't do that...don't—" He gasped as she bit into his neck. The moment she tasted his blood, she broke free and stumbled back—scrambling away from him, fear in her eyes. "Shae?" Slowly, he sank down onto his ass. "Oh, God..." Kiran passed out at the sight of blood on his hand.

The taste of his blood shocked some sense into her. She stared down in horror at Kiran's unconscious figure. "What have I done?" she whispered, words heavy with guilt.

Panicking, she used her map app to search for the nearest hospital. One result was only a few blocks away. She scooped Kiran up easily with newfound vampire strength. Then she formed a portal on the outer wall, jumped through it, and landed on ground level.

Her vampire speed had them arriving at the hospital parking lot in seconds. Two EMTs were exiting the building and heading for their ambulance.

"Help my friend," she called out to them.

They hustled over with a rolling gurney and she set him on it. But before the EMTs could question her, she was gone.

She wandered onto a busy street, stumbling into young lovers locked in an embrace. They carried on, oblivious to Shae watching them from just a few feet away.

'That should have been us with Nickolas.'

It was such a heartbreaking moment to watch the couple.

'Perhaps we should just suck the woman dry and take the man for ourselves.'

She managed two steps toward the couple, pausing from Nick's conjured voice, *Please, Shae...don't give in to what he did to you! Please...just come home!*

She shook her head and hustled away from the couple. *But I can't go home. Not with you, Nick, or at the Royale Hawse. And I'll be damned if I go back to Jacquain.* She was determined to resist him and the pleasures his presence stirred. But even apart from him, Shae knew she was losing the battle. Without the bond, it was only a matter of time before she became what Jacquain wanted. Spending time with him now would only help speed up the process.

Shae approached a popular late-night club. The door was open, giving a partial view of the colored lights pulsating to the beat as people entered and exited freely. The music drew her close and the temptation of pleasure drew her even closer.

Once inside, she took note of the dancing mass of Civilians who seemed to take up the whole area. Despite the bright lights and jubilant music, a feeling of solemnity lingered in the air as she moved past the couples swaying in their own private cocoon.

The dance floor was packed as she maneuvered through the crowd. She gave no apologies toward anyone who suffered any collision with her body.

A young man appeared and whispered, "Well, damn...this must be my lucky night!" He was tall and handsome, with a playful gleam in his eye. No resistance as he pulled her to an available spot to grind.

She rested her head on his shoulders, their bodies pressing tighter together. They swayed to the music, and she counted the pulses of the vein in his neck to the rhythm of the dance beat.

Her smile faded. Gerard crossed his arms in a stern pose at the edge of the dance floor. *Is he really there? Or am I just wanting him there?*

Gerard pushed his way through the crowd. "May I have this dance?"

"Get lost." The young man didn't even look at Gerard.

She would have been amused at the boy's audacity if not unnerved by Gerard's presence. Purposely, she gyrated with the boy. The entire time her eyes were locked with Gerard. She saw a vein in his neck twitch, and his eyes simmer. Taking it further, she whispered into the boy's ear, "How 'bout we find a secluded spot?"

The air in the room seemed to shift. Gerard's gaze intensified, his face an unreadable mask. With one last glance, she grabbed the boy's hand and began moving toward the exit.

He paused. "I know a perfect spot. C'mon!" He snagged her hand. "See you later, loser!" He never once looked at Gerard.

Before she disappeared into the sea of dancers, Shae glanced back, but Gerard was already gone. *I'm surprised Jacquain didn't behead him on the spot. Does he already know my plan?* She returned her attention to the boy.

He guided Shae into the darkness beyond the lit dance floor. Hearts beat wildly as they passed through a door that led into a narrow short hallway. They continued past another set of doors. Fresh air greeted them as they paused in a dimly lit alley between buildings.

He set her against a brick wall and initiated a heated kiss. He broke from her lips and trailed a sloppy path to her neck, their chests both heaving. In that moment, she felt his façade slip away, and an unbridled passion took its place.

"Do you even know who you were talking to?"

As the boy moved from one side of her neck to the other, he asked, "No. Should I?" The vein in his neck pulsated.

Shae rested her head against the brick wall as sharp fangs emerged. *Should you?*

If she wasn't so hungry, she would have continued the conversation. Instead, she snatched a handful of curly hair from the top of his head and twisted his head to the side, unconcerned with his shout of surprise. "You should have, then you would have known the danger you were with." Her other hand grabbed a fistful of his shirt and tugged it down, exposing his neck. If he realized now she was a vampire, she didn't care. Fangs pierced his neck. His pitiful attempts to free himself only made her grip him tighter. The clouds drifted over the moon sending gossamer light down onto the trash cans nearby.

"Mighty impressive, my Queen." Shae didn't flinch at the sound of Jacquain's voice filling the alley.

Shae broke her hold on the boy and tossed his now-drained body aside. The noise the body made as it fell against trash cans failed to disturb either of them. She hissed, "You don't own me, Jacquain." *You won't ever own me!*

He didn't appear phased by her anger, his silent approach radiated a smothering obsession. Once he was close enough, his bony hands extended out.

She sidestepped him and leapt away from his two accompanying lackeys. "You spoiled my fun in there."

"I'm terribly sorry. But—"

She whirled to face him, fury boiling over with venom, "What do you want from me?"

"My Queen is displeased?"

"Stop calling me that!" As Shae moved toward the end of the alley, Gerard sighed and barred any attempts at escape.

"Let me go."

"Where are you off to in such a hurry?" Gerard frowned.

"What's it to you, Jacquain?" She wavered from the fact that Gerard was her enemy. "And how'd you even know I was here?"

"My Queen...please...your anger toward me is unnecessary." Gerard motioned to a lackey behind him, "These...gentlemen...are my eyes and ears." He held out a hand. "Why do you resist me and the royalty that I am offering you?"

She chose not to answer him. *Because it's your*

fault, Jacquain, for my separation from Nick. This obsession of yours is ruining so many lives.

"You think of him?" Gerard shifted his stance, placing a hand on his hip. The expression he presented flickered sour for just a moment before becoming a malicious grin. "But he knows what you are. And I'm sure his wife and child fear you now."

"I don't care about them!" She turned away, fingers clenching so tightly they turned whiter than the lies she spat.

"Let's not worry about them right now, Shae."

It's no good anyway. I ruined the prophecy. What's the point of wanting Nick now?

"Well, don't be so hasty to disregard his importance to us."

And what of Kir—

"He's not important. We can't let outsiders interfere."

Shae's expression exhibited confusion. *Outsiders? Kiran is not—*

"Just trust me about this."

"My Queen?"

A tear trickled down her eye. She quickly tried to wipe it away. "Leave me alone, Gerard."

"I cannot."

"WHY!? Why did it have to be me?" She faced him while more tears fell. Gerard enveloped her into his arms. Shae cried softly into his chest.

"Do you hear that, Shae? That is my heart—it beats only for you." His sincere words stopped her tears. "Please, reconsider my offer."

"To be by your side?"

"As my Queen." His hard gaze softened and he

extended his hand once more. "You know it's best."

A cool, light breeze swept through the alley as she struggled with a heart heavy from an internal urge for power too hard to ignore. She gazed into Gerard's eyes, stumbling toward him as if pushed by invisible forces.

"Take his offer."

Despite being torn between a growing love for Kiran and an overwhelming desire for power, Shae finally relented. In the biggest decision of her life. She slowly raised a trembling hand toward Gerard.

Gerard's grip was tight as he sealed their deal with a kiss. "Come now…you should get a good rest. When the night falls tomorrow, I shall give you the official tour of your new home."

Chapter 11

As promised, Gerard gave her the grand tour. He walked through the foyer with a purpose, his long strides leaving her struggling to keep up. She followed, hesitantly, as he made a sharp turn down a wide, mahogany-lined hallway. Oil paintings in gilded frames acquired through shady means decorated the wall.

Finally, they reached the den. She schooled her features as they stood between the chair and retro record player. There was no need for Gerard to know how much the memory of that night with Riley still affected her.

She had seen his vast collection of books in the library and study with its heavy mahogany desk, carved and embossed in extravagant motifs around the edges. The game room with its stunning brass chess set and billiard table.

Shae paused at the chess set.

"The queen. Pick it up."

She picked up the black chess piece.

"That's you, Shae. The most powerful piece on the board."

She noticed the white version on the opposite end. *But that's a queen as well.*

"The weaker version. That is the you now. At least while Gerard is still alive."

"My Queen, do you want to learn this game?"

She felt unnerved by the whole conversation in her mind and quickly set the piece back down. "No. Let's just…continue the tour you promised me." She moved away from the chessboard just as Gerard placed his hands on her hips from behind.

"Very well."

Next was the dining room with its grand table and credenza. All of the windows swathed in heavy, velvet maroon drapes. She gave a noticeable pause in the dining room. However, when Gerard attempted to discuss the memory of her transformation, she turned away. With a sigh, Gerard continued the tour, moving to the kitchen and pantry, state-of-the-art.

She followed him past the stairs that led to the second floor, returning to the hallway with the oil paintings. "Why are we going this way again?"

However, in the middle of the hallway, Gerard paused in front of a door they had waltzed right past earlier. "I saved this room for last on the tour of the first floor. My private room."

"Where is the door handle?" She looked at him as they stood at the large oak door to the room.

"There is only *one* way to get into this room." Gerard placed his hand on the spot where a doorknob should have been. She watched it light up. He pulled his hand away to reveal a circular leaf pinwheel glowing in gold. "I've set it to recognize your hand. You just need to let it get a reading so it will permanently record it."

Shae watched as a faint light appeared on the panel, followed by a soft beep. Gerard motioned for her to do the same. She reached out hesitantly, mimicking his action. A soft beep indicated that the hand imprint was registered. She waited until the light faded and then performed the action once more. "Very impressive."

Gerard smiled and pushed the door open as he escorted them into the room. "It's amazing what Civilians can create when you threaten them." The windows reflected the furniture in the room, but not them. "If I cannot be found, then it is because this is where I am."

Shae nodded, gazing at the enormous canopy bed and sitting area next to a row of windows to view the hedge maze and garden outside.

He swooped forward, lifted her into his arms, and whisked past the various guest bedrooms on the second floor. She was already familiar with one bedroom— his—having slept there once already.

"We'll return here soon enough."

"A blind fool he is. But we'll let him have his fun with us."

"I'm fine enough to walk on my own." Shae squirmed out of Gerard's embrace, hoping he couldn't sense the uneasiness in her tone. '

They paid a brief visit to the section of the mansion appointed for his lackeys and servants, arranged like military barracks. The servants slept in the cots at night and the lackeys during the day. And then it was time for a tour of the outside grounds. They quickly passed the garden shed, as he was eager to show her his exquisite botanical garden.

Gerard led the way back into the sunroom after a round of adult hide-and-seek within his garden maze.

"Excuse me, sir." A lackey bowed to him and then to Shae. "My Queen."

Shae was fine with Gerard using that endearment, but she seethed at the lackey. "I'm not your queen."

126

"I have ordered them to address you as you are entitled."

She rolled her eyes. "Fine." She sighed as Gerard kissed her knuckles. She leaned up and kissed him on the lips, only to have the lackey force a cough to interrupt once more. "What is it?"

"Uh...phone call..."

Gerard stepped forward then, his dark clothing making his pale face appear almost ghostly in the waning evening light. His eyes were unreadable but his voice was surprisingly gentle. "My Queen," he began, "the time we have just spent together is a treasure I'll remember forever. But alas, I must leave you now to attend to some pressing matters."

He reached out and brushed his fingers through her hair, before trailing his bony fingers down a silky pale cheek. He kissed her forehead before following the lackey down the hall.

"I'll go find something to do then," Shae shouted at his backside. Once alone, she glanced around for inspiration on what to do now. Two hours before sunrise and she made her way to the front door of the mansion.

Conflicted, lost, and half aware of the intended destination, she emerged from a portal. *No. I shouldn't be here.* Shae willed her feet to take her away from Nick's house, but instead, she walked up the steps compelled by an invisible force, onto his porch.

Shae shed a few tears and placed a hand on the door. But there was no glow similar to the door of Gerard's private room. No glyph would light up. She closed her eyes and stroked the bond as if it were a newborn animal. It was still there, weak and faint.

There was no longing or hope in it anymore, just pain and sorrow.

I want to come back, but I'll never be accepted here. I'm sorry, Nick. We cannot go back to how things were. We cannot.

Yet, Shae circled the back of the house, stopping at Nick's bedroom window on the first floor. Riley's room was the window above, on the second floor. Through a crack in the blinds, she could see him—sleeping peacefully, his arms wrapped protectively around Diane. More tears fell as Shae wished that it was herself, not Diane, lying so peacefully next to him.

She quickly wiped her eyes and roughly shook her head as she recalled the kiss with Kiran at the market event. *I liked it. Kissing him. So, I don't understand why I felt so much fear of him.*

But then an intense craving for Gerard, increasing now, second by second, since the moment she gave herself willingly to the feared vampire, began to pry its way into her thoughts. A craving for more than just blood.

"Let us take his soul, Shae."

"What?" She shivered with dread upon hearing that dark voice again. Hastily scrambling away from Nick's house, she stumbled backward, landing safely into a portal. Ironically, it released her onto the cement stairs outside Gerard's door. The cement surface seemed cold against bare feet. Sadness shifted to a familiar dark desire as she climbed the steps. It was like a velvet curtain cocoon.

Despite having a fully staffed mansion, an eerie silence permeated the area. She rushed straight to the master bedroom and inhaled the soothing scent of

Gerard on the sheets. Through all the inner turmoil, exhaustion slowly settled in like a warm, heavy blanket until suddenly—pressure on one side of the bed jolted her awake.

She turned to the window of the French door and calculated one hour until sunrise. "Gerard?"

"I apologize, my Queen. You've fallen asleep while waiting for my return." With assurance, he pulled her to him. "The sun will rise soon, but I wish to…"

She hushed him with a finger on his lips. "My dear Gerard," she mumbled, allowing him to focus on the sensations of hands gliding upward on his chest.

His hesitant expression broke into a pleasured smile. "I am filled with much ease…to know I have finally found someone who knows what I say…without me ever having to say it."

"But it's not telepathy, Shae. We just all want the same thing right now."

"My Queen, are you all right? You are much too quiet and so distant at this moment."

She distracted him with a lustful grin and heated eyes, a hot breath whispering in his ear, "Take me…I am yours."

His eyes exposed how those words completely melted his need to control situations like this. He may have initiated the kiss, but she deepened it. Their tongues danced, exploring each other's mouths as they lost themselves in the passion of the moment.

Shae moaned into Gerard's mouth, feeling his hardness pressed against her thigh. Without a word, she removed the thin, silky lingerie and tossed it aside. Her once olive-tinted flesh had faded to a creamy white hue, further enhancing the savory sculptor of a warrior's figure. Fully awake now, she played coy. "Do you like what you see?"

"More than you will ever realize." His response earned him a seductive smile. "And now…" He stood up. "I shall return the favor." Wiggling free from his blood-red boxers, he didn't bother returning the question—especially when her breath quickened.

She willfully relented control back to him. Gerard motioned his finger, completing two full circles drawn in the air. She scooted to the edge of the bed and rolled onto her stomach—feet planted on the hardwood floor.

He pulled her ass up in the air, angled just how he liked it. Then he swiftly claimed her, right there at the side of the bed, gripping her body tightly as he pumped fully in and out. The squeaking of the bedsprings amidst their heavy moans filled the room. Only after her body yielded to his coaxing thrusts did they shift again to lay together in his bed. They snuggled briefly, both basking in the intimate afterglow during the intermission.

With just minutes left until sunrise, they trembled with anticipation as their bodies entwined—an intimate tangle of limbs and desire. Gerard marveled at the curves, softness, and warmth as he entered her, fastening them together in a tight bond.

Shae savored his weight on top of her, captivated by the intensity of his gaze. As they continued to move together in perfect synchrony, the rhythm intensified with each thrust. Groans surged from deep within him as Shae's moans echoed throughout the room. Gerard's roaming hands sent sparks of electricity, igniting every nerve ending.

Reaching the pinnacle of pleasure, they jointly

cried out each other's names in a chorus of euphoria that filled the air around them. With one final exhale, they collapsed onto the bed in an exhausted post-orgasmic bliss. Shae nestled into Gerard's chest, cocooning within his warmth as she listened to the soothing sound of his heartbeat.

****

Shae approached the row of windows in their private room, lithe figure illuminated in the waning light. Beyond the glass, the gardens stretched out in a sea of dusky blues and greens, the muted colors framed by the silvery night sky. Soft petals of datura and hydrangeas opened in the moonlight.

"What are those?"

Gerard's cold body enveloped her in a powerful embrace from behind. His chest was still slick from their quick, intimate romp in the canopy bed. "Those are datura's, often considered moonflowers, also known as devil's trumpet."

"Interesting."

"Isn't it?" He chuckled.

"I didn't take you for a man of flowers. No matter what they are called." Shae studied the large, showy trumpet-shaped blossoms of many shades: purple, pink, yellow and white. "They are beautiful."

"Not as beautiful as you."

"You're sucking up, Gerard."

"Just don't confuse datura's with Brugmansia—angel's trumpets."

She laughed heartily. "As long as you don't confuse me with one of those Civilian hussies you used to entertain."

"I wouldn't dare." He moved to block the view of

the flowers.

"Tonight is a perfect opportunity to find someone to play with," she murmured, her darkened voice barely more than a whisper.

His eyes grew dark and serious. "Shae?" The intense staring contest between them lasted a few seconds. "Who are you?"

She raised her hand, cupping the side of his face. "I am the side that you asked for." A haunting, eerie giggle escaped her lips. "My dear Gerard, am I not your queen?" Her gaze bore into his.

Slowly, he nodded. "Yes. Of course. You are my queen. But, I do have some last-minute business details to finalize."

"You would deny your queen her pleasure?" Shae's voice was dark and she tilted her head in an odd way at him.

"I could never deny you, my Queen."

Feeling satisfied, the darkness receded.

Gerard retrieved a robe and slipped it over her shoulders. He adjusted his shirt and trousers for the sake of the others in the mansion. Footsteps echoed off the floors of the foyer as they passed through.

He stepped closer to Shae and slipped his arm around her waist. Together, they ascended the stairs that led to the guest bedrooms. On the second-floor hallway, gold-leveled lamps lined the walls, and mini-chandeliers glittered from the ceilings.

Shae studied the numerous lights. "Is this you making up for not having access to the sun?"

He chuckled. "Requests from the Civilian staff. This part of the hallway is much too dark for them without all this light."

"But this is your mansion. You aren't bothered by all this light?"

"No. I've grown to ignore it." He motioned toward one chandelier and one gold lamp. "The deco is very intricate and fitting, don't you think?"

She stared at the curves and the chain that anchored the chandelier to the ceiling. "Yeah, I suppose." She approached the walls. "Although, I do so appreciate the visual texture more."

"I am glad you are pleased."

Once in the master bedroom, Shae waited to see what he would wear. They each chose garments with hints of fiery velvet and raven leather, allowing flexibility in their movement. Shae's outfit had more tantalizing views of exquisite flesh.

Gerard admired her curves. "Ready to paint the town red?" he asked, smiling mischievously and offering his arm.

"Let's go."

The conjured portal delivered them from the rooftop patio of the master bedroom to the circular cement stairs of the front entrance.

"Such an odd mode of transportation, my Queen." He had to lean close to be heard over the lively atmosphere of the street. Musicians playing on the corner of an intersection to a crowd sitting or standing nearby on an outside bar patio.

Shae's brow furrowed upon assuming one of the customers resembled Kiran. "Gerard, let's pick a different street."

"Very well."

They weaved through the crowd unnoticed as they veered toward a much less crowded block. Most of the shops were closed, with a few getting ready to end the business day. She kept her hand in his as they walked past storefront windows—her gaze more at him than at the stores.

"What troubles you, my Queen?"

Shae blinked but didn't glance away. "Since my first return to the Royale Hawse, they've filled my head with words coloring you in a negative way. But after spending time with you, I believe they maligned you."

He turned to face her, causing them to stop in front of a card and novelty shop—which was still open. "But I've killed many."

"So have I," she insisted.

"For pleasure?" He took her other hand.

"For survival." Shae stepped closer to him. "And the same can be said about you, Gerard—on some level. So many fear you and twice as many want you dead."

"And Battle Realm brought you pleasure." He tenderly caressed her cheek.

"Considering how much time I spent there, yes, it did." She closed and opened her eyes. "They wanted to make me untouchable to you—if we ever were face to fang. But I am yours now."

'For now.'

She ignored the ominous threat of the voice.

"I have bonded us together, so it would be universally difficult to come between us now." There was an unnoticeable flinch from her at the mention of the word bond. Any other reactions were overruled when Gerard tenderly pressed his lips to hers. Slowly, her arms raised and rested loosely on his shoulders around his neck.

"You sick fucker! How many more girls are you going to leave dead and drained?!"

Gerard spun to find a shotgun pointed at his face and the owner of it glaring angrily from behind the barrel. Shae simply stepped back instinctively and arms dropped to her sides—a little miffed that the kiss was interrupted as she was about to deepen it. Just as he was about to reply to the Civilian threat, Shae stepped forward. "I'll kindly ask you to remove your weapon from the sight of my lover."

"Lady, he's just going to kill you…leave you dead!" The man didn't waiver as Shae glared at him.

"I wouldn't do such a thing."

"Don't listen to his lies, Lady…he's just trying to fool you! But I know better!" the man protested.

Shae folded her arms and stepped between the point of the gun and Gerard. "Obviously, you don't." Without warning, she snatched the shotgun and tossed it away as she advanced on the Civilian. "I love him…and I will not stand to have things I love threatened." When Shae flashed her fangs, the Civilian gasped in shock. She moved behind the man and captured him in a headlock.

"You love me?" Gerard looked at her in bewilderment.

"Don't do it, Shae!"

Shae ignored Rozette's interruptive plea as she snapped the Civilian's neck. The body fell like a rag doll to the pavement as she resumed her place at Gerard's side. "Rozette…how nice to see you."

Rozette's eyes glinted in anger toward Shae's mock greeting.

Shae continued. "Let me introduce you to—"

Rozette turned to Gerard. "Bastard."

"Roz, such hurtful words." He smiled menacingly.

Shae purposely ignored the name Gerard was called, "Are you here to save me, Rozette?" She stepped back onto her heels. "Or are you here on a kill order?"

"I will not kill you, Shae," Rozette replied. "But him—"

"I won't allow it." She hissed and clenched her fists, ready to attack.

"Stand down, Shae!" She whipped her gaze to the left and noted Verties approaching them. Rozette stepped back.

Gerard glanced at Verties with a smirk. "I must have displeased your leader if you're out here." Teasingly, he slid his arms around Shae's waist from behind and planted a kiss on her cheek as he purposely cupped the underside of her half-exposed breasts. "Oh yes…now I remember what I did."

"Gerard…be nice," Shae playfully scolded him and broke from the embrace and circled Verties and Rozette, ready to pounce at any slight movement from them, "But honestly, what does she hope to accomplish by sending Verties out? Does she think the sight of *my father* would cause me to feel ashamed for fornicating repeatedly with a monster?" Shae stepped toward Rozette, but Verties intervened.

"Rozette, head on back to the warehouse. I'll handle this." Verties wearily eyed Shae. With a sigh, he turned to Gerard. "Do you know what you've done?"

Gerard tilted his head at Verties. "I think someone misses you, my Queen."

"Well, he'll just have to deal with me wanting you

now, Gerard." Shae looked squarely at Verties.

Verties shook his head. "You're still the loser, Jacquain."

"Oh? How do you figure?"

While they began swapping insults, Shae walked away from them. She tuned out their verbal squabble as an odd sensation stirred. Something prickled at her awareness, like a lingering odor or annoying buzzing. Colors and sounds seemed to waver as if seen through a haze. She staggered further away from the two arguing figures, fading from reality. Blinking didn't help—the blurriness remained. One misstep on the crackling and uneven sidewalk sent her stumbling into the brick wall of the card shop. A trembling hand scraped against the bricks. Molten hot dizziness erased any coherent thoughts and feverishly spread through her body. This was certainly different from the mind attacks Gerard used to instigate.

Summoning every ounce of willpower, Shae managed to shift, leaning back against the brick wall, slightly hunched over. Limbs twitched with a barely contained energy, body hunched over. Instead of the sidewalk, she envisioned herself on a precipice over an endless void.

All around was only darkness and silence. No sound of the faint music from a block away. No Gerard or her father arguing. Even the wind seemed absent.

Fingers flexed in frustration, desperate for a target. They twitched and burned with an intense desire to destroy; her mind screamed for mayhem. A vampiric crush just waiting to be unleashed!

"Uh…Shae?"

She glanced up, seeing Kiran standing there with

worry in his eyes and an innocent plush teddy bear in his hand. *Why am I only seeing him...in this...void?* She noted his turtle-neck sweater. *He's trying...to hide the...bite.* When she stepped to him, he stepped back. "Get...out." The conflicting fear and anger in her voice made them both pause.

"Been wanting the chance to tell you I forgive you for biting me." Kiran was the first to act. "I even got this for you, hoping we can make amends. He's holding a little knitted pumpkin. See?" He held out the teddy.

"Kiran?" Her body was shaking. She put a hand to her head, eyes closed tightly, and whimpered.

"Scare him off, Shae."

"Your hand is bleeding." He fisted around in the pockets of his jeans and pulled out an unused, crumpled napkin. "Let me clean that up for you."

"Get rid of him NOW!"

She flinched from the shouting. But there was no time to question why Kiran made the voice fear him. "Kiran, don't. You need to go."

"You don't look too good. Let me take you to the hosp—"

"Listen to her, young man." Verties moved in front of Kiran, just as Shae tried to lunge for her Civilian friend.

"But I...you—"

"Kiran...just go." She held on long enough to watch him reluctantly leave with the teddy still in his possession. Then she groaned as another flash of pain erupted within and she crashed to her knees.

"Shae!?"

"I wouldn't if I were you, Jacquain." Verties scooped Shae in his arms, only getting as far as the small, attached parking lot of the store before Gerard was there to separate them.

"Unhand her this instant!"

There was a minuscule break from the searing sensation coursing through her. "Stay away." Her voice was strained and cracked.

But Gerard dared, putting a hand on her shoulder. "Shae…relax, it's just me."

A feral growl pierced the air. Eyes alight with rage, her voice dripped with malevolence as she spoke, "You are of no use to us." Shae frantically scrambled backward, seeking a more innocent victim to corrupt. Though vampiric healing kicked in. Tears formed just as the kill sensation began rising again. She called out, in an anguished voice, "Father…"

Verties hustled past an annoyed and angry Jacquain to kneel at Shae's side. He pressed a hand on her forehead and mumbled a magical spell in their native Deviant language. Shae's eyes glazed over, and her breathing slowly evened out. "It has passed."

She glanced up at him, attempting to question why she was on her hands and knees in a parking lot. But she shook it off and stood—moving back to Gerard's side. "It's getting crowded here, Gerard."

"Wait…what did you mean earlier? I am of no use to you? But you said us?"

She ignored his question and walked away.

Chapter 12

"Are you sure you're all right?" Gerard questioned for the fourth time as they entered the main foyer of his mansion.

"Yes, my love." She reached up and coiled her fingers within his shoulder-length dark locks. "I had a change of wants."

"And what is it you want now?" His hands slid around her waist as he leaned close to her.

"Time alone with you…" Her hands caressed the sides of his neck. "doing something that no outsider can interfere with."

"As much as I'd like to, I don't think you should over-extend yourself."

Her mouth twisted into a half smile. "I am more than well enough to make love to you again, but I respect you need an ample amount of time to recharge," Shae said, as if she knew why. She pressed her lips to his in a simple, sweet, brief kiss. "There are other ways to indulge in our pleasures together, my dear Gerard."

"If you insist. I cannot deny anything you ask of me, my Queen." He suggested an alternate activity. "How about a game of some sort?"

"Something like our game in the garden." She pulled away from him but latched onto his hand to lead him down a hallway to the game room. Once there, she paused to decide which game to play. The pool table caught her eyes. "What game is that?"

"Ah, so you'd like a round of pool?" He grabbed two pool sticks, handing one to her. He explained the game as he set it up. "The object of this game is to sink all sixteen of these balls..." He held up the solid red ball and the striped green ball for emphasis. ". . . into any of these six pockets." Shae approached him, taking the red ball. With a mischievous grin, she formed an exact duplicate in her other hand. Gerard shook his head. "I hope you intend to play the game fairly, my Queen."

She snuffed out the fake red ball and handed the real one back to him. "I am a queen." She picked up the pool stick and rolled it in her hands, a reminder of the sword and the life she left behind. "And as a queen...I must uphold..."

"Shae?"

"It seems so long ago."

"What does, my Queen?"

"The blur of days on the battlefield."

He trailed a finger under her chin and took the pool stick from her hands; she made no move to take it back from him. "Do you miss it?"

"I was wrong."

"Wrong?"

"I should have never left." She moved to another spot in the room.

"How so?" Gerard stepped back into her line of sight.

She finally looked at him—or possibly at a bookshelf behind him. "I wanted to find him."

"You have me now." He tried to sway her again, back into his favor.

"I tried to reconnect with him, but everything was wrong."

"That heathen Civilian is a threat to you, my Queen." Gerard shook his head. "You don't need him."

Shae fell silent for a moment. *It is YOU that I don't need, Jacquain!* She looked down at her hands, now enveloped by Gerard's. *You are suffocating me. I cannot be held back anymore.*

"Shae?" He loudly gasped when he gazed into her eyes.

Calmly, she pulled free, already turning away. She would have left then and there if he had not put his hand on her shoulder. "I should thank you for the gift you have given us."

"Gift?" his voice rasped.

She kept her eyes fixed on the door, hiding the hungry smirk. Her tongue rolled over her fangs—yet it wasn't blood she was after. "I think I shall show you how appreciative of it I am."

But he ignored it. Gerard whisked her around. "This is not the game I wish to play with you. Now cease this at once, Shae!"

The jerking movement had shaken her free from the hold of the Darkness. She glanced up at him, rubbing her thumb on the palm of his hand. "What is wrong, my love?"

He shook his head. "Perhaps you are tired—more tired than we both realize." He wrapped an arm around her waist and escorted her to their bedroom.

A lackey had the audacity to approach them at the stairs leading to the second floor. "Master Jacquain…there is a call for you concerning the Percy exhibit for the art show."

Shae heard the last of it and glanced up. "Art show?" She glared at Thomas and then at Gerard. "Is this like the last time a call interrupted us?"

"Nothing to concern yourself with, my Queen." Quickly, he kissed her temple. "Shall I have Thomas escort you to our room?"

She waved him off. "No…no, I can handle it." She gave him a smile of assurance.

"All right." Gerard turned to Thomas, who handed him the phone before following him to another room.

Shae watched their retreating backs with a pained expression, before slowly trudging up the towering staircase. With each step she took, emotions rose in tandem like an overflowing volcano. Dizzy and lightheaded, she crumbled at the top of the stairs. Hands twitched with the familiar, unbearable burning to destroy. *So…overwhelming…but I…must…resist.*

After a few minutes, her eyes snapped open.

Logan, a shorter, stockier lackey nudged her shoulder. "My Queen, are you all right?"

"What's wrong with your eyes?" Jonas shook his head and moved around her. "I'd better get Master Jacquain!"

She stood up. "That would be unwise, Jonas. My dear Gerard is busy with a client and you know what will happen if you disrupt him." She stepped toward Logan and seductively ran a hand over his chest. "Logan…" She drew closer to him, wrapping her arms around his shoulder and burying her face within the crevice of his neck to breathe in deeply.

"My…uh…my Queen, what're…?" Logan broke out into a scream when her fangs pierced his neck— creating a deadly gash.

Shae heard Jonas' retreat and caught up to him at the bottom of the steps.

He backed against the railing, not bothering to hide his fear as he trembled. "Wh-why…why…?" Shae could hear the footsteps of the others coming to investigate. She kept her focus on Jonas, hungrily eyeing him before diving into him. He suffered the same fate as Logan.

She then moved quickly, ambushing servants and lackeys from room to room in an endless raging storm. With her ability to portal, the entire second and third floors of the mansion were slaughtered before those on the first floor became alarmed. She had saved the hallway of the glyph room for last. She emerged from a portal with a servant in her grip. After the portal closed, she finished draining the servant before tossing the woman aside.

A lackey dashed past her from behind. But she made no move to snag him or give chase. Instead, she spotted a figure in the doorway.

Gerard's demanding voice rang out, "What is going on?"

The lackey froze, unable to resist addressing his master. But he began babbling, oblivious of whom he was talking to, "…completely snapped…it's horrible!!"

"Who is coming this way?"

The lackey turned his head to see Shae closing in on them. "Lemme go…she's gonna kill me!!"

"Hello, my love."

Gerard glanced up to see Shae standing before them.

She mock frowned when the lackey struggled from Gerard's grip. "Aw, you don't want to play with me?"

"Shae?" Gerard gaped at the amount of blood that covered her.

She ignored Gerard and snatched the lackey from him. "If you stop screaming, I'll promise to pleasure you beyond your wildest fantasies." The lackey could not be swayed into silence. She latched a hand around the lackey's throat. "Would you just...shut...up!?" With a twist of her hand, she crushed his vocal cords. The lackey fell to his knees, screaming in pain. She glanced over to Gerard. "I'll be with you in a moment, sweetie..." Her voice was seductively teasing, laced with a neurotic madness. "...I just must finish one thing." She reached down and tugged the injured lackey to her.

Gerard watched as his once sweet queen ripped into his precious lackey. He fled right back into his private room and shut the door.

She tauntingly called out to him, "Oh, my dear Gerard...is this how you show me you love me?" Then she ran her nails across the door. "I told you I wanted to thank you for giving me these gifts!" She cooed and giggled. When she kicked the door open, the lackey with the crushed throat fell into the open doorway. She stepped over the body and entered the room.

Gerard motioned to the lackey in the doorway. He put his hands on his hips. "This senseless slaughter upsets me. And I will not stand to have my queen acting like a whore!"

She said nothing until she was right in front of him, touching him. "Oh, but it is just so much fun to play around." She trailed a finger around his face. "But right now...there are more important matters..." She fisted a section of his shirt in her grip. "...such as giving you the ride of a lifetime." When Gerard attempted to escape, she used her vampiric speed to block his path.

"What do you want?" His voice carried a hint of impatience.

"I believe I owe you a dance, my love." She snapped her fingers and a small radio next to the canopy bed flicked on. The room was filled with the melodic voice of Leona Lewis performing the latest hit, "'Bleeding Love.'"

"Now is not the time for this." Yet he still willingly danced with her.

"We're immortal now, my love. We have time." She heatedly chuckled.

"This is not what I changed you for, Shae."

She growled and stepped away from him. "Poor little Gerard. He'll never get the pleasure that he seeks. Not from a Civilian," She paused from traipsing around him in mockery and then glared at his backside. "And certainly not from your queen." She gave no warning when she snatched the back of his collar and yanked him over to the bed.

"Your eyes…they…they're black."

Shae watched the realization surface on his expression.

He clutched her wrists when she straddled him. "You're not my queen."

"Then what am I?"

"You've taken her." He tried to sit up. "I must warn them."

She slammed him back down onto the mattress, ripping open his shirt and digging her fingernails into his flesh. Blood oozed out from the fresh wounds. "And ruin all my fun? I thought you would be proud. Your fledgling indulging in her own pleasure!"

Gerard winced and narrowed his eyes, staring deep into hers. After a few seconds, he shook his head and tried again.

She burst into laughter. "Oh, that is so cute. But your mind attacks won't work anymore. I've been feeding off your powers this whole time. Why do you think you were so quick to avoid sex with me?"

His eyes went wide. "I've played into your hands, haven't I?"

"They all have, Gerard. The prophecy that they believed in wasn't to protect me from you. If you would have helped me with Nickolas, then I might have spared you. But how could you have known that?" She gripped his throat. "It has really been so much fun pretending to be your queen." She bared her fangs and mumbled a paralyzing spell. He complained of not being able to move, but Shae only giggled before ripping into his neck. While she drained him of blood, the Darkness siphoned away his remaining life essence.

After a while, Gerard's struggle stopped. Shae enjoyed the silent moment, entertained by her lover's dead body. She tousled his hair, running fingers through it lovingly. A noise from the hallway caught her attention. She sensed the blood with heightened excited senses. "Oh, now that is not nice…hiding from me this whole time!"

She carefully crawled off Gerard and trailed after the frightened servant.

The chase was on. The servant ran recklessly through the echoing hallways of the mansion, desperately trying to outrun Shae.

She caught up to the woman servant in the

backyard. "I hope you know the consequences of making me work to ease my hunger."

She was surprised when the woman pulled them both down to the cement patio. "How could you let this happen?" the woman wailed, managing to get free for only a split second.

"That is something you'll have to take up with Gerard," she teased back and dug fingernails into the woman's face—causing her to scream in intense pain. "The only problem is…he's permanently unavailable to help you with your situation." She grinned wickedly and leaned down, piercing her fangs into the shoulder and draining the woman dry.

She sat up quickly upon feeling her shoulder burn and looked to the sky. *Damn sunrise, fun's over.* She scanned the surroundings. *Too far from the private room, although it's ruined now. And no one is alive to secure the master bedroom. Should have let them show me how the system worked. The garden shed will have to suffice.* Inside, she glanced around. *No windows. Well, aside from that tiny glass block window at the very top of the wall.* She ransacked the area inside for a blanket and arranged a section for her to hide in. By the time she finished, Shae had collapsed again.

****

Shae flung the musty blanket off and stumbled out of the garden shed into the dark mansion grounds. *Why am I not in Gerard's bed?* She passed a patio table on the deck and stumbled over a Civilian body splayed out in a pool of congealing blood. *Did my father move me to the shed before launching an assault on the mansion?* "I have to find Gerard!"

Heart pounding, she rushed into the mansion, only

to find more corpses scattered at the bottom of the stairs. Three lackeys and one servant lay strewn about, slain with brutal force. With mounting terror, she hurried up the stairs to the master suite. *What kind of nightmare have I stepped into?!*

Once inside the room, she rushed to the bed. "Gerard!" The two figures were bloody, unrecognizable, but they didn't fit the shape of Gerard. Out on the private second-floor patio was another mess of bodies. Shae's heart raced as she surveyed the scene. The mutilated bodies barely resembled human beings, but none were Gerard. She fought the urge to vomit as the stench of death hung in the air.

Slowly, she made her way back down to the first floor, weaving around bodies on the way to their private room.

The events of the previous night trickled into her thoughts. "I killed them all!" The door was off its hinges and she had to step over another body. She found another lackey wedged in the open door, now only hanging upright by one of its two hinges. The lackey's lifeless eyes stared at Shae accusingly. She gulped and stepped over the body, entering the room. Her eyes trailed over to the canopy bed. "Oh god...Gerard..."

The moment her fingertips grazed his skin, he dropped to the floor like a puppet with its strings cut. She scrambled to his side, aghast at the sight before her. The air around them seemed to stand still as she stared in disbelief at the body that had been so vibrant and alive the previous night.

Since his blood flowed in her veins now, she felt a smidgen of loss. *What's gonna happen to me now?*

'Good riddance.'

"Shae? What the hell happened here?"

She glanced up in tears. *Kiran?* He stood just outside of the door, holding a large, thick postal envelope in his hand. His work shirt collar barely covered his bandaged neck.

She wiped the tears with the back of her hand and stood up unsteadily. "Gerard's dead." She took a deep breath, trying to steady a shaking voice. "I did it. I killed him."

"And the rest of the bodies?" His face paled, daring to glance down at the body he stepped over as he entered the room.

"Yes." Her voice was a mere whisper.

"Holy shit, Shae." He bravely pulled her into his embrace without dropping the package.

She clung to him, sobbing uncontrollably. The weight of the events of the previous night crushed her with every passing moment.

"It's okay, Shae. Someone was bound to kill him," Kiran whispered, rubbing her back in soothing circles.

She flinched and then noticed the package. "What's that?"

"Not sure what's in it. But it's addressed to Gerard Jacquain. Guess I'll bring it back as undeliverable." He nervously chuckled.

"Let's get out of here," she said, wiping away stray tears.

Chapter 13

Kiran cautiously led the way to the front circular stairs, bracing himself for any sort of aggressive reaction.

She simply moved ahead and sat down on the steps. "I'm scared of myself, too."

He hesitantly followed suit and draped an arm around her. "Oh, I'm not worried that you'll bite me again. I mean, yeah, you could…but—"

"I'm not supposed to fall in love with you."

"What?" He pulled back to stare at her.

She avoided his gaze, biting her lower lip as she repeated in an exhausted tone, "I'm not supposed to fall in love with you, Kiran. It's dangerous."

His expression grew more serious from the gravity of those words. "What do you mean, dangerous?"

She turned to look at him directly, eyes now filled with fear and uncertainty. "I mean, there are things about me that you don't know. Things that I can't share."

"What kind of things? What can you not tell me?"

"Kissing you at the market—"

"NO!"

"I haven't been able to stop thinking about the way you bolted after we kissed." He tucked a finger under her chin. "You shouldn't be afraid of me. I kinda liked the kiss." He was leaning in.

"Please don't," she whispered. "I'm scared of what might happen if we kiss again."

Kiran felt a shiver run down his spine as he looked into her haunted eyes. "Jacquain...were you kissing him when you killed him?"

Shae shot upright.

"Please, don't run away again."

His pleading voice tugged on her heart, and tears threatened to fall. Disturbing images of the previous night replayed in her mind. In a flat voice, she grunted, "I don't want to talk about it." Both of her hands checked the pockets of her outfit. "I need to call Nick but I can't find my phone."

"We can use mine."

She recited the number to dial.

When Nick answered, Kiran put him on speaker. "Hello?"

She hesitated to answer back.

Kiran spoke up on her behalf. "Nick, you probably don't remember me. But I'm with Shae right now." He paused. "She just had an emotional situation at Jacquain's mansion...but I'm not so sure you should come here. We could meet up at your place."

"Woah, slow down," Nick's exasperated voice cut in. "Just stay there. Whatever happened, we'll deal with it once I get there."

"Nick..." Shae finally spoke up, just as the call disconnected.

"He'll be here soon, apparently." Kiran stuffed his phone back in his pocket. "Want to wait in my delivery truck until he gets here?"

"Yeah." She stood, wobbled, and approached his truck in the circular driveway. He opened the passenger side door and she settled in the seat. He left the door open and stood next to her. "Kiran?"

"Yeah?" he asked, looking at her with concern in his eyes.

She reached out and took his hand, giving it a gentle squeeze. "Thank you for being here with me."

He smiled softly, intertwining his fingers with hers. "Always, Shae. I'll always be here for you."

The air grew heavy with electricity as she leaned over to him. His dark eyes were so captivating, despite her internal raging war. Desire and fear coursed through her veins as he stared back with a smoldering gaze.

God, he's so damn dreamy. Despite the earlier conversation, she noted his similar love-struck stance.

Their lips finally met in a passionate embrace. His strong arms pulled her in close. In that moment, everything else melted away, leaving them in a blissful cocoon of love. All worries about the past and the future faded away as they lost themselves in the kiss.

Vile anger churned until her legs and arms violently vibrated. *No, not now. Why can't I kiss him?!* She struggled for breath, eyes pleading for relief from her boiling insides.

"Shae?"

Suddenly, an unmarked van sped toward them and screeched to a halt behind Kiran's truck.

Verties jumped out of the passenger side of the van. "Step away from her, young man."

"Who are you?" Kiran stood defensively in front of Shae.

"Father?" Shae's voice cracked, head sweating profusely as if she just inhaled the hottest pepper.

Dorian scrambled out of the driver's seat, and

Rozette emerged from the side sliding door.

"Sedate her, NOW!" Verties commanded.

Rozette approached with a syringe in hand. Shae struggled for freedom as Dorian grabbed her arms.

"What the hell?" Kiran was pushed aside, dropping to his knees in the commotion.

Rozette injected the sedative into Shae's arm, and she immediately fell limp in Dorian's arms.

"What are you doing to her?" Kiran demanded, fear and anger coursing through his veins.

Verties stepped forward. "We're taking her with us."

"Who are you people? What do you want?"

"It's not your concern," Dorian sneered as he scooped Shae into his arms.

"Please, just let her go," Kiran pleaded, slowly rising back on his feet.

"Kiran…" One moment in a voice so weak, then shifting to unfathomable anger, "Must…kill…"

"Wait, what?" Kiran blinked.

The whine of a car engine filled the air, followed by screeching tires. "You guys again!" Nick dashed over to them, daring to wrestle Shae from Dorian's hold.

"Nick…don't," she pleaded.

"Ow, Shae, let go of my wrist." Nick stared down at the death grip.

"The both of you should just leave now. We'll handle this." Verties struggled to unclasp Shae's fingers.

"Let me have him!" The panicked squeal of her voice sounded like nails on a chalkboard.

Kiran reluctantly backed away, not wanting to

cause any more harm to Shae.

"What the hell?" Nick stood firm, staring at Verties.

Shae's head lolled to the side and an arm sprung out toward Nick. Fingers bent in a grip motion as she swiped air while reaching for his arm again.

"We're running out of time, Master Crimshon," Rozette spoke up, nervously.

Verties scrunched his brow in grim displeasure. "She slipped and had an episode last night. No one was spared."

"Not even Jacquain?" Nick crossed his arms.

"I did it," Shae's weak reply shifted into an alarming growl.

"What do you mean, you did it?" Nick asked, his voice laced with confusion.

Her eyes flickered to Nick, and she wickedly licked her lips. The sound of a zipper was unmistakable over her soft cackling.

Nick glanced at his fly in alarm, fighting against an unseen force for control of his zipper.

"Time to go." Verties cleared a path so that Dorian could load her into the van.

Kiran spoke up, gaping in horror from Nick to Shae to Verties, "Where are you taking her?"

"The plan was to get her home, but we've wasted too much time."

"You can use a spare warehouse building. I work there," Kiran offered.

"Then lead us, quickly now. We'll follow you." Verties then glared at Nick.

"I'm coming with you." Nick boldly climbed into the van through the open sliding door.

Kiran quickly got into his delivery truck and sped off, leading the unmarked van to the warehouse building.

"Nick?" Shae reached out for him as he cradled her into his arms. "You shouldn't be here."

"I'm not exactly sure what's going on, but I'm not letting you go through this alone."

She just stared at him, struggling to reach for his face.

"Just relax, Shae."

Suddenly, she whimpered as ripples of shivers racked her body.

Nick held her tightly against him. "What can I do to help you?" he whispered, brushing sweaty strands of hair away from her face.

"Your role in this is no longer needed. Jacquain is dead," Verties solemnly replied.

Dorian glanced over to him. "The prophecy was wrong?"

"I don't know." Verties sighed.

Shae savored how foolish Nick was to hold her so tight. She began weakly grinding against him and leaned up to lick the side of his face.

"What are you doing?"

"Roz, another sedative."

Shae grunted at her father's attempt to pry Nick away.

"On it, Master Crimshon." Rozette pulled out another syringe from the left pocket and a bottle from her other pocket. She loaded up the syringe.

"You…will…not…stop…" Shae's voice rumbled into a monstrous growl, fading after the effects of another sedative worked its magic.

156

****

Shae stayed motionless, eyes still closed, focused on the sensation of being lifted into the air and cradled against a warm and solid chest. For a moment, she almost thought she was dreaming. However, the smell of motor oil and metal were too strong for a dream.

She cracked an eyelid, peering out from crusty eyelashes at a row of wooden crates. She quickly closed her eyes again.

"Dorian, put her against the wall. Roz, keep her pinned down." Verties' voice echoed in the large open area.

"Yes, Master Crimshon." Rozette's feet scuffled on the cement floor.

Within moments, the paralyzing spell settled in effectively. *Roz is the only other one to know this spell.*

"We shall wait a moment before we undo it."

She opened her eyes slowly. Through the high windows, streetlights illuminated a beam across part of the room.

Dorian stood guard nearby, his gaze sharp and focused. "She's awake."

"She's been awake since we arrived." Verties sighed.

Rozette paced back and forth, glancing at Shae with sadness. "Oh, Shae...I never imagined this happening." She wiped her eyes. "Hey, remember the time when we first hung out in your room back at the Royale Hawse? You bumbled to explain the lack of furniture and we both laughed about it. We became best friends that day. That was the only time I heard you laugh, too."

Shae stared maliciously while Rozette talked.

Dorian then added, "And how about our first time in Battle Realm together? Hard to believe I protected you." A strained chuckle at that memory escaped his lips. "You logged more hours there than the rest of us Deviant trainees put together."

"So, you plan to bore me with trips down memory lane now?" Shae sneered.

Rozette's expression turned to one of hurt, while Dorian's hardened.

I don't want your damn stories or your pitiful, heartbroken gazes. Give me my freedom back. Her eyes wandered the area. *Where's Nickolas?*

"No, Shae. It's just that we care about you," Dorian said sternly.

Shae spat, "You're only here because you have to be. Because *my father* ordered you to be."

"That may be true, but it doesn't change the fact that we care," Rozette spoke up, her voice shaky with emotion. "We're still your friends."

Kiran then spoke up, "Nick and I…we're your friends, too."

Shae's angry gaze shifted from the two Deviants to the two Civilians. "Well, look at me…bridging the gap between Deviants and Civilians!" She then burst into unsettling laughter. The echo of it eventually faded. "This has been quite amusing, but I'm getting bored now." Shae glared at the group. "Does anyone else have any more stories they wanna share?" She waited a moment. "No? Okay."

As she began moving her lips, Verties' eyes grew wide. "Oh no!"

Shae burst free from Rozette's spell and she tackled Nick, landing slightly on top of him. She quickly waved her arm, sending the others on their asses. Then she smirked menacingly at Nick, "You and me have some…unfinished business to attend to." They both disappeared in a portal, reappearing in Nick's backyard.

Riley rushed out the backdoor. "Dad!"

Nick tried to scramble to his feet. "Riley, stay back."

Shae pulled him back down and crawled over him, straddling him. She leaned in and licked his neck. "Mmmm, so tasty."

"Sh-Shae?" Riley's voice reeked of fear.

She glanced up, seeing Diane holding Riley at the shoulders from behind. "Greetings, Diane."

"Stop it, Shae!" Riley broke free and dared to approach Shae.

She was rather curious now, using her hands to keep Nick pinned on the lawn. "You should have listened to your father."

"And you will listen to yours," Verties voice boomed as he emerged from a portal, with Roz, Dorian, and Kiran behind him.

Her smirk faded. "Just how did you know where to find me?"

Kiran stepped forward. "I told them."

Her gaze turned to him and he took a step forward. She flinched back and he halted in his step. "Leave me alone."

"Never," Rozette said.

"Hmmph." She grunted and stood up before jumping into a portal—disappearing from Nick's backyard.

****

Shae returned to her usual haunt—the nightclub. She was mesmerized by the large Sunday night crowd that had assembled. The temptation of the music beckoned, promising to erase the painful events of the past few days—if only for the night. She ignored the unmoving line on one side of the entrance, monitored by a large, muscular bouncer.

"Hey. You can't just walk in there. You have to wait in line like these guys," the bouncer's deep voice bellowed.

"No. I don't think so." She stared hard at the guy.

The bouncer grabbed her arm when she tried to enter once more.

"Let go of me," she hissed, fangs protruding from her upper lip. The bouncer stumbled back; fear etched on his face.

Shae took advantage of his momentary shock to slip past him and into the club, weaving her way to the dance floor.

The club was a familiar sanctuary, but chaotic energy filled the atmosphere. The bass thumped through her entire body, and Shae let her guard down. She was here for the same reasons as these Civilians—pleasure.

The lights swirled around the room in shades of red, gold, green, and blue. As she danced, a sense of freedom coursed through her. Her body swayed from side to side as she moved through the crowd of dancers like a serpent swimming through water. Everyone stopped to watch Shae dance. They parted and kept their gaze locked on her graceful form as she glided across the floor, propelled only by music.

Suddenly, she felt a hand on her waist. She spun

around to find herself face-to-face with a handsome stranger. His dark hair was slicked back, and his piercing blue eyes seemed to look right through her.

"Mind if I join you?" he asked, a hint of a smile playing at his lips.

She hesitated for a moment, but then shrugged. "Sure, why not?"

They danced, their bodies pressed together. She couldn't remember the last time she'd felt this alive. The stranger's hands roamed over her body, and she didn't resist. Her hands rested on his shoulders as she felt a second figure joining them from behind.

She turned to see another man, this one with long hair and a mischievous smirk on his lips. He pressed his body against hers from behind, effectively trapping her between the two of them. They danced in perfect rhythm, their bodies moving together as if they were one.

By the time the third song began playing, Shae was now surrounded by three men, all vying for her attention. They swayed as one, their bodies meeting and parting, creating a sinuous dance that flowed with the music. Their hands wandered over her body, leaving goosebumps in their wake, and she lost herself in the sensations.

She felt lips on her neck, and she moaned softly. One of the men had leaned in, the scruffiness of his beard tickling her chin as they made out. His mouth was full and sensual. His hands gripped her hips. Another took his place—his searing kiss tasted of ash and alcohol. The third man—grinding his erection from behind, trailed kisses on her neck. With each kiss, each touch, came a new wave of pleasure, and she wanted it to last forever.

The music at the club was entrancing, a mix of electric and acoustic sounds blending into one another as if they had been choreographed. The room throbbed from the bass as bodies swayed and spun in an almost hypnotic fashion. The smell of sweat mixed with the sweet scent of perfume and cologne mingled in the air.

Every so often, a new song would begin, and the energy in the room seemed to build even more. This time it was a jazzy, funky track that called out to her. She felt almost possessed as she grooved to the beat, hips moving in perfect tandem with the rhythm.

During the next song, the bearded stranger usurped a solitary dance with her. The remaining guys took the hint and found other dance partners. She flowed with him, swaying and bouncing to the sensually fast beat. When the tune shifted to a pulsating trance beat, the bearded man's grip was oddly reassuring yet strangely exciting. She looked up into his deep brown eyes, caught in a trance as he stared back.

They grinded hard, gyrating to the beat and his thick erection became hard to ignore. Their clothed intimate mating spread amongst the other dancers like an infectious trance.

"Best get him in private before he explodes."

She leaned in, prepared to accept his unspoken invite to retreat to the back of his truck for further intimate fun. But then, the record scratched and the music went silent.

"I think it's time you all left now."

Her gaze drifted up to the booth in the loft. There stood Verties, with the house DJ next to him ranting about the intrusion. She silently agreed with the guy.

She turned apologetically to her dance partner. "Sorry. Gotta go." She slipped into the crowd as the music started up again with a new track.

Verties blocked the path to the front exit. "Don't you know when to quit?"

"Hello, Father. Did you enjoy the show?"

Verties' face contorted with a mix of shock and helplessness.

However, a shadow darted between them and a figure appeared next to Shae. "I think you should let our queen have her fun."

She looked up at the stranger who had just come to her defense. He was tall and muscular, with an air of authority that demanded respect. His jet-black hair was styled in a rough, rebellious manner, and his eyes glinted dangerously in the dim light of the nightclub. *The fact that he called me his queen...*But she didn't recognize this vampire at all.

"It's a little bit stuffy in here, don't you think?" He turned to her with a grin.

The vampire stranger quickly hustled Shae through the crowd and out the familiar back exit. Their footsteps echoed in the alley. She followed his path, darting up the side of the building with ease.

Once on the roof, Shae's eyes gleamed with curiosity as she wondered where he was taking her.

After roof hopping a few more blocks, they finally reached their destination—a dojo rooftop that overlooked the city. She glanced around, taking in the breathtaking vista before her. The city lights twinkled like stars, and the moon hung heavy and low.

"Who are you and how do you know me?" she finally asked.

"Forgive me, my Queen. There wasn't a moment back there to properly introduce myself." He bowed to her. "My name is Hendrix." Then he stood up. "I am one of Gerard's allies. He isn't the only vampire leader. His domain is Jupiter. I'm from a few cities away— Okton."

"Oh." She moved to sit on a random wooden crate, most likely left behind by a roofing company. Civilians had called Okton, Oakland, while they knew Jupiter as Los Angeles.

"Yes, my group knows a lot about you. Gerard talks highly of you." Hendrix sat beside her, his dark gaze intense.

"He's filled your head with nothing but an erotic image of me."

"Poor Gerard could not hide his obsession…even though you are our enemy."

"Was," Shae corrected him.

"Excuse me?"

As a demonstration, she flashed her fangs.

"Ah, it's a pity he's already gotten to you."

"Not a pity if you aren't against sampling what he's already tasted." She shifted and placed a hand on her hips seductively."

Hendrix tipped his head respectfully. "I'm afraid I cannot."

"Why did you come to my rescue then?"

"I was in town for a visit, knowing full well that Gerard often frequented that nightclub for his fetish." Then he nodded. "Yes. The other leaders know of that." Hendrix's lips lifted in a smug grin. "But I certainly was surprised to find you in the exact euphoric trance that often claimed him. From watching you on that dance floor—you certainly know how to enjoy yourself. You're even more stunning up close."

A heated flush crept up her neck at his compliment.

Hendrix leaned in closer, his warm breath brushing against her skin as he spoke. "Gerard's helped me plenty in the past—we've become very good friends. So stealing his queen would be ill-befitting of me."

"Hendrix, just how good of friends are you with him?"

"Gerard is like the brother I never had."

Not the answer she was hoping for. "I understand," she said, a note of disappointment lacing her words. "But allies can still have fun together, can't they?" She leaned in, lips hovering just inches from his.

Hendrix's eyes flickered with desire, but then he pulled away again. "I value Gerard's friendship too much to risk it for something as trivial as temporary pleasure." His voice was firm, but Shae could hear the desire he was trying to suppress.

It would be best to keep Hendrix as an ally, rather than another enemy.

She stood up, feeling deflated. "I see. Well, I guess it was nice meeting you, Hendrix."

He stood up as well, his gaze lingering on her for a moment longer than necessary. "It was a pleasure as well, my Queen. I hope we can meet again under different circumstances." She nodded, turning to leave the rooftop.

Chapter 14

Gerard's mansion. As she exited the portal at the bottom of the circular cement stairs, she glanced at the front of the mansion, illuminated by the bright full moon. *This is mine now! The house, the land...although I'll have to make new servants.* Shae gasped as she entered the main foyer. All traces of her carnage had been erased—the bodies were removed and the splattered blood had been wiped clean. She frowned at the prospect that an unwanted visitor was sauntering around the premises. Two lackeys strolled in from the dining room, their faces unfamiliar—and yet somehow familiar too. Her fists clenched in anger as she watched them.

They stood, transfixed, before having the sense to kneel. The one to her left adorned in biker gear—a leather vest and jeans—spoke with a quivering voice, "My Queen, we never thought we'd see you again."

"You may stand." She motioned and they stood up.

"We cleaned up the mansion for your return."

She turned to the one that explained the situation to her. He seemed young and frail in the oversized Goth jacket, but she assumed her view of him was misleading, knowing the strength he possessed.

"What are your names?" Her eyes narrowed in their direction.

"Bruce." The biker lackey bowed his head again

for the third time.

"Michael." The goth swished his long, black bangs aside—only to have them fall back into place. He didn't seem to mind.

"How did you survive the massacre?" She hadn't yet revealed that it was her doing.

"We were out of town." Bruce leaned on the banister of the stairs that led to the second floor. "Errands for Master Jacquain."

"Ex-master," Michael chimed in.

"And you don't question the dead bodies?" She circled them—like a hawk—and noticed it made them nervous. "As Michael pointed out, Gerard is dead now." They masked their fear quite well, but she still detected it—and it excited her.

Bruce still was slow on the uptake. "It's still unclear who killed him."

"None of that matters now, Bruce," Michael said. "Our service is to our queen, not him."

She stopped right in front of Michael, lips twisting into a pleasured grin. "Just the answer I sought." She inched closer to him—a look of lust and hunger crossed her features. He flinched and then tried to act tough.

"How can I be of service to you, my Queen?" he said, throwing his shoulders back in a display of calmness.

She moved in front of them. The chandelier overhead threw a shadow across her profile. Moonlight pierced the window. Her left hand cupped Michael's cheek, while her right hand mirrored the action on Bruce's cheek. "I remember you…" Shae stared pointedly at Bruce. "You were the one that manhandled me while delivering me to Jacquain. I believe you called me...little birdie." Bruce visibly gulped but stood ready if she chose to punish him. She noticed but ignored it. "Since it's a role you are familiar with...you may retain your position as lead lackey."

"Thank you, my Queen." Bruce bowed in gratitude.

She then stepped away from them and they followed her into the den—where guests were often entertained. "Now then..." In the center of the room, she turned to face them again. "I shall explain how I desire to run things around here."

At that moment, another figure entered the room, covered in blood, as she plopped her ass down on a leather two-seater sofa. "Hey, Michael and Bruce and..." She noticed Shae and scrambled to her feet. "Holy shit, it's you!"

Shae tilted her head in amusement at this young woman. "What's your name?"

"Natalie." She was nervous now. "Ya know...I didn't mean what I said earlier. I was just startled to see you again."

Shae dismissed Natalie's apology. "Now, where was I...oh, yes." She narrowed her eyes. "The only thing you'll have to worry about me is...I won't kill you as long as you blindly follow me." She glanced at each of them for emphasis. "Meaning...never question what I say or do, kill anyone who even dares breathe a threat to or about me...and from here on out, I am *the only one* that matters to you." She hesitated, letting her rules sink in. "Do we have an understanding?"

"Yes, my Queen," they answered in unison. "Your pleasure and well-being are our priority."

"Good. Be sure to inform the others about my

rules." She playfully patted their cheeks before moving away from them. "Anything of Gerard's is now officially mine. And any reference to things being his shall now only be addressed as mine." She lifted one foot onto the stairs. "Everything else can be business as usual." Natalie left the mansion again to spread the word.

Michael caught up as she put her foot on the second step. "There is one thing, my Queen." She faced him, left hand still on the elaborate bronze railing, amused he had the audacity to touch her right arm uninvited.

"Yes, Michael?" She broke his grip, only to take his hand. She absently rubbed his palm with her fingers.

The gesture made him hesitate. "Uhh…" He paused. "Jacquain gained an art exhibition. But now you're in charge—"

"An art exhibition?" She wondered if this was the Percy deal that Thomas had once interrupted her and Gerard about. "When is this?"

"This weekend," Bruce interjected, having walked up behind Michael.

She gazed hard at Bruce. "Take care of all the details, but make sure I learn the exact date, time, and location." Bruce left to attend to his duties. She moved again up the stairs, tugging Michael along with her. "Michael."

"I love the way you say my name. And my blood is yours, whenever you need it. If I'm sleeping, just wake me up."

Shae rolled her eyes at his sappy comment.

They remained silent on the trip to the master bedroom. Her moves were the same as others—one foot in front of the other—yet she exhibited power in sleek steps.

Her eyes caught him in the act of obsessively gazing at her ass. "You seem troubled."

He glanced up from his fixated stare of her ass, his eyes sheepishly meeting hers, "What…uh no…" He gave a timid, nervous grin. "I was just thinking…"

She stopped at the door to her room and leaned seductively against the door frame. "What thoughts do you entertain, Michael? Share them with me."

Michael half bowed his head, apprehensive that he was about to admit something sensitive. "I…was part of Bruce's group to bring you to Jacquain. But when I saw you…" Michael trailed off, bracing himself for her reaction.

She took a step toward him, closing the distance between them. "When you saw me what?" She trailed a finger down Michael's chest, watching him tremble slightly.

"I couldn't do it," Michael said in a hushed voice, unable to break eye contact. "I couldn't let them hurt you. Instead of doing something about it then, I fled."

"So you weren't doing an errand for Jacquain." A complex range of emotions briefly crossed her thoughts before she settled into a small, secretive smile.

"No, I wasn't," Michael confirmed. "I couldn't bring myself to do it, so I left without telling anyone."

She tilted her head, studying Michael with a curious expression. "Why are you telling me this now?"

"I want to be loyal to you," he admitted.

She stepped even closer so their bodies were pressed together. "I appreciate your honesty, Michael. And your loyalty." She ran her hands over his chest, sending shivers down his spine once again. "But I need to know that I can trust you completely."

"You can," Michael said firmly.

She trailed her hand down his arm, coiling their fingers together. Then she tugged him into the master bedroom. Once in privacy, she spoke. "I'm going to let you in on a little secret that the others here don't know about."

Michael's eyes widened with anticipation. "What secret?" he asked in a quiet voice.

Her soft chuckle of amusement interrupted him, even though she wasn't thrilled to be talking about Nick when she'd rather be having fun right now. "Dear Michael…" She seductively cupped the side of his face in the palm of her hand. "Has Jacquain ever mentioned anything about me and a bond?"

His eyes glanced down for a moment as he thought about her question. "He did mention something about you bonding with a heathen that would make you untouchable to him." He made no attempt to hide his confusion. "But here you are…and Jacquain is dead."

Her flippant sigh made him pause. "That heathen has a name." However, Shae refused to say it. Then she half smirked at Michael. "I had given him plenty of chances to fulfill his duty, but his devotion to another hinders his indulging in corrupt pleasure." She mock-frowned to play on Michael's emotions for her. "Is it wrong that I must mingle my body with his while his lover bears witness…to stay in permanent control?"

"Anything I can do to help you, my Queen?"

"Prove to me just how loyal you are and I just might let you in on another secret."

"I will be your worthy confidant."

"Good." She stripped him of his oversized jacket and flung him toward the bed. He fell back onto it and she was instantly rising over him—straddling him. Shae leaned over and licked his neck. As she rose back to a sitting position, he quickly discarded his tight black shirt. She eyed his scrawny upper build.

Michael trailed the fingers of his right hand down her left thigh. Then he dared to trail his hand upward and cupped her breast.

She snatched his hand and pressed it hard against the pillow. He tilted his head to the side, exposing his throat. Her fangs descended into his flesh and drank of his blood as if he were ripe fruit hanging from a tree. Together, they made sounds that only untamed animals could mimic: quiet grunts of exertion and pleasure; small whimpers of pain and delight; moans, sighs, and whispers like the night wind through the canopy. After a few moments, she pulled away.

"I've been fed on before...but with you, that was incredible—almost better than sex!" His voice was soft; he had lost more strength than normal from the feed.

Shae rolled away from him, body quaking with a sudden intensity that sparked a raging wildfire. An irresistible craving for violence and destruction seized her.

Michael tenderly wiped the crimson blood from her lips. "Ready for another round?"

"I must leave now," she said in a haunted but firm tone, sauntering toward the French doors.

Michael's breath caught at the sight of her illuminated by the moonlight. "Do I get to come?"

She opened the door that led to the rooftop patio and glanced at him, seeing his bulge. "No. You must stay here."

He remained sitting on the edge of the bed, his hand shifting over his crotch—trying to alleviate some of the sensations of his erection.

She walked back to him and kissed him on the lips. "My sweet Michael." She teased him by rubbing her hand over his erection before pulling away and walked out onto the patio.

"I'll wait for you, my Queen!" he called out to her.

She leaped off the edge of the patio and conjured a portal before hitting ground level. *Ah, the card and novelty shop. The perfect familiar spot to begin.* The neon sign buzzed at full force as it lit up the area around it. However, instead of lingering to hunt here, she walked several blocks until she eventually reached a section by the river. There was an area of a parking lot attached to a bar roped off for an event. The mass of huddled bodies swaying to the beat of a live band drew her toward the tented area. The moment she reached the perimeter of the smaller side of the tent, lips moved in a whisper of the Deviant language.

The band's bass drum exploded like a thunderclap, sending everyone into a panic. There was no hope of escape as they tried desperately to race out from beneath the tent, only to slam into an invisible wall, trapping them in a dizzying labyrinth of terror. Shae was determined that none of them would get away alive.

After feeding until full, she slaughtered the remaining partiers. However, there were still about a dozen left when sirens filled the air—getting louder each second. She narrowed her eyes, taking in the positions of the remaining dozen victims. A dark red orb formed in the palm of her hand. With a whisper in the Deviant language, the orb separated into twelve equally sized orbs. She straightened out her palm flat, and the orbs shot out—connecting with each of the victims. They exploded on contact.

That was fun! The sound of squealing tires and car doors slamming signaled that it was time to leave.

Not enough time to deal with armed men. She portaled to a nearby rooftop of an auto parts store.

The rising sun's invisible fiery tendrils singed the side of her face. Across the street, she noticed a mini market. Shae portaled to street level in front of the market. Daylight slowed her down. She stumbled to the door, squinting against the light. Her hand hovered over the doorknob. *No, wait. The alarm might go off. The cops would get tipped to my location.* A second portal gained her inside entry.

The rising sun singed the flesh on the back of her neck. She stumbled down an aisle toward the back of the store to a door marked Employees Only. She jiggled the knob and stepped into the inky shadows of a supply closet. Stacks of boxes surrounded her. Shae locked the door, sank to the floor, and fell asleep.

****

Shae returned to the mansion, cloaked by a dark sky. With the craving satiated, there was no danger posed to her loyal vampires. A news crew van parked in the circular driveway by the cement steps to the front entrance was packing their equipment.

Bruce met her as she snuck in the back way with advice to lay low. "They love showing up randomly, hoping to catch something juicy."

Bruce must have been Jacquain's advisor. He had

always paced himself, the way he spread out the trail of women in his quest for pleasure. If the city gets too wise about me, then my fun would be ruined.

As she reached the end of the hallway, she heard the sounds of laughter and classical music coming from the ballroom. Curious, she opened the door and stepped inside.

The room was dimly lit with candles, casting a warm glow over the dancers moving to the music. The air was thick with the scent of perfume and sweat, with couples locked in passionate embraces.

Michael was standing against the far wall, watching the festivities with an unreadable expression. With a subtle murmur, her casual outfit magically shifted into one that matched the mood of the festive event. She approached him, elegant heels shimmering in the candlelight, clicking on the marble floor. The deep burgundy gown flowed like it was part of her, stopping mid-thigh.

"Enjoying yourself, Michael?" she asked, voice low and sultry.

Michael turned to look at her, his dark eyes scanning her body appreciatively. "Always a pleasure to be in such beautiful company," he replied smoothly, his voice deep and velvety.

She smirked, knowing the effect she had on him. "I see you're still playing the quiet observer," she teased, stepping closer to him.

Michael chuckled, his hand reaching out. "I prefer to watch. It gives me a better perspective," he said, his thumb caressing the back of her hand. She felt an electric shiver run down her spine.

As the music slowed down, Michael pulled her

closer, their bodies swaying together. "You look absolutely stunning tonight," he whispered, his lips brushing against her skin.

"And you stand out in your goth outfit." Desire pooled in the pit of her stomach. She tilted her head back.

He took the hint and trailed kisses along her neck as they danced. She let out a soft moan, unable to resist the sensations created by Michael's roaming hands.

Their bodies pressed closer together, and Shae could feel his arousal growing. She broke away from the dance to take his hand, leading him toward one of the side rooms. "Let's continue this elsewhere," she whispered, a seductive smile on her lips.

The room was small, with an elegant table for two. The candles, as a centerpiece, provided the only light in the room. Each chair at the table was cushioned at the back and bottom with plush velvet.

He eased her into a chair before sitting across from her. A server entered the room, placing a glass of wine in front of each of them.

"Would you like to order anything from the kitchen?" The balding man stood stoically, awaiting further instruction.

She glanced at the man before turning back to Michael. "No, thank you. We'll just have the wine," she said, her voice soft and sultry.

The server nodded and left the room, closing the door behind him. He raised his glass, his eyes never leaving hers. "To a beautiful evening," he said, clinking his glass against hers.

She took a sip of the wine, savoring the rich taste. "To a night full of pleasure." His eyes flickered with mischief. She let him have his fill of the first sip before setting their glasses aside. "But first..." Her stance shifted from intimate to business. "...it is time to reveal that other secret to you."

He raised an eyebrow in interest, his gaze never leaving hers. "I'm all ears," he said, curiosity tingeing his voice.

"Regarding Jacquain." Her eyes narrowed. "I'm the one that killed him."

Michael's eyes widened and scooted his chair back in alarm. "You *what*?"

From outside the door, the music paused and murmurs could be heard.

She heaved a sigh of displeasure. "Hush, Michael."

There was a timid knock on the door. Annoyance flashed across her face as she stood to answer it.

"Is everything okay, my Queen?" Bruce's face creased with concern.

She rolled her eyes, irritated by the interruption. "Everything is fine, Bruce," she snapped. "Just some unexpected news."

Bruce's expression remained worried as he stepped into the room. "What news?" he asked, eyeing Michael warily.

She shot him a warning look, gesturing for him to keep quiet. "It's nothing that concerns you, Bruce. Please leave us to our privacy." Then she added, "Just make sure everyone out there enjoys themselves."

Bruce hesitated for a moment before nodding, and slipped out of the room, closing the door behind him.

Chapter 15

Alone once again, Michael leaned forward, his expression intense. "You killed Jacquain?" he repeated, his voice low and urgent.

Shae nodded, refusing to be intimidated. "Yes, I did. And I don't regret it one bit."

He studied her for a moment before leaning back in his chair. "Did you kill him for me...or for that heathen?"

Her hand lashed out, gripping the collar of his jacket, tugging his face against the clothed table. The candle remained upright, but the wine spilled. "Did I not inform you that I am not to be questioned?"

He trembled, forced to stare at the tablecloth up close. "My apologies, my Queen," he said, his voice barely above a whisper. "I meant no disrespect. I just want to understand your motivations."

She held him there for a moment longer before releasing him and settling back into her chair. "Jacquain shared his gift with me, and he was no longer useful."

Michael sat up and dared another question in a jittery voice, "W-what gifts?"

"Immortality." She could see he had a third question in his eyes. She wiggled a finger at him. "That is all you get to know."

He leaned back in his chair; his eyes still locked onto hers.

She leaned across the table, her eyes boring into his. "But let this be a warning to you."

Michael swallowed, his eyes flickering with fear. "I understand," he said, nodding quickly. "I am yours to command, my Queen."

"Good." Shae leaned back with a thoughtful expression. "Now, let's put that unpleasantness behind us and continue with our night of pleasure." She reached out to take his hand, pulling him toward her. "I want to show you just how much I appreciate your loyalty and obedience."

His fear melted away as desire took over. He leaned closer, running his fingers through her hair. "I'm yours, my Queen," he whispered, lips hovering over hers. "Do with me as you please."

She smiled at his submission, enjoying the power that came with it. She pulled him in for a deep kiss, tongue tracing his lips before diving inside. Michael moaned, dipping his hand under her dress to caress her thigh.

The sound of music and laughter drifted in from outside the door, but they paid no attention to the world beyond. At that moment, there were only the two of them, lost in pleasure.

As they broke away from the kiss, Shae gazed deeply into Michael's eyes, her own filled with a hunger that only he could satisfy. "Come with me," she said, standing and pulling him along.

They exited the small room and she stopped the balding server on his way to deliver food and drink to another room.

"I apologize for leaving a small mess in the room. See to it that it gets cleaned for the next couple."

The man nodded and shifted course to finish her assigned task first.

Once in the master bedroom, she locked the door to avert any interruptions while he quickly stripped down to his boxers.

She pushed Michael onto the bed, lips trailing down his neck. He gasped as her tongue flicked over his nipple, sending shivers of pleasure down his spine.

She kissed down his torso, hands roaming over his body. Her hand settled on his waistband. "May I?" she asked, while squeezing his thick erection in his boxers.

He nodded eagerly, his breaths coming out in ragged gasps. She smirked and then slowly slid his boxers down his legs.

She admired him before climbing onto the bed and straddling him. Michael's hands roamed over her body, working their way up until they found the zipper of the dress. He pulled it down slowly, flesh exposed to the cool air.

Shae moaned as his touch sent waves of pleasure throughout her body. She leaned forward, bracing herself with one arm while unclasping her bra with a bit of magic.

"Cheater."

"You better watch what you call me."

"Please accept my apologies…my Queen."

She tossed the bra aside.

"Thank you." Michael took in her naked form before his hands moved up her thighs and his lips found her sensitive spots.

Shae's breath caught in her throat as his lips traveled up her neck and across her collarbone. Her skin heated in anticipation as she rocked against him, the friction between their bodies sending fiery sparks through her veins.

Michael gasped as she moved faster, his hands gripping tightly around her hips. His lips trailed down her neck and a low moan escaped her lips as she reached her peak, head thrown back in pleasure.

"That was incredible," she said, voice still rough from the climax.

He grinned, eyes still clouded with pleasure. "Fuck, yeah," he agreed, voice still husky.

She leaned down and kissed him, lips lingering on his before she settled beside him. She curled up in his embrace, cradling her head in the crook of his arm.

****

Michael had proved to be a pleasant distraction. Yet, Shae craved Nickolas. *A wise decision or not, I can't afford anymore wasted time. So tonight's the night to claim him—hopefully willingly in front of that blasted wife.*

"Such a tantalizing dress for the Art Exhibit tonight." Michael appeared suddenly at the bottom step. Or had he been standing there this whole time while she descended the stairs?

"Cancel it." Her arms and backside were the most exposed and each step she took revealed tempting leg views through the slit in the bottom of the dress.

"I'm afraid we can't cancel this close to the event time," Bruce announced from the open front door.

"Fine." She heaved a sigh of annoyance.

Michael dared to run his finger along the neckline of the dress.

But she snatched his hand before he could touch her breasts. "Not yet, my dear Michael."

Again, he squirmed as he shifted his growing erection. "It's a storm out there," he warned. "But I arranged for a servant to make sure we're covered." She noticed a servant holding an umbrella standing obediently on the circular staircase outside.

"You're too good for me." Shae smiled as they settled in the back of the limo and it drove away from the mansion.

"I'd rather be naughty for you."

"How much time before we arrive at the event?"

"We should arrive in less than nine minutes," the driver responded.

"Thanks." Shae pressed a button to raise the diving window for privacy. She glanced at Michael with a mischievous twinkle as hands glided over his chest and stomach before settling on the bulge in his pants.

Michael slid down slightly and spread his legs a bit more to give her better access. Then he unbuckled his trousers as she dipped her hand within and caressed him. "Your hands are amazing, my Queen." He grew hard and thick.

Since they didn't have much time to waste, Shae increased the speed, determined to bring Michael pleasure.

Michael retrieved a sock from the suit coat pocket for this purpose.

"I see you expected this."

"I know my place. I'm just here for your pleasure."

"And such an answer pleases me. Though not as much as this." She motioned toward her pumping hand just as he released into the sock.

The private window lowered slightly. "We are a block away, my Queen."

"Fun's over." She smirked at Michael, leaving him to deal with the soiled sock.

The limo passed by the front of the building. Despite the storm, the crowd was large and eager. He noted the malicious twinkle in her eyes. The limo turned a corner to drop them off at the private back entrance. The only 'crowd' there were Civilian servants devoted to guarding her life with their own. When the servants noticed the vehicle, they radioed to the group of servants in front to let the spectators in. Shae exited the limo and headed inside with her entourage to take their positions for this event.

Off to one side of the main showroom were stairs designed with a half-landing that went to a small second floor of offices and storage. That is where Michael stood as he called for everyone's attention.

"Ladies and Gentlemen…I would like to extend a gracious thank you for attending this event. Now.., you may wonder where the star of the show is…but sadly, she had lost the rights to this show to my previous boss, who then lost it to my current boss. But enough of this…let me introduce you to the main event." Michael then grinned, glancing up and over his shoulder, seeing Shae sitting precariously on the second-floor railing.

She gave a nod, the official signal for the other lackeys posing as wait staff to seal off all exits. When the large doors simultaneously slammed shut, there was an alarming murmur amongst the crowd, but no one was yet worried. She leaped off the railing, landing gracefully upon the half-landing where Michael stood. A low mumble erupted from the crowd—panic was rising. Slowly, her eyes scanned the frightened crowd. "My dear guests, your worry is quite touching. I promise…this won't hurt…" Shae turned her sly gaze to Michael. "…much."

She was the first to select a victim—the signal to start the feeding frenzy. The woman clutched her date as Shae eyed the man hungrily. "Mind if I borrow your date, ma'am?" Tossing the woman into the arms of a loyal lackey, Shae pulled the man close. The man pleaded for his date and for his life. While the chaos erupted, she took the time to savor the man. His effort to obtain freedom amused her.

Shae finished him, and a child huddling against the stair railing caught her attention. A random lackey pulled the child into his grip and Shae strode over to them. "Find someone else." He took one look at her and scurried off.

The child huddled into a ball and began to cry. "Where's my daddy!?"

She frowned at the child. "You must be well educated to be attending an art show." She snagged the child by the collar and pulled him close. "Mitchell?"

"Shae?!" He tried to be brave, despite her scary face. "Why are you doing this?"

She stared hard at the boy, sensing his inner fear. But she was shocked enough by his presence for the hold of the Darkness to ripple. "What are you doing here?" She wouldn't say his name now while struggling to secure the gaps caused by the ripple to eliminate the chance of either her humanity or her animalistic nature to surface.

"My dad brought me here…to make up for missing my birthday." Mitchell wiped his tears, keeping his gaze on her and not the bloodshed around him.

The memory of that day slipped through one of the

gaps—of how she gave Mitchell the pep-talk in order to get him to go back to his party, of how after the party when she spent cherished time with Nick. *I wonder what Nick is doing now.* Seeing Mitchell here stirred her humanity. The Darkness may have consumed it, but it was still there—very, very faintly there.

Michael broke her thoughts. "My Queen, do you wish to spare the boy?"

She shook from her reverie, glancing from Michael to Mitchell. "None shall be spared this night." She didn't even give Mitchell an apologetic glance while sucking him dry. Once done, her hand clasped Michael's. "Let's go. The others will clean up." They returned to the mansion. No time was wasted in taking immense joy in intimately ravishing his body from a different hunger.

****

She leaned against the second-floor patio railing, pondering all the options available as her gaze landed on the servant in the open French doors.

"My Queen. You have a visitor in the den."

She turned to face the servant. "Tell whoever it is I'm not interested in visitors tonight."

"He says his name is Hendrix."

Her eyebrow raised. "Hendrix?" she repeated, curious as to why he would be visiting. She had not seen him in some time, and their last encounter had not exactly been pleasant. But what harm could come from seeing him again? She gave the servant a nod. "Very well."

She descended the stairs deep in thought. *He must have had a change of heart since our conversation on the dojo rooftop.* She licked her lips, excited for the surprising opportunity to bring him to the master bed. *Sure, playing with Michael was fun, but he wasn't a leader like Jacquain or Hendrix. I just know he will not disappoint. But would he be a better lover than Jacquain?*

Shae walked into the den and saw Hendrix sitting in one of the plush armchairs, a glass of blood in his hand. He turned to look at Shae, his eyes narrowing slightly.

"To what do I owe the pleasure of this visit, Hendrix?" she asked, taking a seat across from him.

Hendrix took a sip of his blood before responding. "Our previous meeting was short, but very sweet and memorable. I was hoping we could continue our conversation."

Shae raised an eyebrow. "I have a better idea than conversation." She motioned for him to follow. Along the way, they passed a servant. She stopped the woman. "Find Michael, Bruce, and Natalie. Tell them to meet us in the game room."

The servant nodded and hustled up to the servants' and lackeys' quarters.

Shae continued leading Hendrix to the game room. Her stride was like a hunter approaching its prey, careful and quiet. He breathed in her rich lilac scent as he followed.

"It's been a while since I was last entertained in the game room." Hendrix revealed he knew where they were headed. "Many meetings and deals were conducted over his chessboard."

"Very interesting." Shae showed no surprise at his comment. She slid open the pocket doors and entered the room. As she passed by a leather chair, she noticed

Michael sprawled out and asleep.

His pants were down at his ankles—leaving his half-limp member exposed—and his shirt and jacket were off, revealing his pale chest. The thin line of blood dribbled from his lips, down his chin, and onto his chest, before continuing over his stomach.

Shae sighed. "Well, we found Michael." She leaned over and patted the side of his face rough enough to stir him awake.

Without opening his eyes, Michael grabbed Shae's waist and she settled into his lap. Her hand collided with his growing erection as his lips smothered hers.

Quickly, she cupped the side of his face in a free hand, pressing sharp, dark maroon nails into his cheek.

"Wha...?" His eyes flailed open. "My Queen!" His gaze became apologetic. "Sorry." Then he haphazardly yanked his pants back up, but not bothering with his upper nudity.

"If this was any other situation, I would have enjoyed that greeting. But we have a guest now." Her voice had a disappointed edge to it.

Michael bowed his head. When he raised it, he gazed at the guest. "Hendrix?"

"Shouldn't be surprised you are familiar with him."

"Yes, I know this one. But never really knew his name," Hendrix confirmed.

"From your dealings with Jacquain."

"Did a lot of errands for Hendrix's visits," Michael said.

"Ah, well. That's nice." Shae brushed off that bit of conversation as two more figures walked into the room. "Bruce, Natalie, thank you for joining us promptly."

"What is it that you wish of us, my Queen?" Bruce bowed to her first.

Natalie had her eye on Hendrix. "Hey, you." She attempted to cozy up to him.

Shae moved to block the vamp's' path. "You. Sit." She pointed to one of the chairs at the chessboard.

"Uh…" Natalie hesitated but then rushed to sit down. "What exactly am I to do?"

"An impromptu game between you and Hendrix." Shae motioned for Hendrix to take the other chair. She then continued upon seeing his look of confusion. "I was a bit bored until a servant announced your arrival. Then I had a fun idea pop into my head. To have a chess duel. And the winner gets to live."

Natalie glanced at Hendrix with uneasiness. "I've never really played much before."

"Then this will be an even match." Hendrix admitted. "I don't get to play as often as I'd like. Running a city is very time demanding."

"Perfect." Shae's smile grew wicked.

"What are we to do then?" Bruce finally spoke up.

"Such a moron." Michael rolled his eyes. "We're just supposed to watch."

"I knew that." Bruce's glare was full of daggers at Michael.

"Enough you two. I don't want to hear another argument from either of you." She turned to Michael. "Be a dear and drag a leather chair over here for me."

"Yes, my Queen."

Once the chair was in position, she addressed Bruce. "You may sit here." She watched him nearly fall over himself to sit. Shae proceeded to scooch onto his lap. Out of the corner of her eye, she witnessed the silent steam of Michael's demeanor. "You may stand next to us, Michael." She watched in amusement as he stomped over to the appointed spot.

"You handle your group quite well." Hendrix chuckled.

"Thank you." She flashed him an award-winning smile. "Okay, so let the games begin." She waved her hand at the chessboard.

"Well, I know that having the white pieces means I get to move first." Natalie raised her hand over the pieces but seemed a little lost about where exactly to start. Finally, she moved the pawn in front of the king.

Hendrix made his move in response, chuckling at her faulty start. A tense chess battle ensued, with both players giving it their all. Fingers were flying over the board, pieces moved and taken, and strategies made and ruined. In the end, it came down to the decision of one man.

Hendrix stared for a long moment at the board before smiling and taking Natalie's queen. "Checkmate," Hendrix announced.

Natalie slammed her hands on the board and pushed her chair away. "That was impossible! How did you get me?"

Shae smirked. "You did rather badly in comparison to Hendrix. As promised, the loser will be killed."

He held up the black queen. "I've defended my queen quite well." He smirked at Shae before he rose to his feet and extended his arm. "Congratulations, Natalie. You played a well-matched game."

Natalie's eyes widened in fear. She scrambled from her chair, glancing back and forth between Shae and Hendrix, a silent plea for mercy hanging in the air.

Shae simply shrugged, a bored expression on her face. "What can I say? You lost. It's not my fault you weren't up to the challenge."

"Please, my Queen," Natalie begged.

"Call me what you will, but you cannot change the result."

Michael stepped forward, "My Queen," —he bowed his head— "should I prepare the execution chamber? Or is there another punishment you'd like to offer?"

Shae's features twisted into a wicked grin as she sauntered over to Natalie, embracing the woman from behind. "Be honored that even a loser like you will bestow one last gift to me."

"What...what gift is that?" Natalie's body trembled. The fear in her voice was unmistakable.

Shae licked one side of Natalie's neck. Before the woman could protest, Shae sunk her fangs deep into 'Natalie's neck.

Hendrix mused at Michael and Bruce, "Our queen comes up with some very unique punishments."

Gulp after gulp, Shae slowly drank Natalie's life away, her fingers running through her hair. When there was nothing left, Shae dropped the drained body to the floor.

"You may dispose of her." Shae motioned to Michael.

Bruce stepped in to help him clear the body from the room.

Hendrix raised his eyebrows at Shae. "My Queen, I'm impressed with your ruthlessness today." He bowed his head.

"Thank you." She straightened her dress. "It is true

that sometimes I can be quite…bloodthirsty." She took the black queen chess piece and viewed it closely, as if in contemplation. The black queen was a symbol of power and victory. *Mmm, that was so much fun.* A wicked laugh escaped her lips before gazing at Hendrix. "A token of thanks for entertaining me."

Hendrix smiled and bowed. "I will proudly display this gift in my personal quarters…of which you are most welcome to visit anytime."

"Since you have offered yours, I will offer mine." She stepped closer to him, running her hands up his chest. "If you are still up for some entertainment, how about a few rounds of dancing?"

"Dancing? A visit to the ballroom then." He tilted his head.

"Hmmm, not that kind of dancing." She evoked a flicker of heat within her voice.

Hendrix paused longer than expected. Then he finally spoke. "As much as I'd like to accept that temptuous offer, I shall take a rain check on that."

She suppressed her disappointment. "Very well. Maybe another time then."

"Perhaps, and I look forward to it, my Queen." With that, Hendrix gave her a low bow before turning to exit the room.

She watched him walk away, a slight smirk playing across her lips. "I already saw how you were breaking down. The next time we meet, I will not expect any more no's."

She stood there for a moment, her gaze lingering on the chessboard. With a sigh, she collected the remaining pieces into their respective compartments, a silent reminder to restock the piece she had given away in case she wanted to play this game later.

Then she glanced around the room.

'Very well done, Shae.'

A rumble of thunder, followed by a flash of lightning, shook the mansion, as if in agreement.

She laughed and glanced out the window, an amused expression growing in satisfaction. Despite the earlier boredom, she had made it an enjoyable experience. No one was safe, not even her favorite pawns.

Chapter 16

The hallway was as dark and still as it had been the past two evenings. The inhabitants of the mansion loitered in a subdued manner. Yet, something had changed. The air now seemed charged. Electricity seemed to course through Shae's veins, and an insatiable urge for chaos throbbed.

Shae sauntered through the hallway, her footsteps sinking into plush rugs and traipsing over the hardwood flooring. Eyes fixated on Michael at the bottom of the stairs, she descended.

"Have we done something to displease you, my Queen?" Fear tinged his eyes and voice.

Shae stepped closer; fingers twitched in anticipation. She continued to hold his gaze as she spoke, her voice low but clear. "Gather who you can, my dear Michael. Tonight…we hunt!" Shae linked their hands and together they entered the main room. There was a large group of lackeys lounging around.

"Ladies and gentlemen!" He called for their attention. They all stood upon noticing Shae.

"My Queen…" Bruce spoke up for the group.

She held out her hand and approached the group, breaking away from Michael. "Boys…and girls…we are going out now." They licked their lips clearly knowing exactly what she meant. As they skittered away from the mansion, her voice could be heard bellowing around them, "Spare no one. Eat to your heart's content! Tonight…we indulge in our pleasures!"

Michael joined her side on the circular cement stairs. "You look ravishing!"

She looked at him and pulled him into a kiss beneath the clear night sky. "Let the Deviants try to stop me this time."

****

She reached the heart of the city within the hour, surrounded by towering buildings. She wasn't alone. There was always at least one or five of her followers nearby and more followed from a distance. They even looked after each other, like a pack. And she didn't mind that Michael had gone off on his own instead of hovering around her like a wild, horny animal.

While the group hunted with fervor, she was more casual. She refused to let thoughts dwell on anyone unless pleasure was attached to it. That meant no thoughts of her Civilian and Deviant friends, her parents, or her recent meeting with Hendrix. *But I do need to plan a clever way to approach Nickolas.*

She turned away from a couple of her lackeys dancing around and toying with a terrified female Civilian. When the woman 'escaped', Shae chuckled. *Far be it from me to not allow them to play with their food as they wish.* Her amused grin shifted into anger and heartbreak as Nick entered the alley she was attempting to leave. She backed deeper into the alley's shadows.

"H-Hello?"

"Perfect time now for us to—"

NO! I don't want to do this anymore. She half expected backlash from the voice for her defiance. But nothing happened. She glanced over, watching Nick turning to leave the alleyway. Her sensitive hearing recognized the scuffling of her lackey's footsteps. Shae lurched forward, clamping a hand over Nick's mouth from behind. "Don't move." At that moment, three female lackeys dashed by. *Triplets changed by Gerard during an out-of-control night of pleasure,* Shae recalled their explanation during the round of meet and greets of the new loyal group of servants and lackeys. "I'm letting go now. Don't scream."

He shrugged free and spun on his heel. "Shae?!"

"What do you think you're doing?" Shae hissed at him, stepping away.

Instead of answering, he tilted his head in confusion. "Not gonna jump my bones this time?"

"Don't tempt me."

"Why do you even care?" Nick stared pointedly at her with a challenging glare.

She huffed as she started to turn away from him.

He shook his head. "I don't get you at all, Shae. The last time, we were in the presence of my family and you were so eager. But now?"

Shae glared at him over her shoulder.

"Now it's just you and me in an alley. No one to interrupt us. C'mon, Shae, what are you afraid of?"

Her eyes then scanned the alley.

"Your Deviants don't even know I'm out here on a movie date night with—"

She faced him in alarm. "With her?"

"Mmmm...would be so much fun to ruin date night then."

She grimaced, struggling to maintain control of this situation. Her eyes narrowed before they saddened, and a bit of humanity flickered. "Nick...go home..." *To her.*

Nick grabbed her by the arm. "I'm heartbroken to see you this way. Shae, please...let us help you!"

Humanity gained traction over fury from his distractive pleading. "Nick...please..." *See me! Hear me! Save me!*

"We're concerned about you...me, your parents, and...Kiran."

Specifying her parents certainly shocked her, but it was mentioning Kiran that made her gasp. She pulled free but didn't move away.

"So now all you can manage is protecting me from a distance?" He dared to step closer.

She tried to step back but he had a grip on her hand, so instead, she bowed in shame. "Yes."

"He told me you bit him."

Her body trembled from having to recall that night.

"Just come back to us." He spoke softly, daring to touch her cheek with his free hand.

She slowly leaned into his touch.

"The cement here is kinda grimy...but let's take him!"

"NO!" She flinched, pulling herself away from Nick's tender grasp. Walking away from him, she purposely let her old icy demeanor wash over her. Just before leaving the alley, she stopped. "I'll make sure that you aren't attacked—but only if you take Diane straight home and you both stay there." Shae disappeared into a portal and trailed Nick as he met back up with Diane.

From the opposite side of the street, she hid behind a tree near the curb, planted there by the city for beautification. She triggered magically enhanced vision and hearing to listen in on his conversation with Diane.

"What do you mean you changed your mind? Does this have something to do with where you disappeared to?" Diane then gasped, "You saw HER, didn't you?"

"Kinda..." He looked at her sheepishly. "Yes." He quickly threw his hands up, "Now before you rant about that...THIS wasn't planned." He lowered his hands as she eased a bit. "But it's good that I stumbled upon Shae. She's brought out the household to hunt tonight."

Diane gasped again but for a different reason. "Hunting!?" Eagerly, she followed closely behind Nick. "We have to get home. What if she goes after Riley!?"

"She won't." Nick unlocked the car once they reached it. "She promised." Nick sunk into the driver's seat, forcing Diane to sit in the passenger side.

Diane's hysteria rose. "How can we ever be sure we're safe with her on the loose?"

Shae tuned them out as they drove off. After emerging from a portal, she hid behind the next-door neighbor's large bush. She secretly watched over Nick until he entered the house with Diane, calling for Riley. She walked out to the sidewalk once it felt safe enough. The house across the street from Nick's caught her attention.

The shape of the house hasn't changed, aside from new windows and siding. I wonder if the in-ground pool is still in the backyard. While pausing on the curb before crossing the street, she glanced over to the last window farthest from the front door of the ranch house. That was her room. Gone were the silly window decorations she always rotated through for each holiday. *Kiran's right. I do love all the holidays. The chance to decorate the houses—inside and out.*

Thoughts wandered to Kiran. About his offer to show off the decorations at his place. As she stepped off the curb to cross the street, squealing tires and a blaring car horn broke her reverie. She flinched back from the car, watching the driver hop out. Her jaw fell open. "I was just thinking about you."

"Way to make a guy feel special, but..." Kiran hustled over to her. "...maybe next time look both ways."

For some reason, she smirked. "Seriously doubt a car could kill me at this point."

But he frowned. "Not a time to joke, Shae."

"Wait...what are you doing here?"

He scratched at the side of his head. "I don't know. I just...had this feeling to drive down this street."

They quietly gazed at each other.

"What about you?" he finally asked. "Are you going after Nick again now?"

Shae's stance shifted nervously.

Kiran dared to touch her shoulder as he lowered his voice. "Was it you that killed those people at the riverfront?"

"No."

"Yes!"

Shae whimpered, putting a hand against the side of her head.

"Shae?" Now Kiran's other hand was on her other shoulder.

"I did it. I killed them all." She gazed at Kiran. Her voice was a harsh whisper when she spoke again as she struggled against the darkness for control. "It's afraid of you."

"What…what do you mean? It? Who is it?"

She sucked in a breath and hunched over. "Please, Kiran…I don't want to hurt you again."

"Do you want me to go get Nick?" Kiran took a step toward Nick's house.

"Yes," she hissed, voice shifting from anger to anguish. "NO!" Suddenly, all four of his car tires burst, the bang echoing through the air, but she nonchalantly rose from her hunched position, unaffected by the forceful blast that knocked Kiran to his hands and knees. She clenched her jaw as she stood next to his fallen figure. "You are getting too close, Civilian." Her voice cackled and fizzled like a broken transmission over radio airwaves. Shae knelt, grabbed him by his hair, and licked the side of his face.

Kiran stared at her. "Are you gonna bite me again?" Fear crept into his voice.

"If I had been in more control then, I wouldn't have made that mistake." She roughly let go of him and stood up. Then, she stepped back into an awaiting portal. "But even so, YOU can't stop me now." She disappeared into the portal and it closed.

She exited the portal downtown on a random street. She walked along the wall of an office building. Shouts of her clan mixed with screams of their male and female victims rang like a cherished symphony. Just as she neared the front entrance of a random office building, she collided with a man.

"Oh, sorry. Are you all right?" The man clutched her arm to keep her from falling. The streetlight illuminated her and his eyes went wide in recognition. "Hey, it's you!"

"Excuse me?"

"Don't you remember? The diner…you were with others, but I only noticed you." He chuckled. She didn't find it funny. He held out his hand. "I'm Keith Ashby. I work in this building."

She looked at the structure and then back at him, to address the memory he stirred. "That was a long time ago."

"Nah." He shrugged. "It was only like a couple of months ago." Shae made a move to leave, but he stopped her. "How about a name to go with your pretty face?"

She eyed the man cautiously, taking in his shoulder-length wavy black hair, and his lean figure in the dark blue business suit. The detailed suitcase he toted around signified his level of wealth. She smirked, noting the lack of a ringed finger. *Good. I so don't need another married man in this mess.* However, she paused. *There still could be a woman in his life. Ah, the hell with it.* "Shae."

He grinned at her simple terse introduction. "No last name?"

She glared at him, making him uneasy.

He coughed to ease the tension, "Okay…then…uh…I know it's the dead of night, but places are still open. Would you care to join me for a late-night coffee and conversation, Shae?"

"Sure."

Keith grinned and led her to his favorite place. He held the door open. "After you."

She reached out and caressed his cheek. "Such a gentleman." There was a hint of amusement on her lips at his old-fashioned ways. She read the sign as she entered the place and approached the counter. "Best All

200

Night Coffee…Bean Shop."

"A title they've held since opening up two years ago." Keith was at her side, tapping his fingers on the laminated certificate she read from.

She shrugged and glanced at the menu. Nothing on the list was appealing, but she ordered something simple anyway—just for show. Service was fast since there weren't many customers at this hour and soon they sat in a booth. She was silent, leaving it up to Keith to break the tension.

"I was hoping that I'd run into you again…but I didn't think I'd do it literally." He laughed at his own joke. She rolled her eyes at him as she looked away. "But seriously, I saw you sitting there…just like you are now and it made me want to get to know you, Shae."

"Why?" She was looking at him again, his revelation sinking into her thoughts.

He shrugged and took a quick sip of his coffee. "I don't know. I seemed drawn to you and I wanted to be the one to erase that sad look off your face." She managed not to roll her eyes in annoyance at a lame pickup line. Boldly, he rubbed her hand with his fingers. "Or did Jacquain already claim you?"

Did he lose someone to Jacquain? She stared at their hands, disturbed by snippets of humanity slipping through. "Not really."

"I don't…"

"Don't worry about it." She placed a finger to his lips to hush him. Without a word, she drew him from his seat and out of the Bean Shop. By now she had him enthralled enough that he 'blindly' followed her up an escape ladder of a random building, onto a secluded rooftop. She had taken the long way so as not to startle him just yet.

The rooftop offered a lovely vista of the city. "Never saw the city from this angle before." Keith waved his arms out at the skyline.

Poor fool is oblivious that he's dinner.

"Hey, thanks for showing me this place."

Shae sat on the ledge, feet dangling.

"Are you crazy? You'll fall!" He rushed to pull her back to safety.

"My hero." She bolstered his ego before making out with him. They shed their clothing, allowing the crisp air to graze their heated flesh. Shae continued the charade, allowing them both one orgasm. "Keith…" she cooed, breaking his flurry of kisses trailing her neck and shoulder as he pounded away.

He noted her fangs and fear immediately etched his eyes. "You're one of Jacquain's vixens!" Shae tightened her grip on him to ensure he didn't escape. "Please, spare me! I have a kid!" With trembling hands, he reached over to his pants. He fumbled to retrieve his wallet, and eventually was able to show Shae a picture of his kid.

She had been ready to lean in, slightly put off by his incessant chatter. She humored him and glanced at the picture. Keith was sobbing hysterically now and didn't notice how disturbed Shae was. She just gazed at him, horrified that she just *had* to pick Riley's biological father to play with.

"Her name is Riley. Great kid." And then he launched further into his hysterical babbling. "I know I haven't visited lately. Not since a group of vampires kidnapped her during my watch. So I purposely avoided her mother's overbearing rant and…"

"I'm nobody's vixen!" She maliciously yanked his head to the side, complimented with a piercing sensation in his neck. He only screamed for a short while as she ripped a gash in his neck to silence him. Swiftly, she rolled over to be on top. His plea for freedom came out in gurgles. In a short amount of time, she rendered him bloodless and lifeless. And by the time she stood up, magic had given her a fresh set of clothes.

She leaped off the side of the eighteen-story building, twisting as she succumbed to gravity, eager to splatter her on the sidewalk. Briefly, she basked in the free fall, arms wide open.

On the tenth floor, Shae conjured a portal, exiting safely to the cement sidewalk below. Sunlight loomed over the horizon and its rays would soon fill the streets. The world was still and quiet. For the moment, she could forget the chaos of life. Shae summoned a fresh portal. The swirling vortex opened up, and with a last look around, she travelled through it, and emerged on the other side in front of the mansion.

Chapter 17

Shae stirred first the following night, seeing that Michael still slept. She silently left his side and stepped onto the attached second-floor patio. Her casual lounging outfit shifted into a sensuous purple and black polyester jumpsuit. She raised a leg on the surrounding cement railing, rising, allowing the momentum to push herself away from the ledge into the open. The portal awaiting her below prevented the inevitable crash that gravity promised.

She emerged from an exit portal in the small, wooded area behind Nick's house. The backyard lights made it easier to spot Riley on the patio swing. Riley busily played a game on her handheld and didn't appear to care about the cloudy, cold night. However, the pre-teen was in the spotlight of an outside light attached to the house. Diane then appeared and talked with Riley. Shae waited a moment longer for Diane to go back inside the house before making a move. "Can I interest you in a game *two* people can play?"

Riley jumped to her feet. "Shae!"

Shae noted Riley's hesitance and wondered what aspect of the current situation Riley feared. "Don't you miss me?"

"Are you here to take my dad away?"

"I came to visit you, Riley."

Riley glanced at Shae.

Shae snatched the girl's shoulder before she could turn and run. "Riley…" She knelt in front of her. "I actually am here to see you." Riley stared a bit longer. "C'mon, it's me—but I don't know for how long."

"Shae?"

"Honorary sisters."

Riley tossed the handheld aside and it landed where she had been sitting. Then she briefly hugged her.

Nick emerged from the back door. "Shae?"

She stood and glanced over Riley's head at Nick. The item in his hand lured her away from Riley, eyes darting from the chocolate cupcake with white icing and a strawberry icing rose on top, to his even more irresistible chocolate eyes.

"Do you know what today is, Shae? It's October twenty-first." His voice was soft and low. Neither of them noticed how Riley silently moved over to Diane's side. Nick continued, "I know I promised you a giant celebration, but I hope you won't mind just a cupcake and a small gathering."

Shae's eyes flickered to Diane and Riley, but enough of her humanity was present then, and she followed the family into the house.

There was a tray of similar cupcakes on the kitchen table.

"Happy Birthday, Shae." Diane flashed her an obviously practiced welcoming smile.

She took a seat at the table, not minding how Riley eagerly claimed the seat next to her. Nick set the cupcake in front of her and Diane placed a single candle in the center of the rose. Then he lit the candle, stuffing the lighter back in his pocket.

Softly, the family sang—with a brief silence after they finished.

"Go ahead, Shae…make a wish!" Riley urged.

…*save*…

"Shae?" The buzz in Nick's head rippled as he picked up the faint sound of her voice.

…*me*…

"Nick, honey…what's going on?" Diane's voice quivered.

Nick motioned for his wife to hush before putting a hand against his head. "Shae…save you?" He glanced at her with anguish in his eyes.

"What the hell is that supposed to mean?" Diane demanded now, clearly ignoring her husband's request.

Shae's gaze snapped to Diane, a low growl reverberating from deep within. However, she suddenly jerked to her feet. "Please…I don't want to hurt you." She glanced to Nick and Riley. "Any of you." She slowly inched back, feeling herself slipping into the Darkness's embrace once more. She turned, ready to run.

"STOP!"

All eyes turned toward Riley, as the candle blew out and the young girl rose to her feet with just as much confusion on her face as everyone else.

"Wha…?" Diane tried to reach out for her daughter, but Riley moved closer to Shae.

"The bad man was a foolish rook, trying to castle a queen." The articulation Riley presented clashed with her pre-teen voice.

"The bad man? Gerard Jacquain?"

Riley nodded at Diane's question.

"Quite amusing for a Civilian child to be talking in

chess riddles."

Shae could only stand there, as Riley's comments reminded her of two significant moments with Gerard. The first being the menacing conversation with the Darkness about the black and white queen during the mansion tour. The second was the night she slaughtered the mansion residents.

"What happened that night, sweetie?" Nick encouraged his stepdaughter.

"He talked a lot about her."

"Oh?" His eyebrows lifted.

Riley glanced at Shae. "His eagerness for an equal to share his indulgences with blinded him. The night he dared attempt to warn his Deviant enemies resulted in *bleeding* more than just *love*."

Shae's eyes widened at the way Riley stressed the song's title the night she killed Gerard. *But how…how does she know this?!*

Diane stood beside Riley. "Sweetie, what on earth are you talking about?"

Riley tilted her head up at Diane. "The white queen slaughtered more than just lowly black pawns. Before that, she first had to bow in resignation to the black queen."

"So…both queens took out all the pieces?" Nick knelt next to Riley.

"Not quite. It was only the black queen that did all the work." Riley stared right at Shae. "The white queen was off the board that night." Then she looked at her father again. "It's quite understandable with all that's happened since that night that you've forgotten that she already confessed to you—when the Deviants attempted to capture her."

Shae noticed Nick rising to his feet.

"Well that's quite enough out of this child."

What? In Shae's distraction, the Darkness seized control once more. Shae lashed out and snatched Riley from between her parents.

"Get your hands off my daughter!!"

Shae's whole demeanor suddenly shifted. Keeping her grip on Riley, Shae turned to face the older woman. "You should be more worried about your husband." She then smirked lustfully. "The way he intimately engages a woman...it's just..." She teasingly shivered and moaned in a display of complete pleasure that shifted into a malicious chucke.

"Enough, Shae!" Nick bellowed. Then he motioned to Riley, his voice desperate, "Let her go, please, Shae."

"That was utterly unacceptable, Nickolas." Shae's face contorted in disgust.

Riley wasn't enjoying Shae squeezing her shoulder and struggled to get away. "Let go! You're not my honorary sister." Riley winced when Shae's nails dug through the thin jacket, sounding more like a pre-teen now.

Shae ignored Riley and gazed at Nick—amused that he seemed so calm. She also noticed how Nick held Diane's hand—for comfort and to keep her from doing something brash. Anger rolled within her, rousing intense bloodlust. She managed to keep it from the surface for now.

"The last time we were naked together..." Shae noticed the way Diane flinched. "Be honest, Nickolas, you were only going through the motions with me...your heart wasn't really in it. You were only willing enough to form the bond with me to keep me from Jacquain." Shae again squeezed Riley's shoulder and the girl yelped in pain. *Let's test how much you and Diane can handle.*

"We weren't naked together!" Nick weakly countered.

"What?" Diane gazed at him in surprise.

"We never got that far!" Nick assured Diane. "We got interrupted."

"You got interrupted?!" Diane's voice rose.

"Oops." Shae put a hand to her mouth and giggled. "I think I might have caused an argument. My bad."

Diane seemed to ignore Shae's comment, sinking deeper into a lover's spat with her husband.

"Mom, Dad...stop fighting!" Riley cried out.

"Ya know, Riley. Your real father was more willing than your stepfather. However, Nickolas is tastier." She smirked when she got all of their attention.

"What?" Riley sniffled. Nick and Diane just looked horrified.

Shae rolled her eyes and sighed. "You need to make a choice, Nickolas. Perhaps I should help speed up the process."

"No!!" Nick protested as Shae bared her fangs and bit into Riley's shoulder. Riley screamed in shock and pain, causing Diane to burst into tears. "Stop this, Shae!" Nick placed his hands on Shae's arm, hoping to free Riley from her grip. Shae grunted and carelessly let go of Riley. He caught Riley's limp figure from falling to the kitchen tile.

Shae exhaled a heavy sigh. *Nick is still choosing THEM over us.* She looked over in time to see Diane joining Nick in a sort of huddle hug.

Diane glanced up, tears in her eyes. "You bitch!"

Shae stared at Nick cradling Riley in his arms, when she suddenly seemed to wake from a stupor. "Nick...Riley? Oh God!" She put a hand to her mouth.

"How could you!?" he spat. "You're a monster, Shae."

Staring down at the blood on her hands, she inhaled a gasp. *I am a monster.* She glanced back up to the family—who was ignoring her presence now. She watched them scoop Riley's limp body and hustle to the garage, Diane snatching the car keys along the way.

The Darkness clouded over her weakened state as a horrified expression shifted into a proud smirk. "I am a monster." She turned and walked out of the house via the backdoor, toward the fence that separated his yard from the woods behind his house.

****

Shae lay in their bed, staring at the top of the canopy bed. *Last night was an utter failure. It's going to be trickier to get to Nickolas now. But I had to silence his child.*

Michael roused in his sleep and rustled the silk-thin sheet between them.

Her expression remained blank as she absorbed Michael's nude figure. *I've had my fun with him, but it's time to move on.*

He shifted again and opened his eyes. "Hey there, sexy queen. How about another round?"

Shae brushed his long hair aside, smirking at the way he addressed her. *Hell, one more romp couldn't hurt.* She clasped around his thickness and noticed the dark, cloudless sky above the garden maze. *Just like my mood.*

Michael moaned into their searing kiss. However, a

servant soon interrupted them.

"Excuse me, my Queen…but I have a message from Mr. Gehring."

She groaned and sat up, hand still wrapped around Michael's visible erection. She chuckled as the servant averted her eyes. "What is his message, Laila?"

"He requests your audience down in the study." Laila kept her head bowed.

Michael tried to coax his queen to resume stroking his hard-on. "Well, you can tell Bruce that we're busy."

"Hush now." Shae shifted off him and, after donning a robe, she motioned for Laila to lead the way. Michael grunted and quickly slipped his clothes back on, grumbling about the biker vamp.

Outside the study, they met up with Bruce.

"Thank you, my Queen, for accepting my request." Bruce bowed.

She shifted back onto a heel and folded her arms. "What is it that was so urgent to have sent for me?"

"Yeah, this *better* be good." Michael threateningly advanced on Bruce until Shae placed her hand on his chest and pushed him back.

"Ah yes, I'm certain you'll be quite amused." Bruce opened the doors. She noticed two random lackeys kneeling behind a figure in a chair, adjusting the restraints.

She stopped short of the sleeping figure in the chair. *Dorian? What? How? I don't understand!*

"You interrupted us for a damned Deviant?" Michael bellowed at Bruce.

"Not just any Deviant. But the one assigned as her husband."

Shae clamped her mouth shut. *Technically, he still*

is. Slowly, she wandered away from them and approached the two lackeys fiddling with the ropes binding the prisoner. "Leave us."

"As you wish, my Queen." Both bowed and spoke in unison before carrying out the demand. Michael and Bruce only continued their argument.

Shae was close enough now to Dorian and timidly placed her hand on his shoulder. Dorian stirred awake as she knelt next to him.

That caught Bruce's attention. "My Queen, what is wrong?"

"Isn't it obvious?" Michael's reply made her hesitate.

"Well, you seem to know...so clue us in, Goth Boy!"

The nickname caused Michael to seethe with anger and he poked his finger at Bruce's chest. "Moron! It's because she hadn't eaten her 'morning' meal yet!"

She felt a sigh of relief that they were oblivious to the real reason.

Again, the two of them resumed arguing. Dorian's eyes captured Shae's attention. She frowned when noticing the numerous small cuts and bruises on his face. Shae stood on her feet, turning to address the quarreling lackeys. "ENOUGH!" Silence filled the room. "I am VERY displeased, Bruce."

"I don't understand."

"Untie him, NOW!" Her anger urged them to act quickly. Dorian was free to leave, but he hesitated to move.

"What have I done to displease you, my Queen?"

"Shae..." Dorian mumbled.

Michael and Bruce glared at him.

Shae forced her cold demeanor forward. "Get this filthy Deviant out of my house." She refused to look at her husband.

"Yes, my Queen." Bruce bowed and moved forward.

This time, Dorian struggled. "Shae…you have to stop this!" He coughed up a bit of blood as he spoke.

She turned and took her new lover's hand. "Michael, let's get back to where we left off."

"Shae!" Dorian staggered to his feet, only to have Bruce shove him back down into the chair.

She stopped on her heel just before the door and made a deliberate display of locking lips with Michael.

A hot, pulsing ecstasy shot through Shae's body as Michael licked her neck and groped her breasts. He ground his crotch against her thigh like an animal in heat. She slipped her hand down Michael's pants in the open doorway.

"Don't stop this time," he whimpered.

"Don't tell your queen what to do." She released him as she turned toward Bruce. "Throw him out and then ready the Rolls." She watched him hustle off, dragging Dorian to the front door before he headed to the garage.

Michael adjusted his crotch. "What? When are we gonna fuck again?"

"You said it yourself. I need my 'morning' meal." She patted his cheek. "Feed first, fuck later." Then she headed up to her room to freshen up.

Within the hour, Bruce pulled the car up to a curb across the street from a popular ice cream shop.

Michael exited the vehicle first before assisting Shae out and onto the sidewalk.

She moved to the passenger side window and leaned over. She didn't care that she gave Bruce such tantalizing views of her half-exposed breasts. "Return home and wait for us there. Michael and I will—"

"Shae, what the hell?"

She stood up as a figure approached her.

"Hey now, what's the rush?" Michael moved to intercept the figure.

"Get out of my way." The figure dropped his cone while trying to shove Michael aside.

"Kiran, are you crazy?! What if these are vampires?" Kiran's co-worker caught up to him, wheezing. "Oh, hey…is this the friend you mentioned?

Michael raised an eyebrow. "I guess I shouldn't be surprised that certain Civilians still think they are friends of yours."

She chuckled and linked her arm with his. "Friends? With a Civilian?" She glanced at Michael. "I hope he doesn't try asking me out on a date again."

Michael tilted his head in amusement. "Our queen has a lot of suitors at her disposal."

She tenderly caressed his face. "Such is the result of partaking in pleasure." She leaned for a kiss. Kiran and John gasped. She glared at the Civilians from out of the corner of her eye. "My dear Michael, I think someone disapproves of our public displays of affection."

Michael looked square at Kiran. "Well, then they'll just have to…LEAVE." He giggled at the way Kiran flinched.

Kiran, in a moment of stupidity, latched his hands onto her shoulder and attempted to pull her aside. "Shae, what is wrong with you?"

"Get your filthy Civilian hands off her!" Michael snarled and grasped the guy by the neck and squeezed.

Shae's smirk faded when Kiran struggled from Michael's deadly grip. The infamous desire to kill clashed with an unsettling need to defend Kiran. "Relax, love." She eased Michael's hands from Kiran before shoving the Civilian against a brick wall. She licked her lips.

As Shae pressed her lips against Kiran's neck in a pre-bite kiss, Michael licked his lips and adjusted his growing erection. "Appetizers…good idea, my Queen."

With Michael's attention elsewhere, Shae whispered to Kiran, "I'm sorry. But you shouldn't have—"

Her attempt to ease Kiran's fear was interrupted as a dagger whizzed behind her and punctured the car's rear passenger tire.

"You guys get out of here!"

"So, you want to play." Shae narrowed her eyes and bared fangs at Rozette. She didn't care that Kiran and John fled the scene. She launched herself upward, disappearing into a portal and appearing on the rooftop of a random building. More Deviants jumped up from their hiding spots and the fight began. She had given in to her rage and carelessly tore into one Deviant after another, uncaring about the bloody mess she made. Some of them put up a good fight before their demise and some were even lucky to wound her—however, those wounds healed just as fast as they appeared.

"Shae!"

She saw Rozette at the top of the escape ladder. The few remaining Deviants backed off, some of them limping.

"Please, Shae. Wake up," Rozette pleaded.

"Shae's not here right now." She launched herself at Rozette, who dodged the swipe of her hand and hustled back down the stairwell.

Unfortunately, Shae took the bait and trailed after her. She caught up to Rozette at the edge of the warehouse district. "You might be an excellent leader, but you always sucked in our practice chase missions." She gripped her by the arm.

Dorian rushed into the alley and tackled Shae to give Rozette aid.

"Hello again, my husband!" Her smile got bigger when she noticed him shiver. "Soon-to-be EX-husband!"

"This ends now, Shae." They swapped punches and kicks, taking the fight inside the warehouse. Dorian lured Shae to the far wall.

"Dorian, are you okay?"

Shae followed her husband's gaze to Rozette, until she noticed Verties. "I'll kill you!"

"No, you won't, Shae." Nick entered behind Verties.

Shae hesitated at the sight of Nick. "My dear Nickolas...do you want to play too?" Her words and body language betrayed each other. Even she was confused if she was flirting, taunting, or hiding fear. Holding back her rage and engaging verbally was an intense strain.

"No, and it is not a game we're playing now," Nick replied, taking a safe step toward her.

"How's your little girl?" Shae hit a sore spot in him, seeing his subtle flinching. Hands twitched to feel delicate flesh tear beneath her fingers.

"She's slipping, Nickolas," Verties whispered to him.

"Shae…talk to me." He ran a hand through his hair. "I know I called you a monster. But you…this isn't you!"

A tear trickled down her cheek. "It hurts so much…the Bond…it's…" For the instant she was herself again, desperately trying to tell Nick the truth about the bond and its real purpose. She trembled, cradling her arms across her stomach and hunched over.

"This has to be done," Verties firmly spoke.

"What?" She never had time to identify the trigger in her father's hand. A thunderous explosion erupted from a small bomb wired to the wall just a little too close for comfort.

Shae crumbled, struggling to free herself from the debris.

Verties suddenly filled her hazy vision. "My dear daughter," he whispered, his voice laced with sad disappointment, "it breaks my heart to have resorted to such drastic measures to shut you down."

Shae grimaced and continued struggling, even as shackles bound her feet and hands.

Verties scooped her up. "Time to go home."

Within the hour, she watched as Deviants quickly attached chains from the wall to her shackles. Then she was alone with her father.

She tested the new bindings—the cold metal shackles limiting arm and leg movement. 'She glared at her father, envious of his freedom of movement. *This is no fun at all, FATHER.*

"Don't bother using your magic. The shackles are enchanted to negate them."

How am I supposed to get Nickolas now? Even though warned, she dared to try a spell. Nothing happened. Then she sneered at her father. "You may have the upper hand now, old man, but I will not be held for long. Nickolas WILL be mine!" She watched in frustration as her father's response was to leave her there—under a strict, watchful guard, of course.

Chapter 18

Shae awoke three nights later to slow, methodical scraping sounds on the cement floor. She raised her groggy head. Nick's backside was to her as he dragged a cot into her room.

A Deviant guard stepped through the open cell door. He bent over Shae and unlocked the shackles at her feet and hands.

What is going on? Her heart raced as she stood up, muscles stiff from days of being chained to the floor. She groaned from flexing her arms, eyes adjusting to dim dungeon lights.

"Don't think of trying anything funny, Princess. Master Crimshon placed a strong spell on your cell to dampen any attempt to portal out of here."

She recognized Lestor's voice as her vision cleared. "Les?"

"Sorry about the fighting earlier. Dorian is actually a great guy. He was picked for you for a reason—because he really was a compliment to your abilities."

She frowned. "Just leave me alone."

"Yeah, quit bothering her," Nick added.

Lestor raised his hands in surrender. "Okay, okay." Then he locked the cell and left the small room.

She placed her hands on her lower back and gave a long, deep exhalation.

"C'mon, get comfy." Nick patted the space at his

side.

Shae moaned in relief at having a softer cushion for her ass. "Why are you here? You shouldn't be here. Leave before I—"

Nick leaned closer, his voice low and soothing. "I know this is all overwhelming, but you have to stay strong. We will find a way out of here. You can trust me."

Shae looked into Nick's warm brown eyes. "You really shouldn't have come here."

"When was the last time you fed, Shae?" He tenderly moved her damp bangs aside.

She honestly couldn't remember now. Everything was a blur. "The last significant thing I remember was your family singing to me." *Really wish I could have eaten that cupcake. It looked delicious and I bet he slaved all afternoon in the kitchen, baking them with Riley.*

Nick raised his wrist but had nothing to create a cut with. He glanced at her helplessly as he held out his arm.

At first, she shook her head no. But eventually, fangs formed.

"I'm not scared of those."

"I hated having to give myself to that bastard." Her soft voice sounded awkward with such a declaration. Finally, sharp teeth pierced his wrist. After three gulps, she pulled herself away.

"Is that gonna be enough?"

"I don't want to risk losing control and draining you," Shae countered while wiping her mouth with her long, gray-sleeved sweatshirt.

"You are so beautiful," he whispered.

"I look like shit," she grumbled.

He dared to kiss her on the lips, careful of her fangs. A move that surprised them both.

Despite feeding even just a little, Shae was still too weak to hold strong when the Darkness rumbled.

"Time to finally lay our claim, Shae!"

No, I can't!

"DO IT!"

She only sobbed.

"Shae?"

"You're making him wait? Fine, I'll do it for you."

Her hands slid around him and drifted up—fingers brushing his upper backside along the way. "Save me…that was my wish."

Nick stilled from the revelation. "I remember. The buzzing in my head." He cupped her cheek in his hand. "I still don't understand how the bond is going to save you now. But if you still believe in it, then so do I." Nick tenderly nibbled on her ear. "I'll make your wish come true," he whispered.

Shae lay her head back, running her fingers through his hair. The familiar scent of his cologne filled the room, complete with the smoky undertone of musk made her heart flutter. She drew both arms around his neck and whispered, "Nickolas…please!"

He removed both of their shirts and pants, leaving them clad only in underwear. He then pressed his lips against the top of her breasts visible from her bra. She resisted the call, blood pulsing in his veins. *No, not yet.*

His hands left a burning trail down her chest and across her stomach—back up again. They were trembling, and as he looked into her eyes, the heat spread throughout her body. His touch was like fire, and yet it felt so good.

Electricity crackled between them like a live wire, sparks dancing up her arms and down his. The force of the connection was almost too much to bear as their eyes locked in a fiery gaze, a shared feeling of standing on the edge of a precipice about to plunge into an unknown abyss. His eyes glazed over with desire, passion, and something more dangerous lurking beneath the surface.

Shae pressed her mouth to the edge of his shoulder, kissing and licking the flesh, pausing when her jaw tingled.

"You okay?" He leaned back and glanced down. "Do you need to feed again?"

"No, just…gimme a minute." *First, we fuck, then we feed.* Seconds ticked by before she spoke again. "Okay, ready."

Nick reached up and curled his finger under a bra strap, sliding it off her shoulder.

She watched as he tugged at the fabric, pulling her bra away from her body and down her arms. Then rested her head on the pillow. "Very sauve, Nickolas."

"Learned that little move back in college." He cupped her breast and massaged it gently, while the other hand moved between her thighs.

A dull, incessant throbbing filled her chest. With the first pulse came the horrifying image of cradling Gerard's dead body in her arms. The second pulse delivered the same image but it was Nick's body. *No, I would never hurt him.* Was something trying to warn her of what was to come? Fear gripped her heart as the dark reality closed in.

The third surge brought a familiar memory of the

card shop. She trembled in fear of the pain from that moment. *I never want to feel that again. It was so agonizing and I couldn't call for help. But…why am I being shown this moment?* Suddenly, a powerful craving for pleasure and blood arose.

Mistaking hesitancy as just simply basking in the moment, Nick carefully lowered himself down, knees pressing into the mattress on either side. As he continued to brush their bodies together, the tip of his erection barely grazed her vagina.

She squirmed and whined in protest. "No…no…"

"Shae? What's wrong?" He froze, prepared to finally enter her.

Delicate fingers dug into Nick's chest—a feeble attempt to push him away. The struggle against the Darkness's domination vibrated the bed. "Nick…" Abruptly, she turned her head away.

"No, Shae. Just hang on…stay with me." He desperately forced her to face him, only to see bloody tears trickle from her tightly closed eyes. "STAY WITH ME!"

"If I stay…I will kill you." Her voice crackled and ominously rippled. The first part of the comment was her pleading voice, while the second part was utterly vicious. She squirmed again, needing to get away before succumbing to the need to hurt. Finally, she pushed hard enough to create a sizable distance between them.

"Shae…"

He settled her back down on the bed and squinted in confusion. "What do you mean?" Shae turned to the side. "Shae…you're scaring me. C'mon now."

"I hurt Riley." The Darkness was testing him now.

"That night…Riley was…what was she talking about?"

"Chess riddles, my dear." Shae sneered at him. "Much too complicated for a Civilian to understand." But in the next moment, her voice shifted back to her own. "Why would you want to be with a monster?"

"I don't really think you're a monster."

"I wanted to!" She held out her hand between them. "There is still the urge to destroy."

"Save me."

"It's so cold here."

"I miss you."

"The darkness is smothering!"

"I need you!"

"The Bond will devour!"

Nick clamped his hands over his ears and hunched over. "Stop!" The echoed voices faded.

She rolled over, curling up slightly into a ball.

Nick gently held her tightly as she trembled.

"Nick, you have to let me go."

He pulled away, eyes wide with shock. "What? No, I can't do that."

"You have to," Shae said firmly, half sitting up. The presence of bloody tears trickling from her eyes again made him see just how much she was straining against something.

"I don't understand," he said uncertainly.

"It's the only way," said Shae, voice weak and her body struggling to sit up.

"Shae, don't." He pressed her back to the bed.

She shoved his hand aside before clasping the side of his head. "If you don't leave, then this will happen…" Despite having first-hand experience with the room's protection against magic, Shae dared connect with the Darkness. *Time to see what I can do with that True Nature spell I stumbled upon before the shit hit the fan.* Using dark powers, she twisted the spell and placed both hands on either side of Nick's temples.

****

She was near Nick's home within minutes. From her distance, Shae spotted him seated on the bottom step of the porch stairs consoling a distressed Riley. Shae caught wind of words such as 'divorce' and 'visitation rights'.

Diane emerged from the house, suitcase in one hand and a duffle bag over her opposite shoulder. "C'mon, Riley. Time to go."

The young girl stood up and sniffled. "But I don't want to leave!"

"Hush up and get in the car." Diane never once glanced at Nick.

Shae sauntered up the walkway from the sidewalk.

Diane noticed her first. "Oh, look, your bitch is here."

Nick grunted, rising to his feet. "Diane, it was one time. A mistake. She came on to me that night Riley was kidnapped."

"And you couldn't resist the hussy in nothing but your shirt?" She quickly turned to Riley. "Go in the house. I have one bag left by the couch."

"I'm afraid I can't let you do that." Shae was suddenly in front of the door, blocking Riley's escape. "Excuse us, but us Honorary Sisters need to have a little chat." She pulled Riley into a portal.

"NO!" Nick collapsed to his knees.

Diane's reaction was to run out onto the front

lawn, wildly glancing around. "Bring her back, you bitch!"

At the end of Riley's street, four blocks from her home, Shae emerged from a portal on the corner. She dialed the mansion. During Shae's request for a car, Riley struggled for freedom. Shae hung up and shook the younger girl. "Stop squirming!" Shae gripped Riley by each arm and knelt. "I will not hurt you."

"Liar!" Riley responded through sniffles.

"I may have done a lot of things, but as a queen, lying is off the list of my attributes." Shae stood back up and maintained her hold on the girl.

"You're not gonna bite me again?" Riley glanced up with questioning eyes.

Shae chuckled. "I apologize for that, Riley. It was a bit drastic on my part." She caressed Riley's cheek.

Riley sniffled again. "Then what are you gonna do?"

"You will see soon enough."

Shae glanced over, watching the child's calm expression. Suddenly, Riley's cherubic face melded into one of ancient wisdom. *Ah, there it is, just like how she looked that night I showed up pretending I was going to rescue her from Jacquain. The moment she began uttering chess riddles, I knew this moment would come. However, I don't regret returning her to Diane and Nick. It made him so emotional that he was easy to manipulate into another romp.*

"You used to be so nice."

Shae jerked up straight and glared at the child. "That me is dead now."

Riley dared to touch Shae over her heart. "Maybe not." The child's eyes and hands began to glow azure, *replacing her irises.*

Shae hissed and shoved Riley to the ground, baring her fangs. "Your tricks are too weak." Shae noticed fear in the girl's eyes and wickedly grinned. "I want you to do something for me.., Riley."

"W-what?"

Shae snatched Riley and dragged her into a portal.

"What is this place?" Riley's feet crunched in the snow. She looked to the left and noticed blotches of red randomly on the snow. To the right was a small, almost frozen stream, with a dead body downstream.

Shae stood, gaze zipping around until she deemed it safe for now. "This is where I grew up." She made a hush motion at Riley. "Keep your voice low, you'll attract them."

"Who?" Riley looked around. The wind rustled only the skimpy branches of the leafless trees.

"Random fighters...others like me, well half like me." Shae stopped in her explanation and stepped in front of Riley.

"Hey..." Riley protested; their conversation cut off by another voice.

"I smell another loser!" A burly man emerged from the trees, wielding a bloody shield and sword.

Without glancing at Riley, Shae gave a command, "Stay low and silent." She paused in confusion. Why am I protecting this child now? *Shae shook her head and advanced toward the burly man.*

"An eager loser at that," the man commented. "Or are you hiding a weapon to surprise me?" The man gave a menacing grin. "Either way, you'll die like the last guy." He raised his sword and charged. At the last minute, Shae stepped aside and tripped the man. He

landed right next to Riley. But before he could make an easy hit on the child, Shae was on top of him, baring fangs. He seemed shocked at first. "The last guy had those too."

When the man tried to lunge forward with his head, Shae forcefully used her hand to stop his momentum. "It's been a while since I got my hands dirty in this realm." Shae swiftly took out the man's right eye. He screamed and swung out, but she wasn't there anymore. He quickly rose.

Quickly, he scooped up some snow to hold over his wound. "You took out my eye!"

"I was being nice," Shae cooed in a mocking tone. Despite the horror of missing his eye, the man's fury fueled his every swing of his sword. Shae ducked underneath the blade, formed an orb, and stuffed it in the man's screaming mouth. Kaboom! The man's body collapsed, his head blown off. "Now I wasn't nice." Shae made a display of dusting snow from her hands, sleeves, and pant legs.

Riley tried to bolt from the scene, but Shae was quick.

Riley collided into Shae's bloody robe. "You...you..." Riley shivered.

"I killed him," Shae stated calmly. After checking that Riley's screams didn't attract any more unwanted interruptions, she motioned for the child to follow. Shae was amused that the child obeyed. "That is the way here...survive or die."

Riley's stare was a mixture of fear and forced bravery.

Hmmm, the ancient wisdom the child displayed is gone now. She must still be too weak to maintain it.

More snow was tainted red.

Riley's sudden scream broke the silence.

And Shae sunk to her knees.

"If you are here, then you know the way of this place. Yet you walk around, oblivious to the surrounding area." The tall, tanned woman pulled the bloody knife out of Shae's shoulder.

"Shae!!" Riley clasped onto Shae's unwounded side as she looked up at the female intruder.

"You appear weaponless, but I won't rule it out." The woman shifted, ready to strike again, snow crunching under her thick boots.

Shae quickly rose, spun, and bared fangs at the stranger. "I am a weapon." Her hands glowed in an eerie shade of red light.

"Shae Taizer…?"

"How do you know me?" Shae snarled.

"It's me, Thaela." The female pointed to herself. "I trained under Master Crimshon after you left…but he brought you in and introduced us."

"After I left?" Shae questioned, her voice taking on an unfamiliar tone.

"For here," Thaela explained, clearly unnerved by the sound of Shae's voice. "Something about you volunteering for two years."

Shae recognized the fellow Deviant, but tore into Thaela.

"Shae! Stop!!!" Riley yelled at Shae from a safe distance.

Shae spun in a crouched position over Thaela's body and glared at Riley. Shae's now bloody hand waved out. "Ya know, my plan was to leave you here and let this place kill you. But I'm too impatient for that."

An eerie blue circle of light appeared around Riley once she was airborne. The circle was circulating and closing in on Riley. "Shae! Please!" Riley's panicked voice rose into a shrill scream.

****

"What the hell was that?" Nick pulled away from Shae, breaking the vision she had shown him.

She dropped her hands and stared at the grimy floor. "I told you."

He stood up. "Killing Riley is what you wanted me to see—"

"If you and I went all the way." Shae finished for him. She glanced up at him and then turned away. "Listen, Nick. Just go home to your family."

"But I promised to save you."

"Please leave before I make you leave." She narrowed her eyes at him.

"But—"

"Go!" Shae jumped to her feet, fresh casual clothes forming over her nudity. "I will not have another marriage ruined."

"What other marriage was ruined?"

She just shook her head at him. "Guard!"

Nick shrugged on his shirt and pants. The guard entered the small room and opened the cell for Nick to leave. Finally, Nick stomped out of the prison chamber, the sound of iron slamming shut behind him reverberating around the dingy walls.

Shae groaned and plopped back down onto the cot. She envied Nick's freedom, unsure if she would ever experience it again.

Chapter 19

Amid her restless pacing, Shae stumbled onto the floor. Her attempts to stand back up were prohibited with a sudden wave of dizziness. *The sun, rising already?* She crawled over to the cot with great effort. *There's no way to track time down here. Dammit.* As she lay on the cot, the coldness set in her bones. *This is the worst. Will I ever get used to how a vampire's body shuts down for slumber?*

****

Four nights of enduring the forced starvation of her vampiric nature. What little blood Nick had donated yesterday was already used. *I can't decide which is more painful: my hunger for blood or losing my autonomy to dark pleasure.* She stared at the bars as she paced in the small cell. *How much longer are they gonna keep me down here!?* Tears formed as she crumbled in a sagging heap on the cot.

Finally, a guard entered the small room, carrying a covered tray. Even with the lid, she whiffed the scent of blood. It didn't matter whose blood it was. Wearily gazing at the guard, she remained seated.

The guard balanced the tray on his right hand, using his left hand to unlock the cell door. Then he set the tray down on the floor before slamming the door shut with a loud clang.

"Relax. I can't do anything." She rolled her eyes at

the way the guard retreated from the bars as she spoke.

The guard motioned to the tray. "I'll be back in twenty minutes to collect the tray." And then he was gone.

She lifted the tray, revealing a small bottle and a plastic wine glass—separated into compartments with a narrow ledge between them high enough to keep each item from rolling around.

Very amusing, Mom and Dad.

She lifted the bottle and rolled it in her hands. The blood inside sloshed around. She used vampiric strength carefully to pop the cork without the aid of a corkscrew. She placed the cork and the screw back on the tray.

She returned to sit on the cot and proceeded to drink straight from the bottle. She was not expecting the blood to be cold, since being used to warm blood straight from a body. However, blood was blood and she was starving, so she overlooked the tangy aftertaste. Within minutes, she downed the whole bottle and left it sitting on the tray by the cell door.

Could have used more, but that will have to suffice for now.

She sat around for the remaining minutes until the guard returned.

"Someone must have been hungry." The guard made a joke with a straight face after picking up the tray.

"Any chance I can get seconds?" she dared to ask.

"Not my call. I just deliver the tray and return it to the kitchen." The guard left without another word.

"Asshole," Shae mumbled. *The least he could have done was ask if I wanted a book or something.* It would be hours until her body's internal clock said it was sunrise again. She sat there on the cot, staring at the other two walls and the bars that made up a third wall.

"If only you hadn't chased dear Nickolas off."

"Shut up," she grunted. "It's your fault I'm stuck in this damn cell."

"Don't deny that we had so much fun. The club. The mansion. I bet right now so many people are missing you."

In heavy concentration, she ignored the voice—attempting to center herself. Calmness set in, creating a unified focus. Slowly, as if out of a dream, the room seemed to shift around her until an infinite expanse of nothing greeted her. Everywhere she looked, nothingness seemed to stretch into eternity. A canvas of pure black shimmering with an ethereal glow. No sign of life or anything in this void. Yet in this vastness, something in the distance moved.

She squinted, staring hard at the spot until a figure, hazy and indistinct, separated from the vast darkness. "What do you want?" she called out, but the figure didn't answer.

It continued to move closer until it was in front of her. As the Darkness loomed, it cast a shadow that seemed to stretch infinitely. An intense fear coursed through her veins. She tried to back away. The figure seemed to be made entirely of shadows, with piercing red eyes.

It's like its gaze is boring into my soul. "What do you want from me?" Shae repeated in a trembling voice.

The Darkness let out a low chuckle. "You know what I want," it replied, its voice deep and menacing.

The figure reached out and clutched her throat as they floated off the ground effortlessly. The Darkness leaned in closer, its red eyes glowing brighter.

Shae struggled against the grip, choking and gasping for air. *I know what you want.*

"What do I want?"

Pleasure.

A low chuckle rumbled through the Darkness and it released her. "You want it too."

"No."

"You are just like him." Eerily, it spoke in Avia's voice, a throwback to the meeting after returning from Battle Realm a month ago.

"NO!"

The Darkness stared with its ebony eyes. Its power was so palpable, like a thousand prickling pins. Its hand shot out again, placing its palm against her forehead.

Flashes of moments unraveled. At the club—Gerard watched her dirty dance with a Civilian. The many romps with Michael—especially the moment with the sock in the limo. The second visit to the club—making out with the three Civilians. The Darkness lingered on the moment of her and the bearded man grinding hard. "Tell me you didn't ENJOY that attention," it said in a voice as smooth as silk.

For a long time, she bowed in silence. "I did enjoy it," she finally admitted, her voice barely above a whisper.

The Darkness let out another chuckle, satisfied with Shae's confession. "You crave pleasure, just like him."

A chill ran down her spine at the mention of 'him'. It could only mean one person—Gerard Jacquain.

"But you killed him." Shae's brow furrowed in confusion.

"*We* killed him," the Darkness corrected her. "You wanted him dead just as much as I did."

Shae recoiled at the mention of Gerard's death, memories flooding back to the night they had taken his life. She remembered the way his blood spilled, the sound of his final breaths as they echoed through the room. But now, hearing the Darkness speak so nonchalantly about it, a sense of guilt crept up inside of her.

"We had to do it," the Darkness continued. "He was a danger to us all."

Shae couldn't argue with that. But still, she couldn't shake the feeling that somehow, they had crossed a line.

"Come on," the Darkness said, breaking her thoughts. "Let's give you the pleasure you crave."

Before Shae could even process what was happening, the Darkness pressed its lips to hers, its tongue exploring her mouth with a fierce hunger.

She softly moaned, eyes closed, as she savored the sensation, only to suddenly shove him away. "NO!" Now she loomed over the fallen figure. "You may have taken Gerard's life, but you won't take mine," she said firmly.

"Don't be so sure, Princess." The Darkness taunted in Lestor's voice before rudely ejecting her from the corner of her mind, where he resided.

Shae's eyes adjusted to her prison room. Sadly, she sighed. *Who knew I'd be grateful to see these grimy dungeon walls?*

She stood and circled the small, confined space a

few times. Boredom was setting in already. She paused and stared at the bars before raising her eyes to the ceiling. *That's not boredom.* Her body flinched forward, arms jerking tightly. *That's sunrise!*

On the way to her cot, she stumbled as her body jerked and flinched again. However, she laid down in time to succumb to her daytime slumber.

An odd light fizzled into the center of the cell, first forming into an orb and then shifting into an azure static figure. The figure rippled with each step toward Shae before kneeling next to the cot. The hand of the figure reached out, resting its palm on Shae's forehead.

In her vampiric slumber, Shae seized for a small handful of seconds before settling still.

****

Shae's astral form fizzled in a few paces behind her best friend.

Rozette passed a few rooms already in use while carrying a half-empty bottle of orange juice. As she passed each one, she glanced in. The first room was teenage Deviants learning swordsmanship, the second room was preteen and teenaged Deviants practicing magic, and the third room was filled with fresh young Deviants studying from the many books about their race. Those Deviants were just shy of getting actual training or had shown they weren't ready for it yet. Shae also caught glimpses into each room as she followed Rozette into the fourth room.

Rozette set her drink on the main large desk. "I apologize for my delay." She moved around to the front of the desk and faced the class. "Okay, first...I want to make it clear that I will no longer field any questions about my friend, Shae."

Shae had been glancing over at the students, settling on one she recognized, but was distracted by Rozette's comments.

"As I have said before, we are not here to learn about her." She paused, seeing the nods from the young Deviants. "And Gilo is not here with us today as his parents kept him home to heal from yesterday's session. I am told he will be with us tomorrow. We will not visit Battle Realm today. Instead, we have a guest."

Dorian heard his cue to enter the room. "Greetings, students." They responded back.

Shae floated over to the other side of the teacher's desk, away from the door, as he gave Rozette a hug in greeting.

"My name is Dorian Kincaid. I'm sure some of you know already, but I am the top-ranking Devi-Magi."

Tera's eyes brightened. "That's just like Master Crimshon and Shae!"

Again, Shae's eyes wandered to Tera. *Maybe I should take my rightful spot when my father 'retires' as their mentor.*

Rozette gave Tera a stern glare in a warning. Then she focused on the class. "Yes, well...I know a few of you are still undecided between weapons and magic. Dorian has information about magic. Tomorrow, we'll have a guest speaker for weapons." Rozette stepped aside and let him have the floor.

"Thank you, Rozette." He then faced the class. "As you know, Deviants are more known to be magic users. However, Lady Chastain is incredibly supportive in whatever path you choose."

"Show us some magic, Master Kincaid!" an older boy called out.

Dorian chuckled and Rozette just sighed. "Sure. I'll show you a few spells." He motioned for the boy who requested it to step forward. "What I am going to do first is safely control you as a puppet." When the boy nodded consent, Dorian uttered a few words. It sounded like gibberish to the students hearing it for the first time, but Rozette knew the spell well.

Shae smirked as the students giggled while Dorian had the boy prancing around the room in numerous ways. Safely, he released his hold on the boy. She also remembered the few times joining Dorian as a guest speaker for this presentation. *We did work well together.* Her smirk faded after 'speaking' the reason for their arrangement.

"That was really cool," a girl exclaimed.

"I wanna be a Devi-Magi!" The boy looked at Dorian in wonderment. "Can you teach me?"

"Well, to earn the right to be a Devi-Magi, one must endure a series of tests. You will get a Devi-Magi as your guide, but you will be doing most of the testing on your own. It's a heavily monitored process, and for the record, no one has suffered any worse than a few scrapes and a bruised ego." The class laughed at his joke. "As of right now, Master Crimshon oversees the test, but when he steps down, I shall be in charge."

"Shae would have been in charge…" Tera couldn't resist exclaiming that little tidbit.

Dorian frowned. "Yes. She would have. But we all know Shae chose another path." He noticed Rozette's look and knew to change the subject. "Okay, who wants to see more magic?"

Shae's astral form phased through the wall and back out into the hallway. *Enough of that.*

"Very well." The azure figure appeared in front of her.

"What?" However, Shae couldn't question any further as she blinked out of the hallway.

****

Even if she had only seen her parents' private quarters at least twice, Shae recognized the intricate wallpaper on the wall. The scraping of silverware against plates filled her eyes. She spun around to find them seated at a small, elegant table set up at the opposite end of the room. Shae kept her distance, preferring to stay by the door that led out into the Throne Room.

Chicken for lunch. Wish I could have chicken for lunch. Absently, her hand poked at the side of her mouth, *Stupid vampire teeth.*

Verties cut a piece of his meal, pausing to chomp the bite off the fork. "I had a most peculiar discussion with a child today."

"Please, my love…share with me of that discussion."

They visited Riley? At school in Jupiter? Shae had to forcibly bite her lip to keep from blurting the question aloud. *Oh, wait, they wouldn't hear me anyway.*

"I paid respects to Riley in the hospital. The wound our daughter gave the child seems to have healed quite nicely. She's been doing therapy to ensure no nerve damage would diminish mobility." Verties held up his hand to assure his wife that it wasn't that bad. "The child was very vocal about Shae."

"Our daughter…" Avia set the wine glass down with sadness. Verties quickly took her hand in his, offering some peace and solidarity in their grieving.

"Young Riley declared that I should speak with her father."

"Nickolas?" Avia gasped again, only in surprise. "No. We will handle our daughter on our own now."

"She is a wise one as well, my dear. The words of a child—Human, Deviant or otherwise—are always more profound and astute."

Avia silently ate another bite of chicken.

"Avia...please..." He set his fork down sternly. "I know you are still upset for baiting our daughter to our trap. The explosion was a last resort—a much-needed last resort."

Avia's fork clanked against the plate in a loud, disruptive echo. "I had hopes we could have reasoned with her. But she was completely out of control."

Shae fought back tears. *Even my parents saw how wild I became.* She stared at them as they stood up and walked out of the room. She sat down in the chair her mother previously occupied, hand gliding right through the plate.

A surge of guilt and loneliness washed over her.

"You are slowly understanding, child." The azure figure appeared in the chair.

Shae stared at the figure. "You...you're the one blinking my astral form around like the—"

"Think of me as your guide." The figure suddenly appeared next to her, hand on her shoulder. "Time for the next visit."

****

Shae glanced around a general hospital room. *Riley's hospital room?* The hum, beep, and click of machinery echoing from the other rooms permeated the air, a constant thrumming sound that pulsed with life. She glanced at Riley. So many buttons and dials and screens flickered with data—it was almost overwhelming. But it was the patched-up wound on the child's neck that had Shae shedding a tear. Despite the tragedy she caused, the family seemed happy at this moment.

"Go nuts for donuts!" Riley's voice shrilled as she slapped a card face down in front of her on the rolling table often used for eating hospital meals.

It's the donut game—Riley's favorite game of choice for family game night. She put a hand to her head. *How did it go? I think it was...a marketplace that was just a row of face-up donut cards that each player secretly voted for as the one they wanted.*

Shae leaned closer to the opposite end of the table. Her eyes scanned the 'market' row, seeing how each donut had a listed action, an ability to shake up the game. The game ended when the draw pile was diminished to zero. The winner was the one with the most points from their donut collection.

I remember that game being hard to resist NOT playing. Again, she frowned. *I wish I could play again.*

"Oh, I wanted the raspberry donut!" Diane pouted, shaking Shae from her reverie.

Shae smiled as a warmth spread inside her.

"Looks like you're out of luck this time," Nick said teasingly.

"It was a great idea to send him home. Just look at him, happy with his family again."

Shae turned to see the azure figure standing next to her. "Just like how they were before I showed up, huh?"

"Well, he did miss you, remember?"

241

"Yeah, I remember," Shae said sadly, watching as Diane managed to snag the last donut card, ending the game.

"Time to count points," Riley announced.

Shae turned away, facing the large window letting in the bright sunlight. "Get me out of here, please?"

"Do you feel ready, Shae?" The figure put a hand on her shoulder.

"Yeah, I'm ready."

"Close your eyes."

"By the way…Who are you?" Shae hesitated for a split second, and then closed her eyes.

"I am the light within you that was blocked by all the chaos around you." The figure leaned in, pressing lips against Shae's closed eyes. "Those three pulses feeding you visions—first of Jacquain, then Azura, and then of your near second attack of Varron—when you tried one last time to sleep with Nickolas. That was me."

Shae's astral form returned to her slumbering body. And she settled back into a fitful sleep for the remainder of the day.

****

"Shae! Wake up!"

Rattling bars and a child's voice shifted Shae's awareness from groggy to alert. Her eyes snapped open and she gasped. The azure figure's voice echoed in her mind and Shae slowly sat up. "Yes, I'm ready."

"Shae? Ready for what?" Again the child's voice spoke up.

"What?" Shae turned her head and noticed the child standing on the other side of the bars. "Hey, you're the girl from the library…at the computer station. You were reading something and then dashed off so quickly. Tera, right?"

"Yeah, that was me."

But then Shae paused. "Wait…how did you—?"

"I snuck down here after dinner." She clutched a ratty, thick book to her chest.

"You shouldn't be down here," she admonished the child.

"Neither should you."

Shae almost rolled her eyes.

"I know what you've done. It's all in here."

Shae's eyes narrowed in on the book. "What are you talking about?" She got up from the cot and approached the bars, now standing in front of the girl.

Tera opened the book, revealing just a glimpse of newspaper clippings with handwritten notes in the margins.

She recognized the headline. "Camden Deli Massacre."

"Yeah." Tera murmured, her voice tinged with sadness as she glanced down at the page.

"How did you know it was me?"

"Well, let me read it to you." Tera began reading. "'Liquor store slaughter.'" She paused and groaned at the picture—Shae's destruction. "'Three weeks before Halloween, 2007 turned out to be more horrific than a filmed horror production. Six visitors to the Camden Deli & Drinks store had no idea it would be their last late-night run for snacks and drinks. And the clerk was unaware that his store was a target until it was too late. There were no witnesses for the police to question and no fingerprints or weapons to find the responsible party. However, police reports state that no money or merchandise was taken—just the blood of the unfortunate victims. Sources say that they intended to question Jacquain. But the feared vampire had not been seen since days before this incident. It is now rumored that someone is seeking to take over Jacquain's domain and make him look bad.'"

"Okay, but that didn't answer my question of how you knew it was me." Shae stepped back.

"My friends would talk about stuff they overheard from their parents. Said that you gave yourself up to Jacquain to save a Civilian child."

Shae's eyes widened. *Never really gave any thought that the others would talk about me.*

"I want to be just like you, Shae."

"No, you don't." She narrowed her eyes at the girl.

"Why not? Most kids choose one or the other, a weapon or magic to excel at. But you…you use both."

Shae remained silent.

"It's horrible what Jacquain did to you."

"I don't want to talk about him. Especially with you." She sat down on her side of the bars and Tera did the same on her side.

"What do you wanna talk about?" Tera thought a moment. "What was it like living as a Civilian?"

She looked at Tera for a moment, wondering whether to indulge the girl's curiosity. She sighed. "Let's just say it was a bigger living area with a lot more danger."

"Maybe one day you can show me around?"

"That's something you should ask your parents—who then would ask for clearance from Lady Chastain."

"Right."

Shae noticed the gears grinding in the child's eyes.

"But don't do it. And you should really get back up there now before someone notices you missing."

Tera nodded reluctantly, standing up from her seat.

As she turned to walk away, Shae spoke up again. "Wait, Tera."

The young girl turned around, eyes filled with curiosity and wonder.

Shae hesitated for a moment. "Listen, I know you want to be like me. But trust me, it's not something that you should aspire to."

Tera looked at her with a puzzled expression, clearly not understanding why her hero was saying such things.

"I'm serious, Tera. I've been through a lot of pain and suffering. And I've caused just as much pain and suffering. If I could go back in time, I would have listened better to Lady Chastain and Master Crimshon."

Tera looked at her, eyes shimmering with tears. "I don't understand."

"And I hope you never will," Shae replied softly.

Tera gave a nod, then turned to leave, only to collide with Shae's mother. "M'Lady! Master Crimshon!"

Shae glanced up as Tera bowed to them.

"Young lady, you know you are *not* to be down here," Avia said sternly.

"I'm sorry."

"That's quite all right, Tera. Run along now." Verties was as authoritative as Avia, but in a softer tone.

"Yes, Master Crimshon." Tera bolted from the room.

Avia turned to Shae. "You certainly have been

quite busy down here, daughter."

She rose, dusting off her pants, and bowed apologetically. "I didn't ask her to come down here."

"That may be true, but it's not the actions I'm referring to."

Does she know about my astral visits or what I almost did with Nick?

Verties revealed the key to the cell door. "Everything will be discussed further…in your room."

She jumped back as the door swung open. "You…you're letting me out?"

"We trust you, Shae." Avia reached a hand out to her daughter.

"To be honest," Verties continued, "with your magical antics, despite the barrier we placed, we have been uncomfortable keeping you locked up down here."

"So I'm getting locked up in my room again?"

"You will be more guarded than before, but you will have your freedom back," Avia confirmed Shae's suspicions.

She surprised herself when instead of taking her mother's hand, she lurched forward and embraced the woman as tears tumbled from each of their eyes.

Chapter 20

"Shae, do you remember when we first brought you here?"

So good to be back here in my room. Shae took a moment, brushing fingers across the desk and pressing her palm against one of the armoire doors before moving to sit on the bed. "Yeah. I was sitting here sulking just like this." Shae demonstrated with a hunched brooding expression, "when Rozette, Keitan, and Dorian walked in."

****

"Hey...my name is Rozette...this is my friend Keitan and Dorian."

Shae glared at them. "I'm supposed to be in your class...but I want to go home."

"You are home," Dorian corrected.

"This is not my house," Shae snapped back.

Rozette jumped between Shae and Dorian. "Hey, guys, relax." Then she turned to Shae. "Look, we understand that you may be feeling anxious and uncomfortable right now. It's totally understandable given the circumstances. But us Deviants gotta stick together."

"Deviants?" She tilted her head at Rozette.

"Yeah, that's what we are. You are too."

"C'mon, we'll be late for our first sword lesson with Master Crimshon," Keitan said.

Shae's eyes widened. Sword fighting? Like in the Hollywood movies I watched with Kiran? *She hesitated for a moment before shrugging and following the group toward the training grounds.*

As they walked, Shae listened to the three of them chatter excitedly—many times trying to involve her in the conversation. But Shae barely gave any answer to their questions, and didn't offer any added comments to theirs.

When they arrived at the training grounds, Shae gazed in amazement. Various groups of people, each practicing their own unique skills, filled the area. Some were wielding swords, others were practicing hand-to-hand combat, and a few were even shooting fire from their palms.

Master Crimshon greeted the group and began their lesson, teaching them the basics of sword fighting.

****

"I remember being a quick learner—even if it was just a pole stick. I was really disappointed not getting a real sword until later. And then Dad gave me my own sword." Her eyes traveled over to the wall where the cherished sword hung back on the wooden plaque.

Both parents faintly smiled at the memory. But it was Verties that spoke, "You were difficult then, as you are now."

"However, it was understandable," Avia finished.

"I know. And I'm sorry." Shae's eyes welled with tears. "I'm really sorry, Mom, Dad."

"We believe you." Avia moved to sit next to her, while Verties sat on the other side.

"It wasn't me, my astral form. Some figure…completely shaded in azure and no distinguishable features, triggered my form while I slept during the day. She showed me how you, Roz, Dorian, and even the Azuras, living their day while I was imprisoned."

"I see." Verties rubbed his grizzly beard in thought.

Shae turned to him. "And I didn't heed your advice to be cautious when I opened the box."

"You get your impatient from your old man." A hesitant chuckle escaped his lips before he reined it in, but Shae only smiled.

"I guess I also get your trait of making stupid jokes in a serious conversation."

Avia rolled her eyes fondly at the banter between father and daughter. "Let's focus on the issue at hand, shall we?"

A quick rap on the door and then it opened. "I heard laughing. Is it safe to come in?"

She jerked to her feet. "Dorian?" She took a slight step forward but retreated when she noticed a woman behind him. "Who's that?"

"Ah, yes, c'mon in." Verties stood up, waving the couple further into the room.

"Hey, Shae." Dorian seemed to stumble to explain his visit. "Oh uh, this is Myra."

Shae wearily glanced at the woman and then back to Dorian. "It's nice to meet you."

Myra smiled warmly and shook her hand. "It's nice to meet you too, Shae. I've heard so much about you."

"Nothing bad, I hope." Shae glanced at Dorian wearily.

Myra chuckled lightly. "No, not at all. Dorian has only good things to say about you."

Shae let out a sigh of relief and then turned her

attention back to Dorian. "So, what brings you here?"

"We wanted to invite you as a VIP guest for the Arrangement Ceremony," Dorian began.

"Your request to have your arrangement with him nulled was officially finalized recently. But with all that has been happening, we haven't had the chance to tell you," Verties clarified.

"Ah, I see." She frowned for a moment. When she turned to Dorian, she attempted a smile. "I'm happy for the both of you. And yeah, I accept the invite." She abruptly turned to her parents. "When...is the ceremony?"

"It hasn't been set yet. Dorian, Myra, and the AC commune will meet soon though," Avia answered.

"No worries, Shae. Myra and I aren't in a rush. We are taking this time to get to know each other first."

Well, at least one marriage has a chance.

"Anyway, we didn't plan on sticking around long. Just popped in to tell you." Dorian took Myra's hand, ready to leave.

Shae nodded, feeling a tinge of sadness at the turn of events. He really was a great guy. She watched the couple leave the room. Slowly, her gaze turned to her parents.

"Are you okay, sweetie?" Avia asked.

Shae bit her lip, trying to hold back the tears that threatened to spill. "I'm fine." She forced a smile. "Just happy for them, that's all."

"Really? Because it looked like you were upset," Verties pressed. "Is there something you want to talk about?"

Shae hesitated, unsure if she was ready to share her deepest thoughts and feelings with them. *I'm just gonna say it.* "I hate that I had to open that box," she began. "I know when I was returned here ten years ago, I was angry to have left my Civilian life behind."

Avia and Verties looked at each other with pained expressions before turning back to their daughter.

"It was a heavy decision to bring you back here," Avia said softly. "We kept tabs on your progress with Nickolas. But we always had doubts about letting you stay with him."

"Maybe it was the azure figure trying to tell you something, like she had done with me when I tried to be intimate with him."

"Possibly." Verties nodded. "But at this point, we will never know now. All we can do is move forward after all that's happened."

Shae sighed. "But I failed the prophecy. I never got to bond with Nick and Gerard...I've become just like him."

Just then, a figure stuck his head in the door. "Maybe I can try to help figure that out?"

"Kiran?" Her jaw dropped as she faced her Civilian friend. "What? How?"

He entered the room, "Friends of yours...ummm, Rozette and Kegan, I think...brought me here."

"Roz and Keitan?" she corrected him. "How did they find out about you?"

"They said that some blue lady told them about me." Kiran grabbed the desk chair, spun it around, and then sat normally in it. "Let me explain." He cleared his throat and began, "I was minding my own business...filling up at the gas station yesterday afternoon when this kid approached me..."

****

Kiran had exited the station building and returned to his car. He moved to the back end, stopping at the side just after the rear passenger door. After unlatching the door, and unscrewing the 'locked' cap, he turned around, removed the nozzle from the pump, and selected his desired level of gas. He noticed another car pulled up at the stall opposite him. A young girl got out of the car but stopped and stared at him strangely. The moment was broken by another woman getting the girl's attention. Then the girl hustled inside. Kiran shrugged and went back to his task of filling the car's tank.

The girl emerged from the building, a purchased snack in hand, andapproached his car. "Is your name Kiran Varron?"

Never having seen this child before, and her knowing his full name, left him stunned. "Uh...y-yes, it is. Who are you?"

"Riley Azura." She announced her name proudly yet sadly. Kiran recognized the last name. "Yes. I have a connection to Nick...and Shae. And so do you. All will be explained soon, but first...you must go to this address at this appointed time. That's when things will begin to make sense to you." Riley handed him a slip of paper over the hood of the car. Before he could question her, she had turned and skipped back to her own car.

****

"I recognized the address as the mansion. When I arrived there, Rozette and...Keitan were there waiting for me and brought me here." Kiran ended his brief explanation. "Of course, I'm still confused about things."

"You and me both, young man." Verties eyes were wide after hearing the story.

Shae sat up straighter. "I think it's time to bring Riley here, Father." She quickly explained the night of her birthday party at Nick's house. "She acted unnatural then, just like how she approached Kiran."

Avia moved to the door. "I will assign an escort to bring her here."

"Nick will probably want to join," Shae warned.

"We will deal with that when he asks." Verties followed Avia out of the bedroom.

"So…" Kiran glanced around the bedroom. "This is your real house?"

"Yes." Shae stood, putting a sizable distance between them. She shifted on her feet, keeping her gaze from him.

A fellow Deviant entered the room. "Um, Kiran?"

He turned. "That's me."

"Ah, I'm supposed to escort you to a room you can use and show you to the dining hall for a meal."

Shae lurched forward. "I can show him." She moved closer to Kiran, her hand almost touching his before she jerked away and moved to the door. "C'mon, I'll show you to the dining hall." She flashed him a glance before leading him from the room.

****

Kiran rolled onto his side on Shae's bed. He wiped the nap sleepiness from his eyes and glanced over to the digital clock radio and mumbled to himself, "Two hours till sunset. And everyone probably got loads of candy already."

"Halloween." She looked over from her seat at the desk.

"Yeah. Do you think your parents would allow a TV in here to watch scary movies?"

"I don't think so."

"Ah, well, didn't hurt to ask." He got up from the bed, visited the bathroom, and washed his hands. He remained standing when he returned to the main part of the room. "Hey, how about a game of cards to pass the time until Nick and Riley get here?"

"Game of cards?" She sat down on one side of the bed.

"Yeah, since I'm a guest here, your parents asked me if there was anything I needed. I gave them a small list." He leaned over to a duffel bag next to him and retrieved a set of cards. "Playing various card games really helps to pass the time." He sat up and wiggled the deck of cards at her.

"I haven't been playing much card games."

"Do you remember any that I taught you? I mean, when you were living across the street from Nick?"

Shae thought a moment. "Wasn't there one with an ace card being either ten points or one point?"

"Twenty-one." Kiran brightened up. He took the deck out of the box and began shuffling the cards. "We'll play like how we used to, no using chips of any sort—just seeing which of us gets as close to twenty-one as possible."

"I remember Nick mentioning that part—called it gambling, like they do in Civilian casinos."

"Right." He set the deck face-down between them. "Maybe one day, I'll take you to Vegas."

"I've heard of that city."

"Yeah, we can drive there—make a weekend trip of it," he informed her.

"I'd like that."

Kiran smiled.

"Uh, are we gonna play or what?"

"Oh, yeah." He sheepishly bowed his head and then flipped over one card. "Oh, I got a six."

She quickly reached to draw a card. "Two."

"Just remember, when we do go, you'll have to make sure not to use any of your magic. Casinos frown on cheating. And I don't feel like getting thrown out and banned."

Shae paused, looking at him. "They would do that?"

"Yeah." He then drew his second card. "Another six. That's twelve for me."

She flipped her second card. "Ace."

"You'll have to stick with counting it as one. If you use ten, you'd be at twenty-two."

"And that'd be one too many." Shae sighed.

"Third card for me is…" He flipped it over, and revealed a queen.

"How amusing is that."

Shae had been ready to draw a card, until seeing Kiran's card and hearing the voice. Her hand jerked, knocking the pile over, with some of the cards spilling onto the floor. She immediately jumped up.

"Shae?"

"Sorry." She turned away from him.

"That's okay. I lost anyway." He shrugged and busied himself by picking up the cards. "We can play something else?"

"No. I'm good for now. Just wish everyone would get here." She began pacing. Kiran just sat on the bed.

A sharp knock on the door suddenly disturbed the

quietness of the room.

Shae was closest to the door, so she answered. "It's about ti—" Instead of Riley and Nick being at the door, it was her parents. "Oh." She stepped aside to let them in, shutting the door behind them.

"They haven't arrived yet?" Verties glanced around the room, noticing the deck of cards. He said nothing about it, though.

"Not yet." She moved to stand by the desk, half leaning on it.

But just her luck, another knock.

"That's gotta be them." Kiran stood up.

Avia was the one next to the door, and she opened it.

Nick entered with Riley behind him. "All right, we're here." He refused to look at Shae.

And she returned the gesture. Her gaze shifted directly to Riley. "Really appreciative that your father let you come here."

"Diane allowed it," Nick huffed. "But only after we gave Riley a few days rest at home."

"Oh. Then I thank her as well." A bit of sadness in her voice as Shae curtly glanced at Nick.

Riley's eyes settled on each figure in the room. "I know why I was asked to be here."

She looked at the small bandage on Riley's neck. She planned on officially apologizing for that later.

"It is time, Shae." Riley then moved to stand next to her. She motioned for Kiran and Nick to sit back down. Then she began. "What Shae has done up until now, shouldn't be our focus. What matters is…saving her."

Shae moved over to the door and wound up closer

to Nick. However, all eyes were on her due to Riley's words. With only one hour until sunrise, time couldn't be wasted.

Nick waved his arms about, demanding attention. "First you show me this wild vision, then you kick me out. Then I get a phone call from your parents requesting me to bring my daughter here. But now I'm regretting that decision."

Seconds ticked by, and she just stared at him. Kiran's hand on her shoulder was encouragement enough to pull through the gaps in the Darkness. Finally, she turned to Riley. "The night you tried to celebrate my birthday; you spoke in riddles."

"Yes. When she bit me, things became clearer to me." Riley kept an eye on Shae before turning to Kiran. "When she bit you, I'm sure you felt something for her."

"Yes, but I still don't…"

And then Riley looked at Avia. "I transcended the Realm of Death to aid my granddaughter."

"Oh my…" Avia's hand went to her mouth. "Mother?"

"Grandma?" Shae's eyes widened.

"Yes, my child. But before we can talk about the Prophecy, we must first hear from your time in Battle Realm. Something you did aside from fighting, and taking naps when you could. I want you to recall one of the places you dared to hide in, when at one point things got a little too chaotic for you."

Shae put a hand to her head. Many seconds of silence passed. "There was a cave."

"NO, enough of this."

Riley dared to force Shae to sit down on the bed,

holding her by the shoulders. "Now is not your turn to talk. It is Shae's turn."

Shae paused. "You heard him?"

"Yes. One of the abilities of the dead allows me to hear the unnatural beings that dare to cross into our realms."

Shae trembled a bit, then continued. "One of the days during my excursion, there seemed to be a scheduled or at least a planned visit. So many showed up that day. And an all-out brawl broke out. I would have participated, but it was so overwhelming. And I was tired and hungry. So I found a cave to hide out in for a few hours—to rest and regain my strength. There was a sign at the entrance to the cave—no words, just a Do Not Enter symbol burned into each side of the wall of the entrance, as well as on the ground and the ceiling."

"But you chose to enter," Riley added.

"Yeah." Shae lowered her head and guilt entered her voice. "I remember entering the cave. And then it was suddenly the day my father came to escort me back home."

Everyone else in the room gasped.

"So…You lost a chunk of time?" Kiran spoke up.

"A whole year."

A shrilled sob escaped Avia's lips. Verties pulled her into a tight, comforting hug.

"It wasn't your fault for that, Shae," Riley then revealed.

"What?" Verties stumbled, eyes wide in disbelief. He apologetically glanced at his daughter.

Riley stood up and faced everyone in the room. "You all played into his hands. Blindly following in the vision he fed to you, Avia." Riley moved to sit down in the desk chair, facing everyone. "Primal is his name."

Shae bolted to her feet. "Yes. The prophecy, orchestrated by me. Yet, I underestimated Shae's will. She may have 'ended' it with Nickolas, and you may all now know the truth..." She then sighed, staring at Riley. "It's sad that your mother didn't join us. But I suppose you witnessing the event would be enough of a qualifier for completing the Bond." Shae then coyly reached out for Nick's hand, slightly tugging him closer to her. "You and me, Nickolas. Right here, right now."

The door of Shae's bedroom kicked open, revealing Keitan and Rozette. Without a word, Rozette tackled Shae. "Finish the 'story', Shae."

She grunted, squirming for freedom from Rozette's hold and failing. "I will not be stopped." Her voice was eerily menacing now. The room itself seemed to become darker, even with sunrise within less than fifteen minutes now—and the room had started to brighten.

Rozette then reached out toward Shae with her right hand. "Time to shut you down, Shae." Rozette used the paralyzing spell on Shae.

However, she smirked and performed the counterspell. "Tsk, tsk, Roz. Not gonna work this time." She then pushed Rozette off and stood up. However, just as she turned around, Avia slapped her across the face.

"Will that work?"

Shae stared at her mother with a stunned expression.

Verties shot a hand out and Shae's body jerked backward, immobilizing her. "Finish talking now!"

That was enough to shake the hold the Darkness had on Shae, but only for the moment. A tear fell down Shae's cheek. "I'm sorry. I tried so hard to…tell you."

"You can tell me now, Shae."

She stared blankly at Nick for a moment before continuing. "It was a false prophecy fed to Avia." Shae's voice sounded distant but steady. "Primal needed me to bond with Nick. One true act of unholiness would have supplied him with enough dark energy to make the binding permanent."

"Us?" Nick scratched the side of his head.

"No. Me and Primal," Shae confirmed. "Just like Jacquain—Primal had a thirst for pleasure."

"So how does Jacquain fit into why Primal needed him?" Verties stood in front of his daughter.

"The blood and fangs were an unnecessary part of it. Primal needed immortality. I would be young forever."

"And thus, infinite pleasure," Riley added, reminding everyone she was still aided by Shae's grandma.

"Correct." Shae nodded at Riley before turning to her parents. "Putting me with Nick as a child allowed me to meet Kiran." Then she shifted her gaze to him.

"My way of trying to avert the prophecy. Rules of the Dead say we couldn't outright intervene." Riley spoke again.

"Hence the riddles," Shae explained for everyone's benefit.

"Okay, so how do we fix this?" Avia moved next to Verties.

"Battle Realm." Shae's head drooped forward.

"We will need a lot of help for this." Riley turned

to Shae.

"Now?" Nick stepped forward, having been quietly listening to this madness.

"No." Riley approached her father. "All Souls Day would be more significant to gather in Battle Realm."

"Then it's settled." Verties eased Shae back into the comfortable bed.

"That will give everyone time to prepare and meet us here." Avia sat down next to her daughter.

"You should rest now." Riley stood in front of Shae now, gently running her fingers through her hair. "You will need the strength for what is to come." Then she waved her hand out to the others. "You all will."

"I'll have another room arranged for you and Riley." Verties motioned for Nick and Riley to follow him.

"I'll get some rest too." Kiran hugged Shae before following the others out of the room.

"Shae, if you're hungry, I'll have your tray delivered up here."

She shook her head before turning toward the window. "But I'm gonna need the window covered to block the sun."

"Right, I'll get on that." Avia left the room to assign someone to fulfill her daughter's request.

Chapter 21

The following night, Shae sat on the bed next to Kiran. The breakfast tray filled the space between them. It was his insistence to be present as she drank the blood from the bottle.

"I'm going to need to get used to this, Shae."

"I know. But it's still awkward." She glanced at him, resting the half-full bottle on her lap and flickered a smile at him.

"Yeah," he agreed, only to then rise and pace around. "So the others should arrive here any minute."

"Are you worried?"

He paused and turned to her. "No. Are you?"

"No." Shae took another swig of the bottle, set it on the tray, and stood up. "I kind of already have an idea of what needs to be done. But with everyone here, we'll flesh it out with no room for question."

An hour later, Shae stepped out of the bathroom, her skin still warm from the hot shower. She noted the figures in the room. Rozette, indirectly chosen as leader of this mission, perched in a chair by the desk, eyes darting around the room at the others. Riley, still the host for Shae's grandmother, was standing in the middle of the room, her arms crossed over her chest as she waited to assist Shae in explaining the plan. Dorian rested against the wall by the desk. Keitan sat on the bed.

Kiran spoke up. "Sorry. Everyone arrived while you were in the shower, so I let them in."

"That's fine." She paused. "My parents haven't arrived yet?"

Just as she asked about them, they entered the room.

"We are here. We were just giving Nickolas a convincing argument to return home to wait for us there."

"So he's okay with leaving Riley in our care?" Shae glanced at Riley.

"Battle Realm isn't meant for Civilians," Riley said. "Kiran will be the only exception."

"What about you?" Kiran asked her.

"My dear, I'm inhabiting this child's body. Clearly she is Deviant levels now."

"Oh, right." He nervously placed a hand on the back of his neck and rubbed a bit before dropping his hand.

"Relax, Kiran." Shae was there at his side. She slipped her hand in his and faced the group. "Okay, this is the plan. My parents, Keitan, Roz, and Dorian will perform a spell—creating a sort of safety zone for Kiran and I."

"And I will keep watch," Riley added.

"What will you and Kiran do?" Keitan stepped forward.

"Being that it is dark here in our realm, Battle Realm will be daylight. Kiran will be focused on keeping me protected from its sun. That will allow me to focus on taking out anyone that Riley spots trying to ambush us."

"So that we can concentrate on the spell." Dorian

stood up straight, snapping his fingers.

"Exactly."

"Good plan." Rozette smiled. "Guess that makes you the leader of this mission, Shae."

"Yes and no." Shae turned to Dorian. "You're the leader for the spell part. You are Rank 2, after all." She winked at him, and he chuckled.

"That is a good call, daughter." Verties stood, placing his hands on his hips. "Avia and I might be older and powerful, but our age is also our hindrance. Dorian's youth will benefit from the power of this spell."

Riley cleared her throat. "We need to be sure there are no surprises when we get into the fight."

"Right…What about…What was its name?" Keitan began.

"Primal," Rozette reminded her husband.

No one spoke for a few moments, then Avia said, "I think we should have some kind of backup plan in case things go wrong. We should have a way to retreat if needed."

Everyone agreed.

Dorian then suggested, "If things get too outta control, we'll have to bail and bring Shae back here."

"If they think they can handle me."

Shae winced, putting everyone on alert.

"What's he doing now?" Keitan instinctively slipped into a defensive stance, his fists clenched and raised in front of his chest.

"Just boasting that you couldn't handle him if he decided to act," She boldly stated, surprised that she was even doing that.

"Right. I hope we don't have to worry about him

ruining the plan." Dorian sighed.

Riley continued. "All right, I think that covers it. Everyone should have a good idea of what their role is and how to best prepare for the battle. Are there any questions or concerns before we adjourn?"

"This plan sounds intense, but I believe in it," Verties firmly said with conviction.

Everyone nodded in agreement.

"I suggest everyone eat and rest for tomorrow night." Avia officially ended their meeting.

****

Emerging from the portal, they found themselves in the heart of the Battle Realm, surrounded by two teams engaged in a fierce three-on-three combat.

"This isn't good." Shae glanced at Kiran, motioning him to stay down. She turned her attention to the group while staying close to him to keep him protected. Not waiting for anyone to attack them, Shae lunged forward to the nearest opponent. Time couldn't be wasted, so she executed him quickly before launching herself to the next. That pattern continued until there was just one last opponent. He seemed to be giving her a fight. Primal took advantage of Shae's distraction. She ripped into her opponent, leaving him more mangled than the rest of his teammates.

"Shae?" Kiran stood up, taking tentative steps toward her.

She spun around, her front side a bloody mess.

Reverberations of death filled the air, and Kiran gasped. His eyes slowly wandered over the mess of bodies. "Woah." He suddenly sunk to his knees, struggling for a breath of fresh air.

She turned to him, her expression unreadable in the

waning light. "Are you all right?" she asked.

He nodded, but remained silent.

"Kiran!" She shook her head as if shaking away the fogginess in her mind and rushed over, helping him to his feet. They moved away from the scene, reaching a cluster of trees. She let go of him and touched one of the trees. "This is the spot."

Sunlight broke through the clouds, a ray of light hitting Shae's hand. She winced from the sizzling. Mistakenly, she turned right and found herself bathed in another ray of sunshine.

Luckily, the others arrived in time.

"Oh good." Kiran did his best to cover Shae with his body, but it wasn't enough. Patches of her skin continued to sizzle.

Rozette rushed over with an extra-large blanket. "Figured this would be needed. I snatched it off Shae's bed."

Shae recognized the quilted blanket.

Kiran adjusted it and then ushered her over to a shady spot between the trees, strategically positioned to maintain clear sight lines to the group.

"Okay, let's get this rolling." Dorian swiveled his finger around in a circular motion.

Keitan, Rozette, Avia, and Verties moved into spots forming an arc and faced the cluster of trees. Dorian filled in the extra-long gap between Rozette and Avia.

"Riley." Shae waited until she had the girl's attention. "Need you on watch duty. Let me know if anyone tries to ambush our party."

"Got it!" She gave Shae a thumbs-up.

The 'Arc' Group raised their arms out to their

sides, and the chanting began. They focused their gaze on the inner part of the tree cluster.

A twig snapped in the distance, followed by rustling leaves from a breeze. The chanting continued as per the plan. Shae's heart raced as she and Riley glanced around. No further sound happened. Riley glanced at Shae with a shrug.

Without warning, a figure leaped out from behind a nearby rock, brandishing a sword. Shae's instincts kicked in as she lunged forward, only to be gripped by Kiran.

"No, Shae…the sun…"

She grunted, having no choice but to stay in her shadowy spot. Riley lead the intruder into her line of sight. "Perfect." She swiftly motioned and the guy's sword flung from his grip.

"What the hell?" He looked around until he spotted Shae and Kiran.

"Busted," Kiran whispered.

She gave Kiran a sarcastic smirk. "Really?" She put her attention back on the attacker. "I'd really like to mess around with you, but right now. I don't have the time." True to her word, she made quick work of the guy.

He managed to dodge a few of the explosive orbs, laughing as he faced her with a sneer. "That all you got?"

"No."

Kiran wasn't able to stop her this time as she lunged at the man. She tackled him and bared fangs.

"Oh, no!" Kiran gave chase.

Shae leaned in and bit into the man—tearing into him like she had done so many others. When Shae sat up, fresh blood soiled her clothes over the dried blood. She quickly flinched off the guy when the sunlight singed her cheek.

"C'mon…" Kiran dragged Shae back to their safe spot.

"Sorry," she mumbled.

Kiran wheezed from the smell of burnt flesh. "Don't be. You had to get rid of him the quickest way possible."

They both settled back into their hiding spot.

"That was close," Riley mumbled.

Shae looked at Kiran with a sympathetic expression. "I'll be more careful next time."

There were still traces of fear in Kiran's eyes.

Another portal appeared, but this portal didn't match the style the Deviants used.

Shae stood up but stayed in her spot. "We got incoming." She eyed the portal wearily.

Two females emerged from the portal. The women had blue skin and white hair.

"And they aren't allies." She latched one hand on Kiran's arm and another hand on Riley's. She tugged them both down. But then remembered the chanting. "Shit. If it weren't for the chanting, those two women would have walked right past us." She sadly glanced at Kiran.

"Stepping out into the sun again?"

She nodded.

"Okay, make it quick." He sighed.

Shae jumped forward, creating a psionic dagger, and lunged at the two women. The taller woman created a shield to protect herself while the other unleashed a flurry of fire blasts at Shae.

She dodged them, drawing the women's attention away from the trees—and the group. She ignored the pain from the sunshine and created a wall of ice to trap most of the opponents before launching a wave of icicles at them.

One icicle struck the shorter woman in the neck. Using her fire ability, the woman effortlessly melted the ice..

"I bet they are tasty. Blood warmed by their abilities."

No. I will not let you help me take care of them.

"But it will be so much fun. You do want this over quickly, don't you?"

Shae ignored Primal. But she did accept his idea. Both women hesitated to return the attack once Shae bared her fangs.

The battle soon became bloody and brutal as Shae drained the two women dry.

Once it was safe, Kiran came running out of the shadow spot and covered Shae in the blanket, ushering her back.

Shae trembled, barely able to contain the mixture of exhaustion and adrenaline.

"You're looking a little wired, Shae." Kiran stared at her in concern. "How much longer is the spell gonna take? I don't think you can keep this up for long before losing control to Primal."

"And the amount of blood you are consuming isn't helping either," Riley added.

Shae breathed heavily, struggling to maintain control. Her predicament had Kiran and Riley only half focused on keeping an eye out for any more surprises.

"C'mon, Shae. Breathe in, breathe out." Kiran did

it a few times as an example.

She joined in, eventually calming down.

"Better?" Riley knelt by her side.

"Yeah. Thanks." She glanced from Riley to Kiran.

Another few moments of silence, aside from the chanting, passed. The entire time, only a few formed clouds passed across the sun, but most of the day had been bright. Then a larger cloud blocked the sun and eerily stayed there.

"What the—?" Shae glanced up, watching the cloud expand to ensure no sun peeked through.

The chanting group glanced up, slightly faltering in their task.

"Guys, c'mon…Keep going!" Shae urged them. She stepped out from the hiding spot.

A flash in her peripheral caught her attention. A young man clad in scarce armor, holding a staff with a crystal at the top, appeared. The crystal radiated and cackled.

Shae braced for an attack, but the man only shook his head no at her. With his free hand, he snapped. More flashes erupted and faded to reveal a sizeable group of vampires. And that's when she noticed a familiar face. "Michael?"

"My Queen," he responded with a sneer to his sarcastic words.

She frowned. "What is the meaning of this?"

"Well, the group decided they wanted your head— for both abandoning us and killing Gerard."

Her eyes widened, scanning over the group behind him, seeing them all nodding in agreement with him. "You told them?"

"Not really. They sort of concluded that once we

found out Bruce was dead. They all had a feeling that you would be Gerard's demise—the way he was so obsessed with you."

Shae frowned, staring at Michael. "Do you want me dead?"

"I convinced them to at least give you a chance to come back to us willingly."

"Not interested," she quickly rebuffed.

"Then I guess my answer to your question is…yes. I won't mind being the one to kill you. Would have preferred fucking you…after all, sex with you was incredible. But…" He paused and shrugged his shoulders. "Group decision."

The vamps spread out around and trapped her in a circle of death.

Shae didn't want to have to fight them, but they gave her no choice.

Michael stepped forward. "Time to face justice for the death of our beloved Master Jacquain."

She remained still and silent. Rozette suddenly appeared from a portal. "Can't let you fight alone, Shae."

She turned. "But the chant."

"This is more important right now."

That's when she noticed a sword in Rozette's hand.

"Time to hack and slash, Shae." Rozette smirked. "Ready?"

Nodding, she clenched her hands that cackled and glowed. "Ready." As she spoke, her fangs dropped.

The vamp army rushed them. Swords clashed, explosive orbs flew, fists collided with faces and screams filled the air. Shae and Rozette handled themselves quite well—matching the vamps speed with their own.

Suddenly, a vamp tackled Rozette, wasting no time tearing a sizeable gash in her good arm.

She struggled against a vamp blockade, keeping her from coming to Rozette's aid.

Michael knelt next to Rozette, revealing a dagger in his hand. He glared right at Shae. "For you, my Queen." He sneered again, before piercing Rozette in the stomach and then yanking the blade down.

"ROZ!" Helpless, Shae screamed as she watched Rozette's figure convulse and blood seep from her wounds.

Michael dashed right up to her. His face twisted into a cruel grin. "Now, Shae, you will face justice. Death will be the punishment. But yours will be worse than what you did to Master Jacquain."

She glanced over his shoulder, seeing the way the other vamps giggled and licked their lips.

"You're going to be so tasty for them." Michael confirmed what she began theorizing as her punishment.

Shae dared to close her eyes. "Go ahead, do your worst." She expected Michael to kill her the way she had done to Gerard. When she opened her eyes, Riley stood defiantly facing Michael. "Riley, what are you—?"

"I will not let my granddaughter fall to a group of vampires," she called over her shoulder at Shae.

"Grandma?"

"Yes, dear. The others are finishing the chant now. Keep watch. I'll deal with this group."

However, Shae hesitated.

"Don't worry about this child's body. She will be

unharmed." Riley turned, "NOW GO!"

"Okay, Grandma." Shae inched back, retracing her steps toward the cluster of trees. She still kept an eye on Riley, ready to intervene if necessary.

Riley bolted into the thick of the vampire group. But as Shae stepped forward in fear that her Grandma needed assistance, vampire bodies flung out from the center of the fight, landing lifelessly onto the dirt.

Body after body launched into the air left and right. *Wow, Grandma kicks ass!* And she smiled proudly. But watching Grandma thin out the group gave Shae inspiration. She turned. "Michael?"

He just stood there, watching the scene before him. "Who the hell is this kid?"

"Actually, it's my grandma, using Riley's body." She shook her head at him. "It's a long story…that I'm not going to share with you." She angrily faced him.

He finally looked at her. "Ya know, that whole punishing you deal…"

Shae gave him no chance to speak. She latched her hand around his throat. "I should end your life here and now. But I know you're not like Jacquain. You're more sensitive, Michael."

"My Queen…please!"

At first, she started squeezing him tighter, but she suddenly let up. He dropped to his knees, gasping for breath.

"That is correct." She scowled down at him. "I am your queen."

"Yes, I understand." He kept his gaze on the ground as he wildly nodded.

"Be sure to remember that." She gave no warning as she bashed her foot into the side of his face, knocking him out cold. Then she opened up a portal to the mansion steps before throwing his ass through it.

That's when she noticed Riley's fighting growing sluggish. "Grandma!"

Riley turned Shae's way.

Shae dashed forward, joining her side. "I think it's time you let Riley go, Grandma. Before you overuse the body. She's not used to this just yet." *Still two more vamps to deal with.* Shae waved her hand out at them, knocking them back with an invisible force to buy some time with Grandma.

"It pains me to leave without having said goodbye to your parents, my child."

"I'll tell them for you." A tear slid down Shae's cheek. "Really wish I had more time with you. Can't you come back again?"

"No. I broke the rules getting more involved here than I should have. But it was great to meet you, even in this brief time."

"Despite the circumstances." Shae sniffled as the azure aura faded from Riley's eyes. *Will Riley remember this?* Shae carried the pre-teen back to the others. "Mom, Dad."

Her parents turned, their mouths agape at the sight of Riley in Shae's arms.

"What happened? What's going on?" Her mother rushed toward them.

"Grandma is gone."

"Your grandmother loved you, Shae. She did what she did to protect you."

Shae nodded, her voice cracking. "I know. I just wish…"

"I know. But she did what she had to do. And so

did you." Verties gave her a reassuring smile.

Her mother wrapped an arm around Shae. "We finished the spell. Let us take Riley home. You and Kiran have to do your part now."

After a quick hug, Shae watched her father carefully pick up Rozette, making sure to not jostle her wounded arm. Dorian opened the portal and then Shae was alone with Kiran.

"How you holding up?" She approached him.

"I'm still, uh…" He shook his head. "I'm good." He held out his hand to her. "Let's finish this before any more trouble shows up."

Chapter 22

The grove of trees surrounding this spot was designed to hide Kiran and Shae's small, cozy cottage. Only those who helped with the spell could cross an invisible barrier into the cluster and see the house. No one else would know of the pocket universe within.

"I have to be the one to lead you into this pocket universe. Once I'm strong enough, I can alter the casted spell to have it recognize you." Kiran just nodded as they entered the cluster of trees. Their new home became visible to them.

The walls of the cottage were made from thick, polished wooden logs, which gave a rustic feel. The interior, on the other hand, continued the rustic vibes around modern fittings, plush furniture, and state-of-the-art appliances.

Every corner of the cozy cottage was tastefully decorated with intricate embroidery, floral patterns, and captivating artwork that depicted serene landscapes, majestic forests, and brilliant sunsets. The fireplace, located at the center of the living room, was cobbled with smooth stones of different sizes and shapes, and its flames bathed the entire room in a warm glow.

The bedroom was just as charming with fluffy pillows, silk sheets, and faux fur throws that added to the overall cozy ambiance of the cottage. The en suite bathroom was equipped with a luxurious rain shower and a Jacuzzi tub, with a large bear rug.

The second floor was a loft with an outer balcony. When they glanced out the window of the living room, they didn't see the cluster of trees from Battle Realm. Instead, they saw the serene and tranquil view of a medium-sized river running just a few meters away. The river was so clear that you could see the colorful pebbles and aquatic plants growing on the riverbed from the full moonlight. The sound of the gentle current filled the air with a relaxing melody.

"Kiran…" He had been standing in the living room, absorbing the area in awe. "We don't have time for a tour. I don't know how much longer I can maintain control." In a low but firm whisper, "I refuse to be consumed by such evil permanently." Her hands trembled as she slowly reached out for his hand.

The excited expression on his face twisted to one of deep concentration. Their hands stayed joined together as they made their way down the short hall to the back bedroom of the small cottage. His lips were both soft and firm against hers, dialing into a gentle electric shock that ricocheted through her body. The caress was slow—almost symbolic—before he led her over to the bed. Thin, high wooden corner bedposts were the pillars that held see-through sheer drapes that swooped low and sparkled.

She sat down on the side of the bed and watched as he pulled out an iPod Classic from his pocket. "Kiran?"

"I'm just going to set this up real quick." He retrieved a cord from his other pocket and plugged his iPod in. "Sometimes, when I'm working in solitude, I plug in headphones and listen to music. Helps make the shift go by faster. But when I heard this song, I just had to save it—in case I ever got the chance to play it for you." He didn't hide the blush of his cheeks as he rejoined her in bed. "However, now is the PERFECT moment." He pressed play and the song began.

Even though it wasn't wise to waste time, Shae listened to the first few beats of the song. She couldn't claim to be even remotely versed in pleasant music, but already this song sounded amazing to her. "You're right, it is perfect."

The first verse of the soulful tune filled the bedroom in the small cottage. She raised trembling hands to the button of her blouse. It took some time, but she exposed part of her front figure.

He unbuttoned his shirt and tossed it to the floor next to their feet. She stared at his broad, toned chest as he started unbuttoning his jeans. Now, in only his boxer briefs, his physique was on full display. He was quite the specimen of a man his age. And his snug shorts left very little to the imagination. Even flaccid, it was more than clear that he sported a thick, long manhood. "Do I have permission to touch you?"

The music was still playing in the background, at a decent decibel, so neither of them would have to shout.

She nodded. "Yeah." The heat radiating from his large palms warmed her cold skin and a spark traveled through her arm. She wanted to lean in closer and bask in the heat, but instead, she accepted his help in taking off the blouse.

He placed it on the pile of clothes nearby. She sucked in a breath, followed by slowly exhaling. He stood back, savoring the moment. After a few seconds of silence, he slowly stepped closer and brushed his fingertips across her exposed stomach. She gasped at the sudden contact. He caressed every inch of her with his fingertips. Her skin prickled with goosebumps. "Still with me?" He ran his index finger along the underside of her breasts.

"Yeah." She gently trickled fingers above his right pec. "I'm not scared of you."

"Thanks." Passion settled around them again. Kiran hooked his fingers into the waistband of both her skirt and panties before slowly sliding them down her slender legs. The entire time he kept his gaze focused on her face. Then he dropped the skirt and underwear on the floor. Kiran softly squeezed her breast.

A whole slew of emotions fluttered across her expression. With a shaky hand, she reached out to him—again touching his lips. His face. Neck, shoulders, stomach. When her pinky finger grazed against the tip of his cock, she froze. She gasped the moment she saw it twitch.

As he pushed Shae back onto the bed, her breasts pressed against his chest. His strong, muscled arms supported her as he moved gently yet firmly on top. He subtly growled into her lips as his large hand traveled over her mound. She hissed in pleasure when he gently rubbed little circles into it. His touch was tender yet electric.

Arousal rose faster than she could control as he kept teasing with his skilled fingers, drawing out each stroke like it would be their last. His lips were soft yet commanding, and she could feel herself slipping further and further into a state of pure bliss.

"Guess now's a good time to mention that I'm no virgin either."

"We both had to experience others to be ready for

this moment," she said with a grin.

He glanced down at her with a lopsided smile on his lips. "Wow, that's…really profound. But you make sense, Shae." Then he continued his foreplay.

Every spot pulsated and rippled in sensations that lured her deeper into this moment. *His growling reminds me of a wolf in heat. Fuck it's such a turn-on.* She slid her hands down his sides and kneaded the flesh of his hips. *I'm so glad I get to enjoy this without worrying about the Darkness.*

Kiran's hands moved slowly, stimulating in ways she hadn't known existed. His fingertips radiated warmth as he sensuously caressed her arms, shoulders, and face. His touch was mesmerizing.

I can't believe I'm so wet and we haven't really done much.

He peppered her neck with tender little kisses. "You can tell me what feels good and what doesn't."

"Hell, it all feels good." When his cock brushed against her inner thigh, sensations of pleasure spiked. "MMM…Kiran…please…I want…" Sparks of desire coursed through her veins.

He paused. "Tell me. Share with me. No matter how silly it might sound. Let me take you beyond pleasure." Kiran's hands traveled down her neck to her breasts, stroking and teasing her nipples until they were hard and erect. With expert precision, his fingers teased and tantalized her until she was almost unbearably aroused.

"Make love to me, Kiran."

"Your wish is my command—"

She placed a finger on his lips. "Don't you dare call me your queen."

His eyes grew wide. "No. I won't do that. I was just gonna try a stupid love nickname for you."

"What…what would that nickname be?"

"Pookums." He tilted his head. "Remember that teddy I tried to show you? Well, the accompanying tag said that Pookums was its name. It just felt…fitting to call you that."

"I love it." She rewarded him with a kiss. "Do you still have that teddy?"

"Yes. Up on a shelf in my living room next to the TV." He then slapped the side of his head. "Oh, I guess I'm gonna have to sell my place if we are living here now."

She pulled his hand away from his head. "Yeah. And I'm sorry I never got to see your Halloween decorations. But maybe later we could collect what you want from your old place?"

"Yeah, later." He spread her legs as his hand wrapped around the base of his shaft. "We're getting off track here, Pookums." Kiran positioned himself right at her entrance. "You ready?"

With a nod of permission, he buried himself deep inside of her, growling uncontrollably as his thick cock met with her hot, wet insides. He bucked himself hard into her and they both moaned.

"Oh my…God. You're fucking…" He paused for a second. "…incredible." He rested his forehead against hers, looking longingly into her eyes.

Shae hissed and gasped for breath as he sank deep into her. His thickness hurt a little, no getting around that, but her body quickly adjusted.

"NO!"

She flinched and whimpered from the pulsating

shock of the voice—working to disrupt her union with Kiran.

Kiran paused again. "Shae?"

"It's trying to come back. Just keep going. Don't stop." She gritted her teeth.

"Okay."

"Stop him now!"

Shae reached for one of his hands, linking fingers in his—sweat building on her forehead. "Kiran..." Absently, she applied too much pressure as she squeezed his hand.

With powerful and passionate movements, he seized control of their union, causing her body to jolt and the comforter to gather in bunches. He slowed his pace but the firmness of each thrust remained constant. "I got you, Shae," he murmured. "And I won't let you get lost again."

Each hard, deep thrust rocked the bed like a boat on the waters. She trailed fingers across his broad shoulders, tracing the contours of his muscled chest. Tilting his head slightly to the side, she pushed her lips against his skin, inhaling the rich cologne. Amongst their moaning, the bed squeaked, and the song shifted into the second verse. Shae moved her lips closer to his ear. "Little faster...Kiran...I feel close...really close."

Soon, the room filled with the subtle sound of flesh slapping against flesh as he picked up his pace.

Through ragged breaths, he whispered, "So am I."

"Kiran!" Her whole insides felt like a euphoric explosion as she came all over his cock. Shae arched her back, overwhelmed by the orgasmic sensations. "Don't stop...so fucking incredible..."

With one last, forceful thrust, he exploded. The

first large rope that left him filled her almost instantly as he growled loudly, unconsciously nipping the tender flesh of her neck. But he was hardly done. Spurt after large spurt left him as his cock throbbed violently. "I love you, Shae." His seed, having nowhere else to go, started sputtering out, staining her thighs and the comforter. He continued thrusting. And then he was done. He was still inside, his face still buried in her neck as he kept saying, "I love you so much."

By now, she was really hot and sweaty, and panting for breath. Her moans, while more strained, still carried an erotic quality.

She leaned in and kissed his lips, his shoulder. Her breathing became erratic. She began sweating, limbs were trembling even worse than when she endured the worst of Gerard's mind attacks.

"Shae?" Kiran pulled out, panic carried in his tone.

Her whimper was the only reply to him. Then her whole body began to glow and levitate. Kiran turned and quickly cut the music from his iPod. The trembling of her body spread out to the room. Framed pictures fell off the walls, items on shelves rattled—even the bed lifted and slammed down.

Her mouth froze open and an inhuman roar grew louder as the shaking in the room stopped. "NOOOOOO!" Suddenly, everything went silent and the bright glow faded. She was catapulted forward into a wall. She hit the floor with a muffled moan. Then she began heaving—once, twice, three times—before she hurled a black icky substance. It seemed like it would never stop until she coughed.

Kiran knelt by her side when she tried to push herself up off the floor. "Shae?"

"It's…it's gone." She sounded lethargic.

"The Darkness?" He carefully scooped her into his arms and stood up. "Let me get you cozy and then—" He was cut off by the sound of bubbling at his feet. The icky goo fizzled out of existence. "Oh, well, thankfully I won't have to clean that up." He looked at her.

With a shaky hand, she cupped his face. "I love you, Kiran Varron."

"I love you too, Shae Taizer." Then he carried her over to the bed, snuggling up with her.

Chapter 23

Valentine's Day, 2008

Even though she now was only one of two permanent residents within Battle Realm, Shae's internal vampiric clock was attuned to Civilian realms—namely the town where Nick lived. The reason being that she was 'born' as a vampire there. So even if she awoke with a few hours of daylight left in Battle Realm, she could remain in her cozy home until nightfall.

There was an hour or two before having to visit the Azura residence as promised. After a brief round of lovemaking, the newfound couple dressed for their 'day'. At the kitchen table, Kiran enjoyed a classic breakfast—eggs, toast, bacon, and orange juice. Shae joined him at the table just for conversation.

"I am a little sad I won't get to enjoy breakfast like that. Or cereal. Or French toast." She sighed but wasn't really upset.

"When did you eat those?" Kiran set his glass down.

"Well, the French toast I had with Rozette. The cereal and eggs were separate days while living with Nick and his family. Diane really did make some great eggs." Kiran just nodded, working to finish his meal. "But, thanks to you…I can finally enjoy my life."

"And I don't mind being attached to someone so

gorgeous." He winked, only making Shae blush. "This bond stuff…I must say, I feel a whole lot better myself now having solved that weird feeling I've had since you first bit me." Shae nodded before sitting on his lap.

"Finding you helped me defeat my vampiric crush." Silence enveloped the moment. The newfound lovers got lost in each other's eyes. "Oh…better get going." Reluctantly, she stood up. Kiran took his dishes to the sink, rinsing them and setting them aside. Menial household chores would have to wait until later.

Once they reached outside of their hidden world and before they could be spotted by anyone, Shae formed a portal. Kiran proudly took her hand, entering the portal on Battle Realm instantly exiting in front of Nick's house.

"SHAE!" Riley gave a less enthusiastic greeting to Kiran as she bolted out of the front door and down the steps.

"Hey, Riley. I hope your parents are still here." Shae gladly hugged Riley before they all entered the home.

"Yeah. It's been…awkward. Neither is speaking to the other." Riley closed the door as Nick and Diane entered the living room from different areas of the house. Nick nervously waved at Shae, but Diane just rolled her eyes.

"Diane. My visit here is mostly for you." Shae moved ahead of Kiran, approached Diane, and convinced the woman to sit down for a talk. "I'm here to come clean about my attempts to destroy your marriage. To make a long story short, my parents—actually, my mother—was fed a false vision. It was so believable that she followed it unquestionably. And since we never dared question her, we believed it as well. While living with you, the truth tried to reach me, but I couldn't listen. I only fell deeper into darkness. And if it weren't for Kiran, then I would have undoubtedly slept with your husband and created the False Bond."

Kiran then chimed in. "Today is Valentine's Day. Shae and I just wanted to make things right. For Riley's sake, and for the fact that Shae believes you still love him…Diane, give Nick another chance."

"Nick is a great guy. And you have been an amazing woman, Diane. The way you put up with me as a guest in your house…" Shae choked up a bit. "The way you both endured my terror on your family." Diane couldn't help but gasp. Shae just turned to Riley before she lost the momentum of her 'confessions'. "And you, dear Riley. I hope you can accept my apologies for trying to have you killed on more than one occasion." Yet, Shae withheld from confessing guilt for killing Riley's father, Riley's best friend, and best friend's dad. Maybe one day, Shae would have the courage to talk about it, but not today.

"You weren't you," Riley spoke up. "But, either way, I'm glad to have met you. I still hope we can be honorary sisters."

Nick was stunned, and Diane couldn't help but sob a bit.

Nick shook himself from the stupor and turned to Diane. "I never stopped loving you. And…I hope you'll let me be a father for Riley again." Shae noticed how hesitant Diane was. She also noted the four wine bottles, two wine glasses, and three coffee mugs littered on the tables around them.

"Diane, you don't have to worry. As long as I have Kiran, I'm no harm to you or your family. Creating the True Bond with Kiran soiled the chance for the Darkness to ever have the opportunity to use Nick. And with Jacquain dead, he can't influence me either, even if he was my creator."

Another long silence followed. Diane sighed heavily, holding her hands up in defeat. "Okay, but, I can only offer him a trial basis."

"Good enough for me." Nick finally smiled but made no move toward Diane.

"That's reasonable." Shae accepted that.

A knock on the door interrupted the conversation. Diane rose to answer the door, grateful for having something to do—as well as have a bit of breathing room from the 'crowd'.

Diane didn't recognize the older couple on the doorstep. "Hello? How can I help you?"

"Greetings, Mrs. Azura."

Riley recognized that voice and was the first to excitedly jump up. "Lady Chastain and Mr. Crimshon!" Shae also stood up then, facing her parents.

"Evening, Riley." Verties nodded at the child, amused at the way she addressed him. He could see Nick's confusion. "Nickolas."

"What are you doing here?" Nick stood up respectfully, but nervously.

Avia stepped forward. "We are here to speak to Riley. But you, Nickolas…and you, Diane…are also needed." Before officially proceeding, Avia and Verties happily greeted Kiran and their daughter. "Now, as not to take too much of your time. Riley, I know it must be confusing, but we are here to explain those weird occurrences you have been displaying."

Verties knelt on Riley's other side. "My wife, she has visions. She also converses with the spiritual realm through these visions and by reading specialized dice."

Diane interjected, "Shae said that the vision about her was wrong. And now you're saying that my daughter has them too?" She reached out, tugging Riley away from them. "Look, on the surface, you all seem like real nice people...but you have brought too much trauma into our lives. Your daughter ruined my marriage and nearly killed my daughter in a tantrum. I would really like you all to just leave now."

Gently, Shae put a hand on Diane's arm. "Please calm down, Diane."

"NO!"

"Mom, stop." Riley shrugged free and faced Diane. "I have been having these strange feelings since Shae came into our lives. And when she bit me, things started slowly making sense. And when she took me to Battle Realm...I wanted to help. I was trying to help." Quickly, she turned to Nick. "And I was trying to help you help her...remember our conversation at the hospital, Dad?"

Nick recalled that conversation. "You asked me where Shae was."

"And you immediately thought about the mansion. But I tried to tell you that wasn't where you should look, that it wasn't where SHE was." Riley tapped her head. "I had this vague feeling then, that the real her—"

Shae then clarified. "I was smothered beneath the Dar—I mean Primal." She turned to Diane. "You see, Diane. Riley is going to be this way from now on."

"I can help guide your daughter to learn how to

deal with these visions and the feelings she gets," Avia spoke up then. "I know I am not perfect. But I have experience. And as a mother, I know you just want her to have a regular life. That's truly why I put my own daughter with Nickolas." Avia nodded at Riley. "We will leave you to your lives here. Contact us whenever you wish."

"Please, Mom. And I wanna visit Shae sometimes too!" Riley glanced up at Diane with puppy dog eyes. Finally, Diane relented. "Woo-hoo!" Riley hugged Shae in excitement.

"I'm trusting you. Break this trust, I will take my daughter and you'll never hear from us again," Diane firmly informed Avia. "That goes for you too, Nick." Avia, Verties, and Nick agreed to Diane's terms. Finally, Nick dared to hug Diane—glad that she accepted it.

"We shall leave you alone then."

Shae graciously hugged her parents before watching them leave the house. "Our visits will take place at the Royale Hawse. Kiran and I now reside in Battle Realm. But when you want to visit, don't hesitate to arrange it with my parents. They will then make sure I'm available." Shae smiled, although it was briefly. She turned to Kiran.

He knew that look. "Shae and I must be going now." He had eaten, but she had not. And he could see the glaze forming in her eyes. Stepping out the door, they disappeared through a portal on the front porch.

Epilogue

Valentine's Day, 2009

Shae snuggled comfortably in a purple beanbag chair as she stared at Kiran across the loft. She watched him setting up another record on the player. The past year he introduced her to more than just music—but also foods and an amazing sex life.

Kiran hadn't put the needle on the record yet when he turned around to face her. "Hey, let's get married!"

She frowned.

"Not the reaction I was hopin' for." He set the needle down and soft music settled in the background of their conversation.

"How can I let myself be happy." She glanced over at him as he settled next to her in his blue beanbag chair. "Nick's marriage failed. It's my fault."

"She's still letting him see Riley." Kiran took her hand, rubbing his thumb on her palm.

She glanced at their hands and then back at him. "You learned that from me."

"Yes. Is it working?"

"Yeah…" Her frown shifted into a drunken smile. "I forgive you for using my tricks against me."

"Speaking of forgiving, I'm sure that Nick and Diane forgive you. Especially after we explained it all to them."

"No, I think that was Riley's doing. Leftover

abilities from my grandma." Shae sighed. "But I'm glad Diane is allowing my mother to mentor Riley."

"Well, that stuff is way beyond me. I'm just here to love you." He sat up straighter. "You haven't said yes or no, yet."

"Yes. I'll marry you."

Kiran jumped to his feet, raised his fist, and hollered, "Luckiest man alive!"

Shae chuckled and then stood up. "You do know I have a failed marriage too."

"Oh yeah, Dorian. How's he doing with…what's her name?"

"Myra? Dorian said he's just fine with her. And the fact that she's pretty good with weapons. Her choice of weapon is a Yumi. I watched the bow and arrow demonstration a few months ago. She never misses the target."

"Wow." Kiran smirked. "But I'll be biased and say that you are still better at weapons."

"Dorian has his hands full. He's also still dealing with my mess. But he's used to covering vampire tracks. He's been doing it on Jacquain's activities for years!"

"Good riddance to that monster." Kiran gave a mock salute. "That's the one good thing you did under the possession of evil."

"I'm just glad the evil is gone." She wrapped her arms around Kiran. Their lips met, the kiss lingering even after the song ended. Neither of them bothered to change it to the next song.

Kiran broke the kiss. "What about the vampires you were in charge of?" He moved over finally to switch records. He picked a random instrumental jazz tune.

"Michael didn't bring them all with him to Battle Realm. Last I heard, my parents created a task force to keep tabs on them. He keeps trying to regroup. I just want to stay away from them. I'd rather be a Pookums than a queen."

Kiran chuckled. "My Pookums." Just as he pulled her into an embrace, her phone buzzed.

"Oh." She walked over to the record player and picked up the cell lying next to it. "Gotta go meet Tera. She's due for her first Battle Realm experience. I agreed to be a mentor."

"And you're gonna be a *great* one!" He quickly kissed her. "Why don't you invite her here for lunch after?"

"Yeah, good idea."

"I do have them from time to time."

Shae kissed him one last time before leaving the cottage.

A word about the author...

Frankie Sutton, born within a Motown/Detroit community, was raised on creativity—starting with music. Her love of reading and writing developed during her school years. However, at the beginning of her high school years, she experimented with many styles of writing. When not writing, she loves bonding with her miniature schnauzer. Frankie embraces her life as a Motown Michigander, ready to share her large imagination with the world.